Bodies and Souls

Also by Tom Stacey

FICTION

The Brothers M
The Living and the Dying
The Pandemonium
The Worm in the Rose
Deadline

NON-FICTION

The Hostile Sun
Summons to Ruwenzori
Today's World

for Eleanor for Christmas 1991

TOM STACEY

from Tom with love.

BODIES AND SOULS

Five Stories

HEINEMANN : LONDON

William Heinemann Ltd
Michelin House, 81 Fulham Road, London SW3 6RB
LONDON   MELBOURNE   AUCKLAND

First published 1989
Copyright © Tom Stacey 1989

British Library Cataloguing in Publication Data

Stacey, Tom, *1930–*
  Bodies and souls
  I. Title
  823'.914(F)
  ISBN 0 434 73504 3

Photoset by Deltatype, Ellesmere Port
Printed in Great Britain by
Redwood Burn Ltd, Trowbridge
and bound by Hunter and Foulis Ltd, Edinburgh.

For Tomasina

Tell all the Truth but tell it slant
Success in Circuit lies
Too bright for our infirm Delight
The truth's superb surprise

As Lightning to the Children eased
With explanation kind
The Truth must dazzle gradually
Or every man be blind –

                Emily Dickinson

Contents

Llan Chernobyl   1

Lady-killer   59

Territoire Inexploré   93

The Lost Poem   133

Dear John   159

Llan Chernobyl

[i]

Something was wrong. There were the sheep: that was obvious. Was it not something more than the sheep? Behind the sheep? Beyond the sheep? Deeper than this Chernobyl thing?

Idris spoke to his dog: a whistle, a syllable. The ewe in difficult labour had taken herself apart to give birth. At his approach she twisted to her feet and trotted reluctantly four yards. When she knew the dog was pointing her, she stayed stock still. He came behind her and as she moved again the crook of his stick was there to trip by the foreleg – just a gesture of the stick, fleetingly surreptitious and gentle. She lay on her side panting, eyes bulging. There was no problem in a man responding to a ewe in difficult labour, no problem there.

But the darkness was in him somewhere, had opened up in him, like a black chasm in the earth not easily delved. He had dreamed of such a chasm on his own land, coming across it to his astonishment, since it did not seem possible after all these innumerable years of intimacy with the land, he and his forebears, treading the ground with their dogs, grazing their flocks. Yet there it was, in his clear dream. And although its presence astonished him, and made him fearful, he supposed it had been there always and somehow he had not perceived it. Or else that it had been present always in the potential, and would reveal itself only as a consequence of some convulsion. North Wales was subject to earthquakes from time to time, that shook slates from roofs and cracked the plaster of town houses; yet never such in living memory that could open a chasm in the *mynnydd-dir*, the mountain land.

That was only a dream. Yet the darkness of it remained, or had been there already, and was on his broad brow now, and troubled his fine eyes. He was a well-cut man, humour and assurance in the face, and a vigour about him too, for he was scarcely yet into middle years, and had sons to retain the youth in him. Yet he was conscious of the presence of the darkness which he did not know how to expel.

He pulled off his waterproof jacket and laid it beside his stick, then he pushed up the sleeve of his sweater and shirt and bunching his fingers to a point insinuated his hand into the uterus up to half his forearm. She groaned. When he had turned the unborn lamb by head and forelegs, his other hand began to press its dam's belly in slow rhythm. His head lay on her fleece so that his tweed cap was pushed askew. He felt the warmth of her on one side of his face and the cold sleet on the other. He loved the scent of his sheep because it was the scent he knew best.

The wise hand working inside withdrew in its sure way – forearm, wrist, the hand itself – and now amid the firm casque of his fingers the neat forehooves and tiny head appeared in the remnants of their cowl, and all at once, in a spasm of rightness, the newborn, immaculate and entire, slid forth. He cleared its mouth with a scoop of his forefinger, and a quavering bleat announced its birth and was answered.

Next, to prevent this human agency making the lamb strange to its dam, he drew it over her back, so that the slime and smell of it was on her. He laid it at her hindquarters on the sodden turf that was half sphagnum moss. He laid it there, not at her head, inasmuch as – in his father's words some forty years ago – a ewe knows it doesn't give birth by the mouth. Sure enough, she turned her head instantly to her own living lamb behind her and pushed herself to her feet to lick it clean. The lamb itself was on its feet and shaking its straggling tail. He released the first dark thick milk from her teats with his finger and thumb, and stood back until the lamb found its first teat, its umbilicus still dangling. He put his jacket back on and straightened his cap, leaving a tiny smear of milk from the teat or mucus from the womb on the peak. Then he took his marker from his pocket and dabbed the newborn's quarters with his flock's tile-red. His lamb. His flock, for what it was worth.

For what it was worth. In midlife now, it was all he had. His animals, and the land they shared with him: that piece of the Welsh hills they grazed, which he knew by every boulder, stain of lichen, clump of bracken, every runnel, gurgle, hollow and bog, every brae, bank, bald top, declivity, at every season in every weather. It was all he had and not much in measurable terms. He had been content with it all his life, insofar as a man has a right to contentment. He knew that contentment was in the earning of it: it was the simple equation of small farming – it gave you back exactly what it demanded of you. That gave it a kind of honesty and integrity which the summertime caravan dwellers from the cities knew nothing about, that barbarian majority of humankind whom he scorned or pitied.

Yet lately the contentment had been elusive. It was to do with the factor that was not measurable, the *capital* factor – the hills and valleys and woods, the land itself, that was in his right from an infinite past to an infinite future. A doubt and suspicion had been worming in there, and that was where something was wrong.

The oakwood rose steep behind him. Some way below, beyond the gully and the tilted pasture with its solitary sycamore where his cows sheltered in the worst weather, his cottage hunched under its knuckle of hill as it had hunched for hundreds or thousands of years. Against the cottage and beneath it, the barns and sheds snuggled there randomly in stone filched from ancient walls and gash oak planks got for next-to-nothing from timber-yards.

Four or five centuries ago, that squared stone cottage with its cavernous smoke-curing chimney had replaced the circular dwelling of his forefathers. For want of chimneys then, the sides of mutton were hung from the apex of the roofs, where smoke from the home fires assembled before escaping through the daub and wattle. His forefathers had cannibalised the earlier dwelling for the base liths of his own squared cottage: Idris had learned this from the traces left by the ancients of how they split stone. Those same giants of men with mere iron bars and charcoal fires had quarried and wrought the menhirs for the stone circles and set them up. One such circle had stood, according to hearsay, above the oakwood on the treeless snow-patched summit of his very hill above the wood, and maybe still lay there, toppled under the turf. With their great circle of erect stone the men of those days made a church of the skies and brought the heaven earthward. He had felt it there on that top, that sacred *moel*, a place of veneration yet.

He looked down through the slant of the rain to his cottage. To this very day it seemed to grow out of the hillside, an excrescence of rock and slate that man had not built but only adapted. All that proved it a home from here was the smudge of smoke which the upper end of the roof-ridge under its knuckle of ground was never without. That smoke was similar to evidence of a soul. When his ancestors with their few iron tools arrived to settle these hills, the land each family was permitted to graze was restricted to that within easy sight of the homestead's plume of smoke. The very terms of the Celtic tongue endorsed the legend.

Idris could see Gerry's red Volvo drawn up in the yard. It was bright and stark against his own grey van. He had seen to his flock now, for the next few hours at any rate. Dusk drawing in, he would be expected home.

[ii]

The three of them greeted Idris through the partition and curtain that divided the cottage entrance from the living room.

'What's it like out now?' Gerry called.

'Sleet higher up,' replied Idris.

He shed his cap and waterproof and wellington boots, and pushed through the curtain into the bright, warm, cramped room. There was his brother-in-law Gerry, and Gerry's wife Myfanwy, and his own angel Mair who was Myfanwy's sister, the younger by a mere hour. He brought the challenge of the hard weather from the hill into their midst, in the firmness of his features and his skin's high colour, and in the unruly freedom of the curly hair released by the cap.

'Well, Idris,' Gerry said. 'Done for the day?'

'Mebbe,' he replied with a pout of a smile. There was indeed one other ewe he was not happy about that he might require himself to tend by lantern-light before he turned in.

Idris crossed the white-washed room, ducking beneath the oak cross-beam, for over the centuries it had sagged and anyway he was tall for a Welshman, and he rinsed the congealed uterine slime from his arm and hand under the spigot of the little tank of warm water alongside the square of open fire. This red coal fire comprised the centre of the low cast-iron range that occupied nearly the whole length of the wall. In answer to Gerry, he said he reckoned to lose one lamb in ten at birth, and this year was inside his average, the foul weather notwithstanding.

Idris spoke in English, as was their custom in Gerry's presence, for although Gerry was a Welshman he had grown up a Glamorgan boy and had taken on little of the Welsh that all of them had here in the north of the Principality. When Myfanwy visited alone or with Vera they used Welsh, their first language.

It had been an encroachment when Myfanwy married out of the language: she hadn't accepted Gerry without consulting Mair who, a year or so previously, had wed the handsome young hill farmer they had come close to competing for. But the encroachment was everywhere already . . . it had been going on for generations, centuries – Saxons, Normans, the unrelenting thrusting forth of authority from London and the south-east. The Welsh monarchs in Hampton Court made English the fashionable tongue of Wales's aristocracy so that before long few of the great landowners knew Welsh unless they got it up as an exercise in quaint condescension, as the so-called Prince of Wales did today. By now the encroachment was scarcely distinguishable from that which it encroached upon, for it was there in the vehicles they drove and the highways they drove them on, it was there in the caravan sites they leased out to the barbarian strangers and in the bed-and-breakfasts they provided them. It was there in the national English press they read and the television they watched. When Idris himself brought home a daily it was the *Guardian*, and the Welsh-language television channel could put on such banality, as if for a remnant of half-wits, that he and Mair preferred the English channels. There in pride of place beyond the end of the cast-iron range stood the big modern colour set. What encroachment was Myfanwy's marriage to all that?

And Gerry took an interest. The well-being of the animals. Prices at market. The mischief of the weather. The twists and turns of the European regulations. The perennial outrage of the Ministry, the Welsh Office Agriculture Department. And now this other thing, Chernobyl, that Gerry knew all about, and that blighted Idris's flock. When they got talking together on whatever sort of topic – like this Chernobyl catastrophe – it would be two good minds at work, as each would be aware. Gerry hadn't the language and professionally they were poles apart, yet he did feel the kinship their sibling wives brought them.

'Let's see the video,' Myfanwy declared. 'Come along. That's what we were promised.'

'Gerry'll not understand a word,' Idris told her, taking up his tea and a slice of sponge cake.

'He understands a whole lot more Welsh than he lets on,' returned Myfanwy.

'Not Dafydd ap Gwilym,' Idris came back. 'That's fourteenth-century Welsh. It's for devotees of the language only. Not for dabblers.'

'Then you can translate for him, Idris,' Mair intervened. 'Show 'im what he's missing.'

'Dafydd isn't translatable,' he insisted, pretending.

'I was waiting for that,' Gerry put in with a smile.

Yet when Idris put on the video tape as he presently did, he did translate as he went – and vividly too. The tape was mostly of himself, a few months earlier, declaiming Dafydd at the eisteddfod at Llangollen: brilliant lusty tales of the poet's own supposed experience, told (sung, of course, in olden times, to the harp) in a self-mocking singular first person, image heaped on wondrous image in a configuration of speech known to 'devotees' like Idris as *dyfal*. Idris had shifted his own rocking-chair to face them alongside the television screen, so that they had a choice of performance. As he rendered Dafydd in English he used the same intonation, the gesture of eye and mouth and sometimes of hand, the same lilt and pitch as the Welsh itself conjured from him, so that the two languages – one out of the screen and the other from the man himself in their midst – became fused. For Idris was no sluggard in the English tongue either. And as he gave it, you could catch in him a wildness, wantonness, a pagan fire, that nothing else lit but this verse, this ancestral Welsh voice. He did not get drunk Saturdays like most of the fellows out of the hills; all he needed was the right words, Mair would say, for his head to go. For Idris's voice, in either tongue, even now, took on a richness, became *invested*, although invested by what Mair could not specify, except that it was not from outside him. It was he himself in an expansion inwards, into himself, no less valid – as her imagination suggested to her – than the expansion outwards by which the poor schoolmaster's son from Criccieth-way had become Prime Minister.

They had all attended that eisteddfod together – Idris and Mair and their two boys, and Gerry and Myfanwy and their Vera. They were all recorded there in the video film, for the camera was handled by each of the boys in turn. Vera was wearing a jacket and skirt in pale blue, chosen for her by her mother for the occasion, to disguise her thick midriff and maybe even spark in her a sense of what it was to feel smart. Every time Vera saw the camera aimed in her direction she grinned at it in childlike delight and tried to move to the middle of the picture. They all smiled now at her antics: there was no guile in Vera. Even Idris's and Mair's clever college boys had learned a patient fondness for their cousin Vera. None of them pretended among themselves that she was quite as other children.

'Idris,' Myfanwy declared when the tape ended, 'you should have gone on the stage. Shouldn't he, Mair? Or politics. You'd have a following in two shakes. Not tucked away up the hills here.'

Mair looked at him and read his face – that the declaration gave him an old, low pain because he felt the truth of it.

'An' if I 'ad a following,' Idris said with his strong smile, 'where would I lead 'em?'

'That's not the first consideration,' Gerry commented, 'for your real politician.'

'I 'ave a following anyway,' Idris added, and under their laughter the compliment went deep into Mair's dark slate eyes. She was his angel, as he often called her. She would even rib him for his wonder at her, though it charged her with delight and he could hardly guess what his strength and straightness were for her secretly. She could be as darkly pretty now at nearly forty as she was at twenty. Both the sisters had kept the looks they had grown up to be famous for in the locality, but while Myfanwy's vivacity bubbled forth in the society of friends and the commerce of daily life, Mair's was shyer and burned in the close circle of the family and farm. And she was fragile-looking, too, though deceptively so, the small bones and transparent skin and delicacy of form containing a deceptive stamina. Indeed, she was never ill: it was Idris who caught the colds and chills. Mair had been up half the previous night helping Idris with the lambing, though no one would have guessed it, seeing her now in her two-piece black suit, neat at the waist, and yellow silk scarf Myfanwy gave her, serving her own sponge cake from the trivet before the range.

And where *would* Idris have a following, except 'up the hills here'? Others had sometimes commented that Idris was 'wasted' working his hill farm with its outside privy and water from the well. Sometimes Mair could believe so herself, not least at this season, when their seven hundred headage of ewes would be bearing nearly half as many again of lambs, keeping them up night after night. Yet, she would say, what would Idris be without the farm, which had been in his family for eleven generations to his own proven knowledge? Idris *was* the farm, the farm *was* Idris, whether or not it kept them nudging poverty by the standards of the times, working day in, day out, with seldom a summer's break or a clear Sabbath.

Only just lately had she grown aware of a sense of futility coming upon Idris. She knew when she had first perceived it, and for months now she had watched it seeping around him, finding gaps in him as if between the timbers of a boat which all his life she had learnt to know only as impenetrably sound. It was a year ago now that the nuclear power station at Chernobyl in the Soviet Union had blown up. This disaster spread a cloud of toxic dust over Europe. Ten days later, tests on sheep across Great Britain found that flocks in the high pasturelands of North Wales and Cumbria were affected by radioactivity to an unacceptable level. Among the farms affected was theirs, and from that day to this never fewer than three hundred and forty farms in the neighbourhood, theirs included, had been designated by the Agriculture Department as contaminated by the blight and were subject by law to their sheep being tested for radioactivity before being sold or slaughtered. For all sheep found contaminated, the Government provided cash to make up the difference between the sharply reduced price offered by lowland farmers prepared to graze out the contamination, and the going price for animals that passed the test. By now, the hill farmers affected were no worse off in income, although they groused and clamoured for better compensation. But there were just as many farms affected as six months ago, and many – like theirs – were still found with as many as a third of their flock above the permitted radioactivity level.

At the first shock of the calamity, when the restrictions were imposed, Mair noticed a sullen anger enter Idris. The immediate requirement was to protect themselves from pecuniary loss. But as that requirement began to be met, the sullen anger did not lift but soured to a kind of dismay that made him grave and meditative, and took away his speech, and kept him rocking in his chair like a man going back to his mother's womb. This was most noticeable to her as those market days approached at which Idris would have sheep for sale, and the Agriculture Department van would call to test the ewes and lambs he intended to take to the town.

Such a day was to occur the following week. They were to take down some store lambs and ewes with lambs at foot. As their guests were leaving later that evening, in cold and driving rain, it was arranged that Mair and Myfanwy should meet up in the town – which lay between the farm and Gerry's place of work – while Idris attended market.

[iii]

Gerry's place of work was Llangower nuclear power station, where he was a senior physicist. Llangower was a complex of mighty edifices built on the shore of its own artificial reservoir amid a wild, unpopulated landscape. Its reactors and its turbines provided half a million kilowatts of power to the national grid, which is to say nearly four per cent of the nation's electrical supply. To cool the condensers of its turbo alternators, it needed one hundred and fifty-nine million litres of water from its own lake every hour. This water was returned to the lake by a subterranean network of channels and settling chambers.

Great pains had been taken by the architect to blend the power station into the surrounding mountain scenery. This architect was one of the most distinguished of his profession in the country, dubbed knight by the monarch on the field of the battle between (as it were) the Will of man and a Nature whose indifference was tantamount to hostility. The precast concrete panels which formed the buildings' cladding were brush-surfaced with the local stone aggregate to blend with surrounding outcrops of natural rock. The pumphouse was put below ground level: the substation was sited in a hollow, and parts of the great expanse of its hard surface were planted with dwarf clover. Trees were planted to screen the view of it from the road; birch, rowan, gorse and heather were reinstated wherever the construction had ripped away the surface of the land. The approach road inflected with the contours; even the embankments of the artificial lake were shaped to give a natural appearance. It was an elaborate manoeuvre of strategic stealth by the knight and his men upon the country which of course, once vanquished, was required still as the dumb force and stuff of the victor's right to exercise his power and his genius. For man himself the vanquished must needs always be humoured.

Twenty-three years after its construction, Llangower still rose there in its grand vale beside its own lake as a sudden, towering, angular intrusion from another order of creativity. It emitted perpetually a complex vibratory hum, containing a high-pitched element and a diapason. This sound hinted at immense power generated and contained.

There was no danger here, of course, of any such catastrophic accident as at Chernobyl. In faraway Soviet Russia, where public accountability scarcely existed, faults in design were permitted that would never be tolerated in a country like Britain. All were reassured on that point. At Llangower, things might go amiss on a paltry scale; but it was proof against any violent overwhelming disaster such as that which occurred on 26 May 1986 when man's irreverence towards those elemental forces upon which he had intruded provoked an eruption of rage that devastated a region and blighted half a continent with its fall-out.

[iv]

The ancient town lay equidistant between Idris's farm and Llangower power station – a road journey of about eight miles from each, and, as the crow flies, less. At the open air market on the edge of the town the knot of farmers clustered beneath the auctioneer who, in his white coat, with his clerk, and raised on a gangplank running all the way down between the pens, might have been a mediaeval pardoner hawking indulgences, and all those farming men, sellers and bidders, as if stepped out of a Chaucer tale or a Brueghel painting – wary, humorous, avaricious, caricaturing themselves. The auctioneer carried a ridged cane which he rapped against the rail of the gangway to seal each bargain at the peak of the bidding. Then his little mob shuffled on to the adjacent pen and his burble-chant instantly resumed, never a pause in its rush to a deal, *fiftei*, *sistei*, barely decipherable save to the initiated and responded to by the bidders with infinitesimal signals – a twitch of a hand by those in front, or the narrowing of an eye from a bidder behind. And among them – as canny, narrow and instinctive as the rest – Idris, his powerful hand, the genetrix hand, cupping a pocket calculator.

Towards the end of the forty-yard row, the little pens contained animals of a different category. As the auctioneer reached this point, the mood changed. Oh, they were sheep all right – last year's tups and ewes with lambs at foot – but these animals were disfigured by a ferocious slash of green paint along the head, which had been shaven to ensure the durability of the mark. This garish scoring vividly bedraggled them. Though outwardly healthy, the violence of the mark, and the way it had splashed on to tufts of adjacent fleece, gave them a blighted look.

And at the same point, most of the bidders had drawn away to chatter among themselves. Each selling owner, as he entered the pen where his lot was to be auctioned, carried an air of confusion, almost of shame. The bidding would begin very low, and the auctioneer must drag it off the bottom against the studied reluctance of the few bidders.

These were 'dirty' sheep, that had failed the radioactivity test the Agriculture Department applied by law to this whole region of restricted farms. The only bidders were lowland farmers or dealers with customers prepared to graze out the contamination over the months and years. When it was Idris's turn to enter his pen of green-daubed sheep, the expression that he wore was that same sullen dismay that Mair had perceived in him lately; and in the dismay, a tremor of disgust that came from the roots of him and had nowhere to go.

★

Elsewhere in the dour, stone-built town, Mair and Myfanwy were meeting at the tea-shop for a mid-morning break in their shopping, and with them was Myfanwy's and Gerry's daughter Vera. Myfanwy was to take Vera to the doctor shortly for attention to the cast in her eye, for there was no optician in the town and here a doctor must undertake not only to diagnose but actually to treat all manner of ailments and malfunctions. Vera was sixteen now and had just left school, from which she had emerged half-literate. Her backwardness was ascribed to a shutting off of oxygen for a critical moment at her birth, which was a difficult one. Not long after Vera's entry into the world, before any impediment in her was noticed, it was felt necessary for her mother to have a hysterectomy, which put paid to her child-bearing.

Vera was not an idiot, only slow and sometimes vacant, and she could be entrusted with small tasks and was a strong, willing, affectionate child. She ate well, and was already beginning to blow out into womanhood with vigorous breasts and heavy buttocks. And somewhere behind the vacancy, or within it, Myfanwy would occasionally glimpse a kind of dumb sagacity which surprised her and even frightened her. It was as if Vera did also have a familiarity with another order that could never be articulated and for that reason was not accessible to the self-aware and intelligent. Yet it had its own pattern and scheme of things, so that sometimes when Vera seemed quite apart and void, Myfanwy would glimpse in her a crowded interiority of active business. This would occur every so often when she had a task for Vera or an instruction to give her. She would perceive her daughter 'swimming back' to her, as she had put it to Gerry, and she would say to her, 'Where were you, Vera? Nowhere?' And Vera would reply, 'Yes, mam, nowhere,' as if *nowhere* was a place of its own with the realism of dreams yet with its own scheme of things and its own sagacity. Moreover, Vera had her certainties that came from somewhere within her, and were not the result of what had been put to her by others or reached from known facts – certainties such as, for example, who was to be trusted and who was not, and even what was permissible and what was not. These opinions did not always tally with the accepted view: she never argued them, of course, and her mother and (less often) her father would become aware of them only through symptoms of sulkiness or of a strange gleaming excitement. Once, lately, she had been taken by some boys to the Bull and got drunk, and Myfanwy knew that none of the scolding she received as a consequence truly reached her. Vera perceived no sin in her experience. Such manifestations were sources of alarm to Myfanwy.

The three of them chatted together in the Welsh language over their pot of tea. Vera ate a sugared cake and the fragment of another that her mother had left over, despite her mother's chiding. 'There's nothing to be done about Vera's waistline,' Myfanwy chaffed. 'Though I'm not one to speak myself. Look at your auntie Mair, Vera. She never puts on a half ounce more than she's a use for.'

Vera grinned happily.

'It's the suburban life you live,' teased Mair. 'All that sun-room nonsense and cocktail patio and central heating.'

She was referring to the smart modern house that came with Gerry's job, in the purpose-built satellite estate attached to the nearest village to the power station itself. It had a garage for two cars.

Myfanwy had always been the bigger eater of the sisters, and when they were children in the manse – for their father took over the Presbyterian ministry of the parish when they were six years old – it was their mother's constant plea to Mair that she should follow her sister's example if she wished to grow up strong and healthy. Yet for all her apparent delicacy, Mair had proved the stronger of the two, her vitality never seemingly sapped, and the two sturdy young men she had mothered were witness to it.

There was always that difference between the sisters, Mair the slighter, and shyer, evoking the protectiveness of Myfanwy with her extra hour in the world . . . though also swifter, mercurial. They weren't ever jealous, the two, being alike in their prettiness, even as children, and each with her own style. Yet for a moment, years before, they were rivals for Idris. Myfanwy withdrew when she perceived that certainty unspoken between her sister and Idris, a certainty that dismayed her. A little later, during her first job in Glamorgan, where Gerry began to court her, Myfanwy would think that her sister had married *back*, into her root kind – whatever the gifts of her Idris in form and brilliance, still *back* – while she would marry *out*, into the new and the forward. She made herself thankful to be spared that peasant drudgery she witnessed in her sister's life, and marvelled at her willingness. Myfanwy began her married life in the south: they did not see so much of one another at first. Then as their children grew, and Gerry was appointed to Llangower, it seemed their offspring rocked the *back* and the *out* the other way, like a see-saw, and she was thankful for the rootedness of Mair's life, though she need never speak of it.

Mair now accompanied Myfanwy and Vera to Dr Roberts's because she herself had some matter on which she wished to consult the doctor privately. On the way, they passed their father's chapel where they still sometimes worshipped on a Sunday morning, though both had chapels nearer to home and Gerry was no chapel-goer. They were to meet there in a month's time at the service of memorial to a farmer whose cancer had carried him away too young, at which Idris had been invited to give the address on account of his eloquence and a natural ascendency among his fellows. The chapel was fronted by a small square, where the town's granite cross stood to the fallen of two World Wars, and it backed on to the field and hills, beyond a wild cemetery. So this chapel was half of the town and half of the *mynnydd-dir*, the mountain land. The sisters fell to chatting about the high incidence of cancer in the locality, and between them they rattled off the names of ten or a dozen families who had lost a member from the affliction in recent years. Was it not on the increase? And if it was, what connection might there be between that and Chernobyl, or the presence of Llangower in the vicinity? Even Dr Roberts was known to have his suspicions. Myfanwy said you could prove anything with statistics, and reminded Mair of Gerry's assurance that the increase in radioactivity due to the presence of a power station like Llangower was negligible, although Gerry himself was never deaf to what he would call 'informed speculation'. The real problem, declared Myfanwy, was that most people still found nuclear power to be mysterious, and that mystery gave force to their fear; while in reality there was no mystery about nuclear power and no need for there to be. Mair heard Gerry talking through her sister, and wondered.

After Dr Roberts had attended Vera, Myfanwy waited for her sister. The examination did not take long. Dr Roberts, who had held the practice since their childhood, wrote out a prescription and told Mair that if the medicine 'did not do the trick' she was to come back to see him.

[v]

The service of memorial was widely attended, for the deceased had been in the prime of life and, as a hill farmer, represented the foremost activity of families in the surrounding hills. Moreover the weather had wonderfully changed, and the whole world was agleam with spring and washed by sunshine. Most of those who had attended the market were present, with their wives and families, although today they looked different. They wore their best caps and their boots shone. It was not only their habit that had improved: their faces too had changed, and had assumed a hard and pious conformity.

As the swelling Welsh hymn died away, the white-headed old minister, father of the sisters, gave way in the high pulpit to his son-in-law Idris. Now Idris had walked across the hills and dales from his farm to attend this worship, for the route was more direct than by the high-road, a mere five or six miles; and the weather so brilliant. He had tied his dog to the fence beyond the cemetery, and left his wellington boots there too, changing into his best boots. Mair had come with Myfanwy, who with Vera had fetched her sister from the farm in her red Volvo; the sisters each had a little smart black hat to wear. Idris had wanted the solitary walk to settle in his mind what he wished to say to the congregation. He wished to speak of the dead man as a friend and as a hill farmer who had served God on account of the very demands of the only way of life he knew, a way of life sanctified by its antiquity.

But when he was up there high above the congregation, framed by the organ pipes whose soaring symmetry all but filled the east end of the chapel, as if it was not so much by Christ as by music that they could reach the Father, he was aware of a new force trembling to take him over – a spirit of *dyfal*, as it were, that would carry the mind in its leaps from image to image and would leave nothing of that which comprised their lives, in fear and drudge and hardihood and joy, unlinked to the whole and without significance. From her raised pew at the back of the chapel, beside her sister and her niece, Mair perceived the difference in Idris, and she could trace its extension from his recent moods of sullen dismay, and from an unwonted reserve these previous forty-eight hours. For as a rule if he had to make a public appearance he would rehearse his text or his ideas on her, but this time had kept to himself.

He opened from the pulpit as intended, his powerful hands still, wrapped over the rim of the wood. He recalled the life and qualities of the dead man and touched upon the grief of those who had survived him, his young family first of all. Only then, at the further consideration of grief, did a phrase he had once read equating *grief* with *ignorance* come to mind. And this released his tongue, yet not in the way that he had felt trembling within him, not the *dyfal*.

He asked, 'If we had released our brother-in-the-Lord not into darkness, where we cannot see, but into light, where we can see, would we grieve so?

'He has been taken from us. We do not know where, though we

trust in our scriptures, which assure us of the immortality of the soul in the kingdom of heaven. We have that enlightening information. It is provided to us in such a form as to oblige in us faith, that death is not what it seems, and that the dead, if taken from us in the flesh, are not taken from us in the spirit.

'But there is another form of darkness, and that is a form that we would be mistaken to tolerate. I refer to the darkness of the *why*. *Why* was this Alun of ours selected so young and taken from us in the flesh? Why him? And why Euryn, and Will Williams, and Gwen Jones, and Pammie Davies, and Dai Pugh, and those several others of our acquaintance in recent times, who have been carried away before the completion of their proper span, whose untimely departure we have lamented in this very chapel? We know of the common cause of their death. But what we do not know is the *origin* of that cause.

'Now, we are also acquainted with the blight on our animals – and we are informed as to the origin of that. It is a puzzling matter, of course, for it is a most persistent blight which we were promised by the experts would pass. Yet it has not passed. It has persisted. If anything it has grown worse. It is a blight not only on flocks but also on our way of life, that has been ours for hundreds upon hundreds of years. We had no knowledge of this blight, of course, until a distant catastrophe provoked the authorities to make their tests. Now, what of this blight?

'I put it to you, is there any connection between this blight and the other? Is there not a region of darkness here, that has remained dark because we have not dared to penetrate it?

'There is no need to subject ourselves to rumour and speculation. The statistics are accessible to us. So are the scientific facts. If there is an angel of death abroad in the land, if a curse has been put upon us, let us penetrate this darkness. Let us – let me – find out how and why, and let us learn how that curse shall be raised. This shall be our best memorial to our departed Alun. Let us go forth from here and bring light to the why and the how. I refer to radiation.'

The effect of voicing from the pulpit that single word was electrifying. That word – the English word, perforce – comprised all the fears and doubts that were circulating among the people. The high pulpit and Idris's conviction all at once charged them with authority to confront what troubled them privately. And here in Idris they seemed to have a champion. Even those most immediately bereaved were lifted and strengthened by the defiance of his speech. All eyes were raised to him in respect – even Vera's were alight with wonder, puzzlement and admiration. They all felt the authority of the man.

When the minister resumed his place in the pulpit, the closing prayers he improvised took up the same theme. He spoke of the heritage that was theirs to defend and the duty they all had on behalf of those who had gone before to those who were to come. He spoke of the power of their history as something blessed, and they all caught his meaning. The sun came in through the plain windows and caught the vase of daffodils and jonquils below the pulpit. And at the close he quoted a prayer of St Francis, giving thanks to the Lord for hiding certain things from the highly educated and intelligent and revealing them to children. For such as these, in whose first language there was no vocabulary for half of what was necessary to know, there could only be the wisdom of children.

The old minister, a widower now, was at the door of his chapel after the service. Several were around Idris congratulating him gravely on his address, for it had brought them courage and it was clear already that they felt they had someone to look towards, namely Idris himself.

'You'll speak to Gerry first,' the minister said.

'That is my intention,' Idris replied.

'Gerry will be truthful,' the old minister answered him, for he was proud of both his sons-in-law.

'I know.'

Myfanwy intervened. 'Gerry will certainly be helpful to you and quite open. But I know his opinion is that radiation leakage from Llangower is negligible.'

'There are still facts to be got,' Idris replied, and both sisters agreed. 'Mair,' he continued, 'I'll be walking home. Are you coming?'

She threw him a little pleading glance. 'I'm a bit done up today,' she said.

'I can run you all home,' Myfanwy volunteered, 'if you'll fetch your dog, Idris.'

But Idris insisted upon the walk, and he turned down beside the chapel alone, and through the cemetery to where his dog waited, and his boots and stick too. Many of the stones in the cemetery belonged to his folk.

It was so sweet a May day. The spring landscape was bursting around him as he entered the hills. The thorn-trees' blossom was so white they seemed like so many brides. There was a masterful beauty about the place, and a secrecy too: living nature and the rocks and hills, the streams and the river below, surged and rejoiced around him as if all were part of a single resurrection. It all reflected in his face. He was moving up now into the familiar woods on the approach to his own land. He was alert to all the sounds of the steep wood of beech and oak. A sudden frantic quarrel among birds halted him, making him frown.

Then he emerged into open grazing, his own land. Here were his own sheep and, beyond, his four black Welsh cows. Suddenly he saw a ewe with a violent green daub on its head. Then another, and a third. These were animals that he was to take to market that week and that had failed the Agriculture Department's test two days previously. It was a green that affronted all the other greens that surrounded them.

Mair had come out from the cottage and a little way along his route to greet him. She wore a cardigan over the dark dress she had put on for the chapel service, and had taken her hat off. He saw how white and thin and very beautiful she was. She leaned on him as they came over the last tump of land before the descent towards where their ancient cottage nestled with its holly and its box. They had always been able to walk like this, she leaning into him, however rough the ground, as if they were one, though he was quite big and she so small. Mair herself seemed to him part of the miracle of resurrection in which everything about him was swept up, except the green-scored animals that had no place on his hills. She for her part felt a new kind of pride in him at this role he had assumed, though there was in it something which alarmed her.

A few mornings later Idris was up with the dawn to put his sheep through the dip, three fields away, before his special appointment. He left Mair sleeping, pale and waxy and restless. It was a misty dawn, and the place had grown most intimate. He was taking the lane that was known always as the Roman road, for it lay in a straight line between two *tomen*, the hill forts of the ancient Celts that survived still as hummocks of earth, and it was also skirted by great upright stones which it was said once lay flat as a firm base for the rolling wagons. It was narrow, though, and skirted too with thorn-trees and damsons that overhung and often touched above. In such a tunnel of growth a sound from close by stopped him – a firm, strong, repeated whistle, tolling from beyond the hedgerow, or within it. He stood and waited, peering, though the mist blocked him. Then it came again. It was only a bird, some bird or other.

Where the old road broke off and for a certain distance disappeared into open pasture, the ground rose and all at once he found himself out of the mist and in the pale sun. A hare got up ahead of him, and ran on, in short sprints, showing him the way.

In the corner of the next field stood his shearing shed, and beside it he had sunk the dip and lined it with concrete. His dog soon had the sheep coralled and ready for the dip. It was a skilled and complex business, dipping sheep single-handed, and it involved two single-animal pens, a rope, a stick and – for Idris – the wearing of an old cricket-pad passed down to him by the senior shepherd of a neighbouring great landowner. This cricket-pad protected his knee from the buffeting it took from the shoving and jostling of the rest of the flock as he let each single animal into the pre-dip pen. Then back with the gate with a tug on the rope, and the prodded plunge into tick-killing solution. It called for strength of arm and trunk and leg, and high co-ordination, and a subtlety with his animals, his care mastering their fear and trust. He disliked the low, sour stench of the solution. He never dipped except in his special overall, kept up there.

Meanwhile Mair had risen to milk the cows. She felt weary and oddly sleepy still, and could not seem to gather herself to overcome the languor of her movements. She sensed a combat with an unseen force, although it was remote from her and perhaps indifferent to her. She rekindled the fire in the living room, and then descended to the milking-shed where the three cows in milk were already gathered. She sluiced the pail at the water-butt and commenced the milking. The languor was on her still, and she propped her head against the animal. As she worked her hands on the teats she felt the weight of her whole body on her head as it pressed against the soft, firm flank. Then it seemed the whole world toppled over upon her, and all at once she found she had fallen on to the straw-strewn cobbles of the byre.

She picked herself up and righted her stool. She was unhurt, but surprised, since she could not make out what had occurred. It had felt to her exactly as if the world had rolled over on her, and not that she had lost her balance. Yet the cow was there, placid as before, waiting. She resumed milking, obscurely drained of strength. Idris and she had discussed seeking a Department grant to install electric milking-machines, but it had seemed hardly worth it for just three or four cows, and all the regulations that went with the grant. They had had the electricity brought to the cottage only when the boys started school, and that was mostly for the television, so that the boys should not be at a disadvantage to the other kiddies. There was no call to rush into all electrical gadgets, Idris had said.

When she had completed the milking, and churned it, she saw Idris and his dog reappearing suddenly through the mist, returning from the dipping. He changed into his pressed trousers and a clean shirt and best jacket before he took his breakfast and drank his tea. They heard the nine a.m. news on the radio. His appointment was at ten. She did not tell him of the world toppling over on her. It did not take on a significance, either then or now.

Idris had allowed himself plenty of time. Mair came down to the van in the yard, to wish him luck. He put the churn into the back of the van, to leave at the gate by the road for collection.

[vi]

You could say that the immediate vicinity of Llangower nuclear power station was demarcated not so much by its outer fence and the notices as by the reach of the many-stranded vibratory hum given out by its transformers and its boilers. That hum told of its mighty, leashed energy. It penetrated all the screening evergreens, and the carefully reinstated birch and rowan, gorse and heather, and reached to the furthest point of the driveway that inflected with the contours of the land. But as Idris approached on foot from the visitors' car park, it was the structure of the edifices that overwhelmed. Behind its high inner fence of vertical steel strips crossed with barbed wire, the central building rose in cold majesty a hundred and eighty feet. Its sheer concrete face was interrupted by a single vast rectangular aperture sited two-thirds of the way up its surface, this aperture being closed off by recessed steel doors that would be opened to receive, by hoist, the canistered uranium fuel and the massive machinery created to handle it. Beyond, lay the artificial lake, and beyond that, in all directions, the Cambrian hills of North Wales, the *mynnydd-dir*. The lights of Llangower power station were visible on a clear night from the high bare hill above Idris's own farm.

He waited at the gate in his clean cap and shined boots, and in a minute Gerry was crossing the inner courtyard.

'Welcome to the temple of Baal!' greeted Gerry.

He clipped the identity tag to his brother-in-law's lapel. It was more than an identity tag: it was a radiation counter.

'You're a member now,' he chaffed, 'contaminated like the rest of us! Follow me.'

Each man used his tag to pass through the turnstile beyond the entrance hall. Beyond the turnstile a man in a white coat ran each of them over with his hand-held monitor scanner. A prominent notice already announced they were in a 'Safety Area', whose meaning was surely its opposite since beside him, fixed to the wall, Idris saw a dispenser containing tablets 'for use in an emergency', and Gerry now led him into a large steel lift adorned with a similar hinted caution, 'Not to be used in a nuclear emergency.'

'You see,' Gerry told him, 'how perpetually conscious of safety we are.' And to be sure, along the corridor to Gerry's office the warnings reminded and reminded that 'The time for safety is ALL the time.'

Once in his office, Gerry settled his brother-in-law comfortably for a comprehensive description of it all. Idris removed his cap and accepted a cup of tea. He took a notebook from his pocket – the well-used little book that accompanied him to market – and opened it at a clean page. He had a pen ready, and wrote a heading on top of the page, *Llangwr*, the Welsh form.

Gerry had taken pains to prepare for this visit. But more than that: he brought to his exposition all the zest and relish of a man devoted to his craft and proud of its results. Idris made no attempt to immunise himself against this zest. For he had not allowed himself to come here racked with the suspicion and hostility of the ignorant. He had come to obtain enlightenment, and to allow the light to shine wherever it would, for he trusted implicitly the present source of this light – his own Welsh kith and his own family kin. In this light he would perceive the facts and maybe then discern the appropriate structure of evaluation. In that spirit had he arrived here. This Gerry Davies was the same Gerry Davies he had known for seventeen years ever since his own Mair's twin sister had brought him into their midst. He did not feel him to be alien or removed from him by the fact of their meeting here, on Gerry's professional ground.

First Gerry laid out the facts concerning Chernobyl. Radioactivity was everywhere: what mattered was the *degree* of it. The Chernobyl disaster increased radiation right across northern Europe: that was incontrovertible. The caesium categories pointed to Chernobyl. Gerry had an atlas out to demonstrate how the flux of upper atmosphere had spread it from the Ukraine across northern Europe and the sea to Britain, where it had descended particularly upon those areas where it rained the weekend of 2–3 May 1986, namely Cumbria and North Wales. As for the power station itself – this one, or any similar – there is always emission of some radiation, but it is marginal, negligible. And he took Idris through statistics, hard upright columns of figures monitored by machines as neutral as God, telling of what the power station's emission could possibly be responsible for, as becquerels, in a growing plant, or a sheep, or a man, or anything that lived, or had lived. Marginal, negligible.

It was no white-wash that Gerry was engaged in but a sharing of knowledge, a vouchsafing of all those compelling secrets of the constituents of matter and man's rightful intervention amid them that had begun with fire. The Promethean right, that raised a man above the beasts, that gave him dominion. They were two good minds at work together. They were kin and kith, cracking secrets like marrow-bones of yore, though no longer in caves or earth forts but in this temple of humming power. Idris felt the enthusiasm of Gerry's enlightenment being transmitted to him: it was like a current of power itself – the lucidity of it, the rationality. And when the briefing was done, Gerry conducted him to the vast turbine hall, one hundred and twenty yards in length, where the four colossal turbines generated so many hundreds and thousands of volts. They surveyed this stupendous source of power from a high gangway; from there they moved to the charge hall with its moveable charge machines, fifty feet high, that fuelled the nuclear reactors below. It was there below, sealed behind a biological shield ten feet thick, wherein matter itself was provoked to power. The atom was split. That which by definition could not be divided and remain itself was none the less divided by intervention of human ingenuity and rendered other. The chosen uranium atom was split, and what was matter became power. That chosen isotope of *matter*, sown in weakness, was by sacrifice raised in *power* – there, right beneath him, now, buried beneath concrete and steel, unapproachable.

That was the heart of it, unseen and unseeable, yet all governed.

The seat of the governance was the control room, to where Idris was now admitted. Here was the cerebrum of the place, governing all to the minutest degree. Here Gerry had his staff of four or five, amid the banks of dials and diodes that monitored every aspect of it, controlling every procedure and process, covering every exigency. As Gerry in his shirtsleeves had a word with a colleague, his visitor in his Sunday best cast his eyes around the panels that told of the performance of boilers, turbines, reactors; the temperatures, the safety circuits, the emergency alternatives, the Coarse Rod Monitor, the Burst Can Detector, the Emergency Gamma Point Map . . .

Oh yes, Idris could perceive the science of it, the verifiable logic of it. He had grasped the functioning of it already, the inevitability of it, the triumph of the man-authority of it. The shape of things to come.

And it was a monster they had made here; they had made a monster and chained him. And here he was in the very brain of him!

[vii]

It so happened that the very same evening a meeting of the Welsh Union of Farmers was to take place in the town, which was to be addressed by a senior official of the Welsh Office from Cardiff. This Office, it should be explained, is a department of central government, in effect the ministry for Wales. The meeting had been called by the WUF to discuss the consequences of the Chernobyl fall-out in this whole region of North Wales. Because of his prolonged visit to Llangower, Idris arrived at the meeting late. The senior official was already nearing the close of his address which, although he bore a Welsh name, he gave in English, his native tongue. From time to time he threw in a phrase or two from the Welsh, but these tags did not fool his audience of hill farmers, who were restive. When he sat down there was not so much as a ripple of applause.

For a moment the speaker looked down upon the audience with a pitying surprise and then blew his nose on a bordered handkerchief which went back up his sleeve for the next emergency. The chairman, who was a local man farming a bigger than average acreage including quite a bit of richer, low-lying land, declared that the speaker had kindly consented to take questions.

The first question came pointedly in Welsh. It concerned the farmers' right to extra compensation for those 'dirty' lambs that might not be slaughtered and so put on excessive fat while grazing out the contamination. The chairman translated. The official responded by quoting the scale of compensation for this disadvantage. Immediately there came further questions about this and other scales and varieties of compensation. The speaker had all the facts and figures at his command: he even had his assistant up there on the platform beside him, a young fellow in a bow-tie, to work out on his little printing-out calculator the precise benefit that could be claimed in individual cases thrown up by the questioners. The official was not to be stumped; the Government had shown its commitment to fair play, had demonstrated its 'deep concern' for the problems created for farmers, which he himself shared. And so on. At one point he mustered the boldness to counter the prevailing mood of hostility with a rebuke. 'Look, my friends, you're all being compensated for anything you lose or might lose – you're getting guaranteed payment. No strings. No ifs nor buts. What have you got to worry about?' This in a tone of patience over-tested.

And his rebuke had some justification. Idris, who had had to stand at the back of the narrow hall (the dance-room annexe to the Bull hotel) because it was a packed meeting, felt a disgust rising within him as much at the questioners as at the speaker. The compensation might or might not be adequate. But he knew that in the first place the problem wasn't about compensation. All that his fellows seemed capable of rabbiting on about was compensation when what was at issue was something much greater, to which they could give no expression.

Then someone asked about the probable duration of the ban. They had been first promised a limit of a 'few weeks', then 'six months', and now it was already over a year and the restrictions had hardly diminished, if at all. Here the speaker seemed to prevaricate. He started to explain about the drift of radioactive particles from Chernobyl – how the fall-out had spread across southern Europe and had come north to Britain from over Spain: he made a movement of corroboration with a curving sweep of his hand.

'I am reliably informed . . .' came a firm intervention from the back of the hall. The speaker paused. Several heads turned. 'I am reliably informed,' Idris resumed, 'that the radioactive particles reached North Wales and Cumbria via *northern* Europe.'

The speaker registered surprise. He bent to the young man in the bow-tie beside him. He straightened. 'Much as I would not wish to disagree with the questioner at the back, the movement was definitely across *southern* Europe. I'm bound to say, there is a lot of inaccurate rumour about.'

'Including from Llangower nuclear power station, apparently,' came Idris's voice again.

'Oh, I really think not.'

'*They* say the radioactive material came across northern Europe.'

'I'm awfully sorry to say you must be mistaken,' said the speaker.

'I'm awfully sorry to say I'm not,' returned Idris, with only a hint of mimicry. 'I've just spent the whole day there, with a senior physicist.'

The speaker frowned. 'I can only tell the meeting what I am reliably informed.'

'Reliably, hell,' said Idris in an audible mutter.

'I beg your pardon?'

'I wish to ask,' Idris pursued in a firm voice, 'if the speaker's

Ministry, or any other ministry, actually tested sheep in this locality before Chernobyl.'

The answer came back smoothly. 'I can assure you that comprehensive tests were carried out on a regular basis, covering a wide field of products, throughout the whole country. I ask you to take my word . . .'

Idris broke in. 'I said, Welsh sheep. Before Chernobyl. Yes or no.'

There was a marked stirring among the audience. The speaker was frowning again. He gave a half-glance to the chairman, who declined to catch it. A joust was developing, a champion emerging.

'Some of these matters,' declared the speaker, 'aren't always as simple as the questioner might suppose.'

'I prefer a man who has the courage to say, "I don't know". Or even, "I do know but won't say".'

The speaker was too experienced to become rattled. 'I can assure everyone present,' he said urbanely, 'there are no facts concerning this issue that are not available to all concerned. Are there any other . . .' And his gaze ranged his audience for some other, tamer questioner. But before there was a chance, Idris was back at him.

'What if the becquerel counts don't come down? What if there are three or four hundred farms still restricted next year, or the year after that?'

'Please feel quite assured,' said the speaker, 'that Her Majesty's Government will not renege on commitments already entered into, by which no farmer affected will suffer any consequent financial hardship . . .'

'That's not what I'm asking.'

'What are you asking?'

'My family have been rearing sheep on my farm for eleven generations to my certain knowledge.'

The speaker leaned back. His head tilted ever so slightly, and the tiniest wisp of humour touched his cheeks. Into the unexpectedly prolonged pause he dropped,

'And so?'

'You don't understand what I'm talking about,' cried Idris.

It was a mistake, that comment. It allowed the other the advantage, which he caught up at once. 'I'm afraid I don't,' he returned, in puzzled condescension.

And Idris had no words, no immediate words in the English language to define his meaning, for in it lay *the* meaning, which was too dark, too secret, to be turned into words that could be readily slung across a hall at a public assembly. Before he could martial this secret depth into a shaped sentence, such as might be a vessel for his meaning if not quite the meaning itself, some other voice from the audience had raised the question about the *reputation* of Welsh lamb: What was to be done about that?

Instantly the speaker was back on his safe ground of money, how Her Majesty's Government was helping to fund a publicity campaign, in co-operation with this very Welsh Union of Farmers. The initiative had slid away from Idris. He felt a surge of anger, and amid mounting blather about money for this, money for that, his mute exasperation turned on his fellows. It was because he, Idris, had for a moment discomfited the speaker that his fellow farmers were after the man now. They scented a weakness in him, but they were in hue and cry after the decoy quarry. Money, money. They would not let the man go: when the chairman attempted to close the meeting, they would have none of it. Some had returned beery from the Bull, and now began to block the exits to the place until some further monetary concessions were made. They had him hemmed in, right there for their taking – or so they supposed in their frailty and their folly. Idris would have none of it, and they, jeering their demands, had forgotten Idris. But of course the official could give no concessions. He was only a puppet. In the end they jostled and bundled and half-frogmarched him into the hotel entrance to oblige him under threat of violence to call the Secretary of State for Wales in person on the telephone in London. This was actually achieved: the Minister took the call in his official car, returning from some dinner party . . . and conceded a vacuous promise to look again at the figures, which the mob took to be some sort of victory. Idris would have no part of it. He got into his van in the thin rain heavy of heart.

As he turned off the public road into his farm track he saw at once that somebody had left the farm gate open. He could have half the flock out on the road! By luck the animals were all further up, away from the road. He shut the gate behind the van.

Four hundred yards further up, approaching the cottage and its farmstead, his lights picked up another car drawn up in the yard. He recognised it as his father-in-law's. It was late for him to be there: something was amiss, he sensed – perhaps it was the old man leaving the gate open at the bottom that told him.

No one was in the living room, though the light was on. He climbed the narrow stairway and found them in the bedroom. Mair was there in bed, her woolly over her nightdress, the father in the chair beside her.

The old man stood to greet his son-in-law. 'Mair was taken bad,' he said. 'I thought I'd come up since you weren't at home.'

'It's nothing,' Mair smiled, and held out her two hands to her husband, which he took. She was so delicately beautiful, and her eyes glittering in her white face.

'She's been fainting,' the old minister said.

'Geraint telephoned father,' she explained. Geraint was their neighbour. 'He was up with the eggs, and when he was here I fainted. I told him it was nothing, just a little dizziness, but when he got home he telephoned father. He shouldn't have.'

'It was the correct thing to do,' said her father. 'And I called Dr Roberts before I left. He said he'll be up here to see her in the morning unless in the meantime I call him to say it's emergency.'

'Of course it's not emergency!' Mair exclaimed, making the English word a portentous intrusion into their Welsh speech. 'It was only breaking the eggs that upset me. I broke four of Geraint's eggs.'

'How?' asked Idris, sitting on the coverlet.

'When I fell over,' she replied. 'Except for that, I wasn't upset at all. I've been a bit dizzy, that's the total of it.'

Idris still held one of her hands, gazing at her, and she looking back at him guiltily, almost naughtily. Above the bedhead was a coloured reproduction of G. F. Watts's *The Light of the World* in a fine elm frame which had been given them by Mair's parents on their wedding.

'What's this "dizzy"?' he demanded.

'Every now and then,' she said.

'You never told me.'

'But it's nothing. It amounts to nothing.'

She was never ill, always so resilient. She had borne her eldest boy John in this very bed, coming into labour so quick: four days later she was about the house again.

'She's been overdoing it,' her father said. 'It's the cows, they're a ball and chain, those cows. And up at nights with the lambing on top of that, it's too much.'

'I'm getting those milking-machines put in,' Idris declared.

He thought she would object, but she didn't, and he was bitterly reprimanding himself for having failed to accept that modernisation, for being the stubborn peasant that he was, to his angel's cost.

'Geraint came up to milk them tonight,' she told him. 'Now then,' sweeping away his solemnity, 'tell us all about Llangower, and just what Gerry said.'

So Idris began to retail to her how Gerry had rehearsed the theory of the process and then conducted him through the technique of it. When he told of viewing from the high gantry the four mighty yellow turbines that sent their power out across the Midlands and fed the national grid, the minister intervened to quote from the temptation of Jesus as told by Luke, viewing the kingdoms of the world from a high mountain, '"And the devil said unto him, all this power I will give thee, if thou wilt worship me."' Mair laughingly chided her father as if he were suggesting Myfanwy had married a devil: they all knew Gerry to be a good man, if not a godly one. The old man gave a little shake to his head, as if to say that the world was racing past him, he knew not what to think; and before long his eyes grew heavy. It was Mair herself who insisted it was time for him to take himself home.

It was therefore only after her father was gone, and Idris was lying beside her in their bed, that he told her of that burlesque of a farmers' meeting, of the slipperiness of the speaker, and how the farmers themselves had shamed their cause. For they barely perceived what their cause was.

[viii]

Mair was already about her normal duties when Dr Roberts called in the morning. He examined her in the bedroom. He considered the possibility of a problem of the inner ear, affecting her balance, or alternatively a touch of anaemia at the approach of middle life. He dismissed any connexion with the aches in the bone that Mair had reported a few weeks earlier at the height of the arduous lambing. He prescribed rest, and a course of supplementary iron. At her father's suggestion, it was arranged that Myfanwy's Vera should move into the cottage with her aunt and uncle for the time being, until Mair had strengthened up again, to help in the home and on the farm.

Vera settled in easily and worked with a will. In a few days Idris had taught her how to milk the cows. It seemed to him she had a natural way with animals, and seeing her there in the byre, her heavy buttocks overflowing the milking stool, it was as if she had been a farm girl all her life. In the evening she was content to watch the coloured pictures on the television, and took a wondering delight in the contests where ordinary people not unlike herself won lavish prizes for the tiniest of feats. Idris would spend his evenings with the printed literature he had brought back from Llangower, and further documents he had sent out for, which went into the question of how radiation falling as rain could affect vegetation and, in turn, the milk and flesh of animals. Gerry himself had truly admitted that much was still to be discovered concerning the transmission and effect of radioactivity.

Mair followed her supplemented diet, and took to resting in the afternoon. Idris now supervised her activities watchfully and tenderly, and made sure she was spared the strenuous work she had customarily undertaken. She took up the crocheting she had not done since the boys were little. But as the spring broadened into summer, she did not seem to strengthen. She was often announcing that she was on the point of recovering her normal vigour, but it did not happen. When the boys came home for the first fortnight of their vacation, before joining a student party bound for the eastern Mediterranean, she busied herself with cooking for them, washing their clothes, tending for them as she always had. Once, in that period, after a big wash, Idris found her struggling – literally struggling – to turn the handle of the heavy mangle with her two hands, and scolded her so fiercely that her eyes filled. He could never remember having brought tears to her eyes. And when the boys were gone, she was exhausted.

Dr Roberts ordered that she should be admitted to hospital for tests. It was a routine precaution, Dr Roberts said. And Mair herself declared it was an adventure, going to hospital: all she had ever been to was the local town's maternity home with her confinement with Evan, seventeen years ago, and that hardly counted. Idris drove her all the way to Wrexham himself in the grey van, and took the opportunity to buy a gross of fence posts in the station yard, a job-lot, at so favourable a price that he didn't risk asking the lad to repeat it. As soon as he got home, he settled down at the table in the kitchen to resume his assembly of all available facts and statistics so as to have them at his command should the local Member of Parliament pay him a visit, for such had been proposed by the branch secretary of the farmers' union.

What did Idris think? The figures were equivocal. Did radiation enter some plants more than others? There were indications that animals grazing the higher ground were more affected than those in the valleys. Yet not all sheep grazing the top were affected. Of course, animals varied just a little in their grazing habits: he'd known that all his life, one animal taking in myrtle leaves or young reeds or even bracken, which another would avoid. Nobody had monitored *that*. The claim had been widely made that the greater incidence of radiation among top grazers was because on the May weekend after the Chernobyl disaster a year ago the rain only fell on the high ground. What rubbish! It had rained on hills and valleys alike. And more than that: it had rained across sixty per cent of Britain that weekend, as the meteorological records showed. So the authorities were demonstrably engaged in fudging when they made out it rained only in North Wales and Cumbria that weekend. They had fudged the fact they had never actually tested the sheep before Chernobyl. They had been wrong repeatedly in their predictions, though they denied it. First the ban was to last 'a few weeks'; the Minister said so in Parliament. Then 'six months'. Now already a year was gone and just as many farms were still restricted. They fudged and smudged because they dared not confess ignorance. His father used to say, 'Only fools or knaves will never admit, "I do not know".'

At least Gerry had had the courage to say, 'There are some things that are still mysterious to us.' And Idris had thought, even in the midst of the light into which Gerry had drawn him, *I should say so*. Gerry had said it in a tone to suggest it was only a matter of time before the mysteries were cracked. Yet what did Gerry and his scientists suppose? Even with all their light-bearing technique, their Lucifer power? That they would one day govern the spin of the earth, master the seasons, create life, stop death?!

Was that not the root of all this blight? That they presumed a right to *solve* the riddle, wipe away the *mysterium*? Did they not remember that that was the *cause* of the devastation across the land – when the sphinx in the ancient story had its riddle cracked? That which may never be truly cracked, but only entered. Why, his right hand that could turn an unborn lamb in the womb could reach deeper into the heart of the riddle than any micro-electronic calculations of the scientists! Why, this lumpish Vera, busying about him now in the narrow kitchen preparing his tea, was closer to the riddle's core by the very cunning of her innocence, than any quantity of laboratories or scientific calculations! She who could scarcely write or read, whose grubby frock – she had arrived with several but would wear only one – seemed to fit her body nowhere.

Idris leaned back in his chair. Oh, he needed Gerry. He respected Gerry. Science had its role. Did he not dip his sheep in chemicals? Yet when it came to the secret things, were they not only to be known *secretly*? And which of them could not do that? When Gerry had witnessed him rendering Dafydd ap Gwilym's poems the other evening, he had taken them as a species of entertainment. But on that matter his brother-in-law would be mistaken, Idris perceived when, after nightfall, settled in his rocking-chair, without his Mair to share his thoughts, he pondered in silence. There wasn't much to be shared with Vera.

'You like rocking yourself,' she said suddenly, 'like a big baby.'

He glanced across at her and smiled. He hadn't realised he was rocking.

'You want to lose yourself, don't you,' she grinned. 'Into where you came from.'

He never knew quite what to make of her, though he was contented working with her. They seldom spoke, now that she had taken his tips, and proved her ease with beasts. Yet she admired his bodily strength – he could tell that – and his sure skill with his beasts. He could share those creatures with Vera.

Three days later the Ministry inspector was to visit to test the sheep Idris wished to take to market for sale or slaughter. It was the same day that Mair was to be released from hospital after her tests, and so it had not been possible for Idris himself to bring her home. The inspector was late coming. Idris was listening out for them when his dog's chain rattled and he looked up to see the white van labouring up the track. Yet as it approached, he saw the red marking on its side. It was Mair returning in a small ambulance!

He had not thought of an ambulance – yet what else besides an ambulance would a hospital have to move a person? Anyway, it was all seats inside. She stepped down so daintily, in that best suit of hers she had worn to go in, and crossed to him immediately, eyes a-sparkle, to where he stood on the threshold.

'Well, you look as if you've seen a ghost,' she laughed. 'Aren't you going to say hello?'

He was putting out his arms for her now, smiling for her, and she found his brown cheek with her lips as he drew her to him and he could feel the vitality of her as of old. Vera came out of the byre below in her boots and grubby frock and called up a greeting to her auntie, grinning. The two of them stood there watching the little ambulance turning, Mair leaning into him, and Idris called to Vera to shut the upper gate after the ambulance. At once Mair began to tell him of the novelties of her sojourn in hospital, of the weird and wonderful fellow patients, whom she took off in little vignettes of mimicry that soon had him chuckling. None of the tests they did caused her discomfort, although one evening and the following morning she was required to fast. And now in any case, she declared, she felt quite well, although the hospital doctor had made her promise not to return to her full strenuous duties until Dr Roberts gave her the 'green light'.

Then while they were still there before the cottage with the warm sun pushing through, she regaling him with her experiences, they caught the sound of the gate by the road. Idris's dog was barking again, and in a moment they saw what might have been the little ambulance returning. 'It's the man from the bloody Ministry,' Idris declared. 'Three hours late. I've had the tups penned up since bloody seven.'

'Don't be so hard on them,' Mair chided. 'What a job to have to do!'

But he felt it like a pall being thrown across his new happiness. He watched the van winding up the track, and Vera opening the upper gate for it. His mind was on the Ministry men, not on what Mair was saying.

As he conducted them on foot along the 'Roman road' and on up to the shearing shed he hated them for their intrusion, for their expulsion of her vibrancy in him. But for them he might have stolen her away upstairs and made love to her, which during her indisposition they had denied themselves. They had filched that moment from them, these intruders. He wasn't going to carry their scientific equipment for them. He refused to volunteer it. The older man – he was Idris's age – was the regular inspector, who had greeted Idris with his practised, shame-faced humour: he carried the clipboard. Vera carried the paint-pot and the torch-like scanning gun. The inspector's weedy youth, who had eruptions on his skin, struggled on behind with the scintillation counter, making heavy weather of it, though it was no bigger than a typewriter of the larger sort. Thus they processed up in silence, only the mew of a wheeling buzzard to accompany them.

The shearing shed itself was raised off the ground, and the tups for market penned in the space beneath. Idris remembered his father building it: he had helped him as a child. It was here they kept all the rosettes they had won at the local shows over the past thirty-five years, father and son – red for First Prize, blue for Second, yellow for Third. There was a whole bank of them in neat rows stuck up on the wall, like a bank of dials in the control room at Llangower. And alongside on the wall was Idris's family tree, beginning eleven generations ago with another Idris ap Owen and stopping at his own two boys, who he dared not suppose might either of them take on the farm when the time came. He had drawn up the tree himself, and stuck it up there for the boys.

The inspector got to work at once, pressing the scanning gun against the hindquarters of each animal as it was released from the enclosure by Idris. Vera held them still. It was hot in there, and heavy with the damp-live smell of the sheep. The youth recorded the radiation readings: if the scintillation counter showed over 210 sieverts the animal was penned off to have its head shaved later and daubed with the violent green paint.

The inspector treated the exercise jocularly, with little hints of apology. To the youth it seemed a tedious chore and an insult to his right to be employed at superior activities or not to be employed at all. He found his relief in smirking at the cricket-pad Idris wore to protect his knee from the buffeting. Then the youth's eyes settled on Vera's heavy young body and thick arms as she wrestled with the tups, gripping their fleece to still them. Yet whether she was aware of his attempt to peer up her dress and multiplied his chance of doing so was hard to tell.

When they were done, and a dozen or more tups shaven and paint-branded as 'dirty', the inspector's eye fell on the pile of printed material Idris had left up there on a bale of wool. He picked up a document headed 'Nuclear Power and Radiation: the Facts', issued by the Central Electricity Generating Board.

'You won't get anywhere with all that,' he assured Idris.

He knew of Idris's initiative: they all knew roundabout. But he had made no reference to it up to that moment.

'I intend to get to the bottom of it,' Idris replied.

The inspector gave him his jocular look. 'There's no bottom to it,' he said.

'That's lucky for you,' Idris returned with a viciousness to his voice, which kept the man and the rest of them silent for most of the tramp back to their van. This time there were two buzzards patrolling aloft, mewing.

One morning a week later Idris received a visit from the local Member of Parliament, accompanied by the constituency agent who had advised him of Idris's authority among the farmers. The MP was a Welsh-speaker, of course, a Clwyd man, a Welshman through and through, open-faced and comradely, quick off the mark and his curly hair brushed up a bit without a visible parting and giving him an inch or two extra on his short stature and a clear Welsh look. It was apparent from a few moments of the start of his visit that he shared Idris's and his fellow hill farmers' concern at the continuing, or even increasing, evidence of radioactivity among the headage of upland sheep. There was no room for doubt about that. His agent had with him a printed résumé of the many occasions the MP had raised the matter in Parliament since the start of it all after the Chernobyl accident, including his two major contributions to agricultural debates, dealing especially with equitable compensation. He knew his farming facts well: he quoted statistics of the heavy penalties some 'restricted' farmers had endured that even Idris had not known of. He seemed at home on the farm. He devoted the greater part of his forenoon to the visit, making a tour of most of Idris's two hundred acres and even going up into the shearing shed where the rosettes were. He scrutinised the family tree enthusiastically. Idris mentioned more than once that it was 'a whole way of life that was at stake', and the MP took the point so readily and gravely that it seemed to Idris superfluous to dwell on it, delve into the meaning of it. He was a man, surely, who had done all the thinking on the subject that it was possible to do: he had taken into consideration every view, every statistic and fact and factor, and even had mapped out, as it were, what was *not* known and might always remain *un*known. He was very much aware of what he termed the 'resonance' of the issue, that element in it which was so difficult to put across to the 'English Parliament', in the mischievous description he used among his fellow Welsh.

He was a man of Idris's age, and despite his eminence with a voice at Westminster and as political spokesman for a whole tract of Gwynedd, Idris the poor hill farmer had begun to feel a real kinship with him by the time he came to take his leave. His interest had not stopped at the farm and its animals, but extended to the progress of the two boys: he himself had been a governor of the college they attended. Here was a man who deserved his eminence; he had earned it.

When Idris returned to the cottage for his dinner, he told Mair, 'That man truly understood what we're up against. It'll make all the difference having him with us.'

'What sort of difference?' Mair asked.

'When it becomes clear what has to be done,' Idris replied.

[ix]

The evening of that same day, Dr Roberts drove up to the cottage. The three of them had just finished their tea, and Vera was clearing away the things. Idris and Mair came out to greet the doctor. He was a family friend of them both – had been so for most of their lives – and only a year or two short, now, of a retirement he knew he had earned. He wore a moustache, and his rumpled tweed suit was of the same colour, like a wintered copse. His sagacity was wintered too, having shed all that was unneeded.

'I thought I'd just come to see how my patient is getting along,' said the doctor as they conducted him into the living room.

'She's improved since Wrexham,' Idris answered. 'Haven't you, Mair?'

Mair smiled, and before she found an answer the doctor intervened, 'How's the lassitude?'

'It comes and goes,' she answered.

They settled in chairs before the range. The doctor had his bag beside him. Vera stood in the doorway to the kitchen. 'How's Vera?' said the doctor, and Vera grinned. 'And how about a cup of tea for me, Vera?'

'Have you got the result of the tests, doctor?' enquired Idris.

'From Wrexham?' said the doctor, oddly vague. His glasses called for inspection. 'Most of them are in. There'll have to be a course of treatment, so far as we can judge.'

'What's the problem?' Idris asked at once. He glanced at Mair, pale and erect. She was not looking at them, but into the fire.

'There's an imbalance in the blood cells that's shown up,' Dr Roberts replied. 'We can't ignore that. It'll need a course of treatment.'

'What treatment?' asked Idris, suspicious.

'In a minute I'll take Mair upstairs and then we'll decide,' said the doctor, taking his tea from Vera. 'Now, Vera can continue on with you for a while?'

'Until Mair is quite strong again?' Idris queried. 'You can stay on with us, Vera, can't you?'

'Oh yes,' Vera said. 'I can stay on.'

'Vera likes the country life – don't you, Vera?' said Mair.

'Yes.'

'That's nice,' said Dr Roberts.

'Will it be long?' Idris enquired.

'Oo,' the doctor said, supping, 'you can't ever be sure. These things can take their time, take their time.'

'What's the name of it?' asked Idris.

'It's one of the forms anaemia can take. Now then.' The doctor put down his tea and picked up his bag. 'Shall we go upstairs for a little examination?'

Mair led him up to the bedroom. Idris remained below. Mair and the doctor were spending a surprisingly long time upstairs. Dr Roberts had imparted no precision. 'An imbalance in the blood cells.' What did that mean? 'One of the forms anaemia can take.' Which form? And what sort of time can such things take? A month? Three months? Yet there seemed not so much amiss with Mair since she had returned from Wrexham, though she had kept her promise and avoided anything strenuous.

Idris sat in his chair, rocking, looking into the fire. Vera came up beside him quietly, bringing a mug of tea – an extra one. She had never brought him a cup of tea unbidden before. He thanked her, taking the big mug, his special mug. She remained there beside the chair, she too staring into the fire. She was a strange girl, Idris thought.

At last the doctor descended the narrow staircase alone.

'Now then, Idris. Be a good fellow and come down to the lower gate with me so that I don't have to open and shut it myself.'

Idris climbed into the little car beside the doctor and they set off down to the gate into the road with the doctor chatting about their boys. Pulling up at the gate, Dr Roberts said, 'Of course, she's a very very wonderful wife to you, is Mair.'

'She is, too,' said Idris.

'She'll need you, this coming period.'

'Why, specially?'

Dr Roberts switched off the engine. 'She's not well, Idris. You may have guessed that.'

Idris felt the blood growing in the neck and around his ears, and when he spoke his voice was already thick.

'You've got something to tell me, doctor.'

'I'm not saying what Mair's got can't be treated. But it's a matter of holding it back, getting on top of it.'

'What?'

'The disease.'

They were sitting in the little car facing the shut gate. Nothing came or went along the country road beyond. All at once a grey squirrel appeared on the gatepost and scuttled along the top rail.

'What is the disease?'

'You've heard of leukaemia?' The doctor shifted round to glance sideways at Idris. He had had to break into English for the name of the actual disease.

'Yes,' Idris said, his face bunched now. 'Does she know?'

'I haven't told her. I see no purpose in telling her. There'll be a long course of treatment. I've readied her for that.'

'And then she'll die?' Yet it was hardly a question.

The doctor was silent for a little.

'I'm not saying that.' He hesitated. 'We all have to die some time.'

The squirrel was back on the gatepost. Idris's eyes were half-blind. He saw the squirrel swimming and squirming along the rail it had first arrived by. He heard his own breath coming in pants.

In due course he said, 'When?'

'You don't want to think of it like that, Idris. The point is, you've to be the strong one. She'll need you all the way through, whichever way it turns out.'

Idris felt a great volcanic rage boiling and welling inside him, and threatening to flood his head so that he feared it should burst. The doctor was speaking again – that some leukaemias proved curable and in others long periods of remission occurred – when he broke in on him.

'Leukaemia is a form of cancer?'

'Cancer of the white corpuscles of the blood.'

'Is there any known cause of it?'

'It's a cancer, Idris. It's not known why one person gets it, another doesn't.'

'The Hiroshima victims. They got it.'

'People get it all over the world with no undue exposure to radiation, Idris. I know what you're thinking . . .'

He was hardly thinking at all. His head was swirling and boiling like the yellow-hot caldera of a volcano.

The old doctor got out of the car and hitched back the gate. He returned to the car, started up, and drove through slowly. He said, 'Have you ever thought of getting a telephone put in?'

'Why's that?'

'I could help you get a grant, for the installation. Without a telephone, you see, it could turn out that Mair would have to – well – spend longer in hospital. Let me know. You'll be needing Vera too. Come down and see me before the week's out.'

The walk back up to the cottage was the longest walk of Idris's life. He stopped by at the byre. Vera had begun the milking. When Idris came in she ceased the rhythm of her hands, and looked at him slowly, one eye holding him, the other eye off to the side. He guessed she knew the truth, whatever it was, though how he could not tell. She did not grin as she usually would. Then her hands began working again. How many million times had Mair's precious hands made those movements in the nineteen years she had been his, and living here? Nineteen years, morning and night. And to what avail? All that patient labour, all that white rich purity, to find the agent of death.

Yet Dr Roberts had not said death, not in a word. What had he said? He could hardly recall any part of the exact speech. He had not said she must die of this thing, this intrusion upon her. And Idris knew that however closely and insistently he was to question him, he would never quite extinguish the right to hope. Yet he knew already that he could not bear to hope, that he must be blind to hope, that if he were to be the 'strong one' – yes, that was the doctor's injunction – his strength could only be that of one eyeless to hope, like the last dark eyeless strength of Samson.

He went on up to the cottage. There was Mair in the living room, at her crocheting. He had watched how beautiful her hands had turned since she had given up the milking . . . this late fortuitous gift of beauty and delicacy that could have been hers always, if he had known she was to be taken from him.

'You were long, Idris,' she said. 'What were you up to? Dr Roberts has given me two boxes of tablets and he says I'll have to visit hospital from time to time for a special treatment before I get quite right again. I've become quite the little invalid!'

He was hearing her across an immense distance, as if she had become a star and was calling down out of a night sky.

'Doctor says I've to cosset you and treasure you and that'll make you better quicker than any medicine,' Idris replied, plumping down beside her on the settee, and tilting to kiss the delicacy of her neck.

'Oh,' she protested, 'you're so prickly, Idris Owen, it's like having a hedgehog down my dress. If that's cosseting, I'd best get better fast.' But he held his face against her, to hide his eyes in her hair.

[x]

A wildness possessed him now. It did not grow in him slowly but was in him instantly. It was all inward, because he must not betray whatever it was he might know concerning Mair, yet they were quick enough to perceive a different force in him, a ferocity, a savagery, a darkness. And he himself was sure that Vera knew, although in what way she knew he could still not tell.

The fruit of this wildness was a burning conviction that Llangower nuclear power station must be swept off the map. The reactors of the existing power station were nearing the end of their approved twenty-five-year life span and the proposal was being mooted by the Ministry of Energy and the Central Electricity Generating Board that a new and even greater nuclear power station should before long be constructed on an adjacent site to replace the old. The prevailing mood among the people of the locality was against it, for most knew of questions unanswered, including that question as to why sites in underpopulated regions of open countryside far from the great cities were chosen for such nuclear plants if the powers themselves knew all the other answers.

So if there was a change in Idris it could be ascribed to the low anger in the air, or when not quite anger, the unease. There was a common suspicion among ordinary folk that they were being duped or palmed off with half-truths and would in the end, whatever their objections, be overridden. In any case, Idris himself sustained his command of such facts as were accessible. One early morning upon another, the little red van of the Post Office wound up the track to the cottage bringing printed material that Idris had sent out for concerning radiation, or Chernobyl, or nuclear power, when in the past the postman would have had no cause to visit them oftener than twice or thrice a month. And every evening Idris would be studying the papers in the living room. Nothing else seemed to occupy his leisure, such as his leisure was. Mair would be at her crocheting, or sometimes at a book, Vera before the television set with the sound off – she seemed to mind little whether the sound was off or on – and Idris at his papers.

The change was observed in Idris by Mair, and also by Myfanwy and Gerry who visited most weekends to be with their daughter. They observed it from certain half-finished sentences, or asides, or silences. It was not apparent in direct discussion. Yet the change was apparent to them: a possession from within, a darkness, a recklessness. The humour had gone out of him, and the zest and relish for life they had known him for. So that when he soon put it to Gerry that he wished to return to Llangower, Gerry found himself to have become wary of his brother-in-law and stalled him, laughingly. 'But Idris, you already know as much about the place as I. What would be the purpose of another visit?'

'The disposal of the used water, for instance. I saw nothing of that.'
'But we did talk about all that. We went through it all.'
'I saw nothing of it.'

'There's nothing to be seen, Idris. It's all underground. You know from the diagrams – it's all quite clear. There is nothing more secret about that part of the process than about any other part.'

'If there's nothing at all secret, then why should you object to my paying a return visit?'

'Oh, but Gerry's not objecting,' Myfanwy intervened.

'Indeed, of course I'm not,' Gerry assured him. Though he was wary.

'Well, then,' Idris said.

And so it was settled, for a certain date.

As for Idris himself, he was aware of the new darkness in him. It seemed to him a darkness not so much made by Dr Roberts's terrible prognosis concerning Mair as *revealed* by it. The source of it was something other than a great grief to come. Idris knew this, and he knew it with a precision because of the picture that hung above the bed where he had slept beside Mair ever since they were first married, that had been given by Mair's father off his own wall. Not only could that bland untarnished Jesus bring him no comfort as the 'Light of the World', but he could not bring himself to look at it any more. Oh yes, there might well be a God of Light with a soft white face, with his calm claim that all would be revealed, given time, given the appropriate circumstances. That would be Gerry's God, if he could admit to one. But what of the God of Darkness? The God of the *ultimate* mystery? Which man cannot dare approach unless he is ready to risk death?

All his life, out in his woods and gullies and high bald pastures, he had allowed himself to suppose that these Gods were one and the same. But now he knew it was not so.

In returning to Llangower he had a special purpose which he did not reveal to Gerry. It may be said that he achieved this purpose. But to what avail?

Gerry, grown wary of Mair's Idris – confused and troubled by the invasion of one world by another – perceived this purpose and frustrated it. The Director, he in the very throne of authority, was not a personage upon whose pattern of life one could just break in. This Director presided in accordance with certain routines of preparation and procedure. If there was one who required to see him he would require first to know why. If it were a stranger, an outsider, he would require to know not only why but who. Moreover, Gerry felt obliged to remonstrate, in the midst of this incomprehension of one world by another, 'For goodness' sake, Idris, where d'you suppose all this is going to lead in any case?' He was in the course of remonstrating exactly thus when his office door opened. The figure who by chance walked in was instantly recognised by Idris from a photograph in a printed article, and Idris – although Gerry's introduction had been one-way only, 'This is my brother-in-law, Idris Owen' – had not let go of the pale, soft hand before declaring, 'I was wanting to speak with you, 'aving some questions that require answers.'

The Director was at once amused and intrigued by the boldness of his Senior Physicist's visitor. He was a large, comfortable man with authority that stemmed from an inherent good order and sage tolerance that sounded in the round Englishness of his voice.

'And what questions are those?' he said right off.

Idris returned a look of astonishment – or was it something more violent? It was Gerry who spoke.

'My brother-in-law farms sheep, just over the hill. He . . .'

'Aha,' said the director. 'So you think it's not Chernobyl at all, it's Llangower!'

Idris was caught – suddenly – stripped of words. 'Not everything is fully understood,' he stammered. 'Is it?'

'And what is not fully understood?'

Again Idris stared at the man, something in his head blocking his words. He wanted to say that the very premiss was not understood. That their light – if light it was – shone out of a darkness as life itself broke forth from a sea of death. Broke forth only to sink back.

But because of his mind's shouting, his mouth was silenced.

The Director resumed gently, 'There's nothing *I* know your brother-in-law doesn't. And very likely he knows a good deal more.'

'Oh, we've had good long talks,' Gerry said quickly. 'Idris knows his way around blindfold, eh, Idris?'

'But it's you I came to see,' Idris blurted out.

'*Me?*'

Gerry said, 'I was trying to explain to Idris . . .' But Idris cut him off.

'It 'ad to be you.'

'Well,' the Director smiled, 'shall we sit?'

He motioned Idris to the chair he had risen from, and settled himself along the desk, equidistant from Gerry. He removed his heavily-rimmed spectacles, polished them, replaced them, and resumed his amused scrutiny of this unusual intruder. He saw the line of delicate white skin along the forehead which the cloth cap sealed against the weathering, he saw the oddly ferocious eyes in a handsome face, the powerful hands, the gleaming boots. 'What is not fully understood . . .' he prompted.

'If the effect of Chernobyl is still with us, why was the time span so grossly miscalculated? We were promised a few weeks. Then six months. Now it's a year and just as many farms are restricted as ever.'

'It's a matter of the speed of the decay of the radio-caesium,' the Director replied blandly.

'We were told in writing, within days of the first tests on lambs after Chernobyl, the radio-caesium decay would begin spontaneously, *at once.*'

'Well, decay has certainly occurred. But we have had to learn about the tendency for radio-caesium to become concentrated in this or that living matter.'

Gerry intervened, 'We've been through all this, Idris.'

But Idris ignored him. 'Caesium 137 takes thirty years to lose half its radioactivity. So what was the Ministry doing pretending that the high counts would last only a few weeks?'

'It was a fair presumption that the dispersal would have seen to that.'

'So they didn't know.'

'To be fair to us here,' the Director said with a sympathetic frown, 'we were not responsible for what was said about Chernobyl. Nor for Chernobyl.'

'And we were also told,' Idris hammered on, as if the other had not spoken, 'that the category of radiation found in the animals pointed clearly to Chernobyl. The fact is, Caesium 137 is exactly what you give your fish in your lake here.'

'After filtration and ion-exchange and storage.'

'Oh, I know all about that,' Idris returned insultingly. 'But what is left is Caesium 137.'

'To a negligible degree.'

'So far as your testing shows.'

'You mean?'

'You test your fish, for instance. You take an average.'

'Of course.'

'And what variation is found within the sample? Those figures aren't kept, or they're kept hidden from the likes of us. But up on the farms, we see it closer. I can 'ave two lambs on the top, born the same day. Three months later one will show a becquerel count of twelve 'un'red, and the other of three 'un'red. What's 'appened? Nobody knows. One side of a mountain 'alf the lambs fail the test, other side of the same bloody mountain they all pass. What's 'appened? Nobody knows.' His eyes burned.

Gerry put in, 'Idris is worried about the incidence of cancer among the local people.'

Idris caught his breath. He turned to his brother-in-law then back to the Director. 'I could be talking about cancer,' he murmured, 'I could be talking about the animals. They're only symptoms, both of 'em.'

'Symptoms of what?'

'Symptoms of what we don't know, mon. What we may never know, unless by inference.' And added, 'By what's sacrificed.'

Gerry furrowed.

'But we know a lot about radiation in the environment,' the Director said, still quite bland, refusing to be riled. 'And its effect on people. We're learning all the time.'

'You're experimenting on a living creation.'

'That's always going to be the case, with any attempt by science to advance us.'

'Advance us to where?'

'Before the beginning of science, life-expectancy was about thirty years of age. Today it's nearly eighty. But I must be on my way.' And the Director rose.

'You forget something,' Idris said, with menace. 'That it's not your creation to play around with.'

The Director threw him an indulgent glance. 'Whose is it, then, if one may ask?' he said, and immediately moving to the door, commented aside to Gerry, on his purpose in calling in, 'Another time, perhaps?'

Gerry said hurriedly, 'Isn't it time *you* were on your way, Idris?'

'When I've answered the man's question.'

Idris now leapt up and placed himself with his back to the door, the poor hill farmer confronting the bland nuclear power station Director.

'Come now, Idris!' Gerry exclaimed, rising too, astonished at what seemed to him a performance of wilful self-destruction by one for whose peasant wisdom he had long ago learned respect.

'Mankind can work with creation,' Idris announced, glowering, his back against the door, 'or he can work in defiance of it. This monstrosity' – and his gesture included the edifices in their entirety – 'is an affront to the gods of our land.' A fragment of a smile touched the lips of the Director. 'They will take the innocent as sacrifice. In the end, they will turn on the perpetrators. And that is you, my friend.'

The Director turned to Gerry and gave him a careful nod. Reading it, Gerry raised the telephone. 'I'll have someone take you down, Idris,' he said, and a moment later was speaking into the mouthpiece.

The Director had turned back to Idris. 'You will allow me, I'm sure,' he said suavely, 'to pass and to attend to my other duties.'

'Your first duty,' Idris told him, 'is to 'ave the place closed down.'

'Well,' said the Director, 'that's a point of view.'

'Don't think I don't 'ave no support, mind. Most of the inhabitants, for what they're worth to you. Our Member of Parliament – there's no mistaking 'im. An' several more besides, 'oo 'ave the power.'

He spoke in vehement bursts, as if from a gun, and was not finished before he felt the door being opened against his back. A thickset man in uniform pushed in. But Idris still blocked the way.

'Time to be getting along,' Gerry said, moving from behind his desk. 'We've plenty of time to talk all this out, you and I.' He was full of sorrow and shame.

'We've no time at all!' cried Idris.

Crossing to him, Gerry took his arm, gently, the guard the other. 'Why, Idris?'

'Why?' Idris's face had gone suddenly hollow, and out of this dark vacuity he peered first at Gerry, then at the Director, then back to Gerry. 'You don't know? My wife is dying.'

'Mair? Dying?' Gerry echoed. 'What of?'

'Dying of all that 'e don't know! Dying of 'is ignorance!'

For a moment Idris seemed as if he might fling himself on the Director, who took a pace back instinctively. 'Aw no. I'm no goin' to 'it you,' he said calmly. 'I 'ave to leave this place of murder now anyway.' And shaking off the guard's hand he set forth down the corridor in his clumping boots . . . just he and the guard; Gerry standing, watching, speechless.

[xi]

Thus began the breaking of Idris upon the wheel; and thus, too, did Gerry and Myfanwy learn the exact nature of Mair's illness, although when Myfanwy spoke to Dr Roberts a few days later he was careful not to rule out the possibility of the treatment's success.

When Idris drove home from the power station he spoke not a word of what had occurred. Mair called to him from behind the cottage, where she was hanging out washing, but he went straight up and changed his clothes, and set off with his stick and his dog for his flock. How he loved her, but he could not touch her now, for she needed every ounce of strength to combat what was within her. How he loved her for her childlike limbs, her narrow child's knees, for the astonishment that her body could never shed, even in its secret sickness. He could not touch her, nor tell her what he was enduring.

He had gone dark and inward, Mair could see. He worked his animals, he fenced and ditched, he repaired his buildings. He was driving himself, she noticed. But he had ceased his private research. The postman still delivered publications and correspondence and research documents on radiation, Chernobyl, and nuclear power, and sometimes these would be left unopened for days. With the long daylight, he stayed out working late, and rose at dawn. He would take the gun in the gloaming very late and come back with rabbits. He took to sleeping in the boys' small room, so as not to disturb her, returning so late, rising so early. But she would hear him. When the boys came home for a week at the end of their vacation and he lay beside her as before, she felt his body to have become sealed away from her.

As for the boys, they noticed the change – scarcely at all in their mother, though they knew she was not well. The change they noticed was in him, a sealing away from them also, as if they had crossed to the other camp and were no longer with him here, in the place that comprised him. Some passing comment hinted not at the pride at their college success that he shared with Mair but at neither being there to carry on the farm when it had worn him out. It was an old theme, the next to inherit, and sometimes a cause of speculation, but never before this dark futility.

Twice during those months of long summer he drove her to Wrexham, and fetched her three days later, after the transfusions they were giving her to treat the 'imbalance' in her blood. She knew she was growing weaker, though there were periods of remission. Her progressive weakening was allowed for in the division of her duties. Vera took on more and more, and sometimes Mair would spend whole days resting in bed. They none of them spoke of the weakening. Instead they talked of when she would be 'strong again', or back to her 'normal self'. Myfanwy came to see her from time to time, but Gerry's duties seemed to keep him away those next few weeks.

It was Vera he had to depend upon. She throve. That summer she swelled and gemmated and ripened out under her cheap frock in secrecy or indifference. The secrecy was always present in her. The dumb arrogance of her body would catch him unaware. Yet she seemed without consciousness of herself. No one ever knew what she was thinking.

Then came the day of the county show. Idris went on his own, with his dog, in his best cap and jacket, and his shone boots.
   It was the big day of the year for the farmers, a celebration, omitting none, and was laid out over two large fields of a grandee's low-lying land, and a third field for the massed ranks of cars and vans and Land-Rovers and the wagons, trailers and boxes that brought the animals. At the far end an inflated jumbo, vast and yellow, with a curled uplifted trunk and a vibrating floor within, and blaring music, provided a focus for the kiddies; and, alongside, for the adventurous young, an abseiling contest put on by the Army trawling for recruits. And between those attractions and the assembly of vehicles, the agricultural show itself. There were cattle of all categories, horses, ponies, show-jumping, trotting, and a double row of tented displays of every kind of farm machinery or service for the modern farmer. Even the political parties had tents erected, with pamphlets galore on farming things, each with its well-attended licensed bar for supporters. But the sheep were relegated to a corner, and once the morning's judging was over, it seemed a neglected corner. Idris had not been minded to enter animals for competition this year and thus had reached the show after the judging, later than his fellows.
   The sheep farmers were drifting in disconsolate groups through the fancy contestants – the breeched young women on their jumpers, the Welsh cobs, the Palominos, the Women's Institute displays and the Carnival Queen. When they spotted Idris they seemed to gather to him, for he was a leader among them. They drifted on, fists round their crooks, a breed of their own in their flat caps high at the back, shrewd-eyed, and once past forty no longer quite straight at the hip. They spoke their own language which till the first pints were downed was half silence, a gapped necklace of monosyllables and tightening of the face muscles.
   They drifted past the Alpine Double Glazing and the Milk Marketing and the Forestry Commission. Then they found themselves in front of the big display of the Central Electricity Generating Board, one of the biggest of all, bent on converting the modern farmer to the use of every kind of electrical gadgetry. But all knew about the CEGB, that operated Llangower. They paused here, in inchoate hostility, feet apart, saying little. There were men up on the platform in CEGB overalls demonstrating this and that – electric

shears, high-pressure hoses. It was quite a little show in itself. A few more farmers came out of the Union tent and joined them, greeting Idris. Then one of them saw a familiar figure emerging from the back of the raised display, where the little pre-fabricated offices were. It was the Member of Parliament. He could have been a farmer himself by the way he was turned out, except that no cap covered the slightly unruly thatch he was easily recognised by.

He was down from the platform in a moment, of course, shaking hands – Idris's among them – greeting them by name. He had a wonderful memory for names. One of them said, 'When are you goin' to 'ave it shut down?'

The MP knew instantly what the man was referring to.

'If I were Minister of Energy,' he told them, 'I'd have the whole policy reviewed. Re-assess the whole policy of electrical generation. That's what we've said in the manifesto. And if we made any electricity for England, we'd make the English pay a proper price for it.'

The farmers had closed in a bunch, to catch his words against the music issuing from the yellow elephant, and the buzz of an electrical machine being demonstrated on the platform.

'A proper price is to shut it down,' another said. 'They've 'ad us flood our valleys for the hydro power. Not content with that, they bloody poison our sheep with nuclear.'

'There's still a lot more work to be done,' the MP said in seeming assent, 'before we know for sure what the consequences are. You're right there.'

'So you've told 'em to shut it down?' It was Idris who spoke, and when Idris spoke the men looked at him.

'Well, Idris,' the MP said. 'Llangower's there. Its existence is a fact of life. You've got to take it from that point.'

'Its existence is a fact of death,' Idris said.

'That's going a bit strong, Idris. Wouldn't you say?' The MP's eyes ranged the ungiving faces. 'Of course,' he hurried on, 'this contamination – that's an issue in itself. We've a way of life to defend.'

'And life itself,' returned Idris.

The MP assumed a puzzled look. 'There's no sound evidence to relate the contamination to Llangower. We mustn't rush in and demand closure only to find our evidence has holes in it.'

Someone said, 'So you support its continuance, then?' to which the Member returned ' "Support" is not what we say. What we say is "re-assessment".'

'A bucket of white-wash, you mean,' said a voice.
Idris spoke again. 'How many does Llangower employ?'
But the MP said he was stumped there. For a precise figure.
'Seven 'undred and forty,' came a voice.
'What's that then?' Idris followed. 'A couple of thousand votes?'
'Well,' declared the MP quickly, 'it's a big employer, you can't escape that.'
'Biggest in the constituency,' someone added.
'A lot to risk – a couple of thousand,' Idris repeated, nodding slowly, almost to himself, so that maybe the Member did not hear, for he was already saying that, naturally, the rights of the employees couldn't be disregarded.

Idris began to move away on his own, his face closed off, towards the yellow jumbo and its drooling blare and whine. He felt a low despairing rage. Only Geraint came up alongside him, his nearest neighbour.

'How's Mair, then, Idris?' Geraint asked.
'Oh, it'll be a while yet.'
'You'll tell me whenever you need an extra hand, like.' Idris was silent. 'She'll be better by bonfire day, maybe?'
But Idris had no answer for him.

Mair was withering before his eyes. She did not leave the cottage for days at a stretch. At the doctor's suggestion a 'day-bed' was made up for her in the living room for her to use when she did not feel strong enough to dress but wanted to stay part of the concourse of the little household, with Idris coming and going, and Vera in the kitchen. Mair could watch the television in the daytime when she was tired of her crocheting. Or she would drop into a light sleep, soothed by the drugs that Dr Roberts prescribed. In the evening, hers was like a voice from a white mask upon the pillow.

The bonfire was to celebrate the jubilee of the Queen's accession to the throne. There were many Welsh that had no truck with such an anniversary, but the hill farmers for the most part were not so minded, for they loved an opportunity to celebrate, and it was proving such a full, rich, fruitful autumn. Moreover Idris himself gave the jubilee his endorsement and when the question rose whether to buttress a queen in London Idris argued the sacred principle of monarchy: it was not a glorification of an arrogant Whitehall and an indifferent Westminster but a ritual of the divinity of monarchy. The Jubilee Committee had confirmed the hill on Idris's land as the appropriate *moel* on which to build the fire, for it had fulfilled such a function down the ages and its light could be seen on a clear night from similar bald summits a few leagues east and west where similar blazes were to be lit. Moreover, the very hill had a sanctity from antique days, as all knew.

It became a colossal pyre. A route for tractors was opened up across Idris's and Geraint's land, and fallen trees and mighty limbs were hauled up there by farmers from the whole vicinity. The requirement of the bonfire took Idris up into his own steep woods of oak and sycamore with his axe, for there was much useless dead wood standing or toppled. He would not take his dog if he went felling.

One evening of peculiar stillness he was there alone, in his steepest wood that overlooked the rough pasture beyond the gully. The autumn sunlight slanted in, dappled by the high cover of ancient oaks and also by the thin underbrush of hazel, and dappled again by the light ground-cover of hemp nettles and enchanter's nightshade. To Idris, the antiquity of man's link with this woodland beneath its venerated summit was as real to his senses as anything he could touch or breathe; and he himself was as intimate a part of the ancient place as all that surrounded him in secrecy and silence. He registered every movement and sound of living things in the wood.

A presence was surely there, not far from him beneath and along from him, but because of the play of light and the complexity of foliage there could be no certainty. No certainty, that is, as to what it was, because of the light's play, but the hirsute hindquarters none the less of a being whose place this was and always had been: a being which, though hooved, stood upright. Yet because of its motionlessness, and the play of light, there was no definition.

Idris was unafraid, for this presence or manifestation was a privilege; and he moved towards it purposefully, his feet slipping because of the steepness of the forest floor, so that sometimes he steadied himself with the haft of his axe. But what he had seen advanced ahead of him. He glimpsed it, surely, again; quite still as before, though he did not fancy that what he actually saw was more than a flank and upper leg.

He halted in wonder. Did he not have the scent of it also? He peered ahead and around him, where the filtered sunlight allowed. He listened to the wood around him, its rustles, its creaks, its snappings, its stillnesses.

When he emerged from the wood's perimeter beneath, the sheep were in the rough pasture unperturbed. He glanced below for his cattle, in case one beast had strayed up into the wood and the lowering sun had brindled its dark haunch. But he saw them all there, all four, far below, across the rough pasture and the gully and tilted field with its single sycamore, and shortly at that distance Vera emerged to drive them in lazily, for milking.

Should he speak of this manifestation to Mair? He was minded to do so, but when he carried her up to her bed that evening and laid her beneath the picture of Jesus with his blazing lantern, the *Light of the World*, he could not do so, because what he had experienced was something other, not known to this Jesus. And afterwards he refrained, too.

Yet it did not leave him, but remained with him like an authority privily bestowed; a power foretold, available in its own time.

[xii]

By the night of the bonfire he knew that Mair was sinking. He could put no time to it, for it had been so slow a draining away. He had never asked Dr Roberts 'How long?' What would have been the purpose? And now he knew she was sinking. Of course, it was the reverse of what they had once pretended, that it was to be by bonfire night that she would be better, that she would be fit to join him in the glow of it at the celebration. But they had not spoken in such a fashion for a few weeks now, and now their question was whether he should leave her side to go up to it.

She still just sustained an outward cheerfulness and from her day-bed in the living room insisted that Vera accompany him to the bonfire: it would be such a great and rare event, and so close at hand, on their own hill summit. She was so insistent that he sensed by not going up he would distress and strain her. The telephone was in now: she could call Doctor if anything were to go amiss.

So he went. Vera had even put on a clean frock for it, and thrown an old coat of Mair's over her shoulders, though it was a warm night for so late in the season, and wonderfully clear.

It was indeed an enormous bonfire, as big as a house. They were all up there, three or four hundred from the surrounding farms and hamlets. They had kegs of beer up there in plenty, and music of their own making. They torched the pyre at eleven p.m. sharp and a few minutes later they saw the prick of light on the far summit eastwards where another group had lit their blaze. Idris drew on the beer freely, as did Vera too, though he soon lost her in the mêlée. They were all gathered round the great fire, men and women and children, in joyous wonder at the power and invention of its upward leaping, the roar and triumph of it, the terrible heat of it that lit their ape-eyes with awe, and shone to a ruddiness the points of their cheeks and noses and gaping blubber lips. They were the primal folk of these hills, making their declaration to the universe in fire and beer. Several carried resinous torches that moved puddles of light among the mob, and here and there dancing broke out since one man had brought an accordion, two or three had fiddles, and another a flute. The dancing caught like the fire itself and in a minute the whole motley was swirling and stamping, feeding on its own frenzy.

Idris saw Vera among the revellers, then lost her again, then a moment later she was beside him. The flames of the fire caught her looking up at him skew-eyed in abominable mischief. She was right against him for a moment, in the throng, thigh and belly and breast, and then away from him, but only a handbreadth, and he felt the power of his manhood leap and harden for her like oak made on the instant. He took her by the flesh of her arm and propelled her ahead of him until they were out of the mêlée and beyond the first circle of light. She stopped suddenly and he bumped her, so that she felt him inadvertently, and she dodged away from him and on towards the darkness. But he was after her fast, and they had already reached where the summit had begun to fall away in hollows of bracken and patches of gorse, and the oaks just below in the steep lea.

He tripped her there as it might have been one of his ewes, though with his foot, and she fell or crumpled to the earth with barely a cry – more a gasp that he heard as endorsement of his blood's intent. For in a trice he was upon her with his rod and she receiving him with her dress pulled up to her dugs and no impediment that he was aware of, no knickers, no nothing between him and the total of her flesh that took his hammering with her own counter-hammer, and each blow with a groan in her throat that was neither pain nor joy but the summit of each together. Until they could bear no more and triumphantly were done. And from where they lay the pinnacle of the great fire and its hurtling sparks were visible on one side and on the other the crowns of the ragged oaks that the fire illumined.

When the boozy farmers saw Idris re-entering the circle of the fire's light, they greeted him as some long lost hero though he had been absent from them scarcely a handful of minutes. He was unaccompanied: Vera had stolen away on her own. The men had more beer for him, for themselves too. He felt the triumph in his blood now, as dark invulnerability. The farmers plied him and gathered to him, and from somewhere the idea emerged and then took on substance that there and then they should descend and storm Llangower. They could see the lights of the power station eight or nine miles below to the west as if it were in reach of them. Idris felt the plan surge in him, and his own invulnerability merging with the invincibility of all of his fellows together, they whose ancient rights upon the place burned with the invincibility of the fire.

The women and children were gone now. The farmers clambered on to the remaining tractors and trailers and farm vehicles. They piled on the last of the undrunk kegs, and with resin torches still aflame set off on the winding descent to the road, certain of a victory somehow.

[xiii]

When Vera entered the cottage and peered from behind the curtain that separated the entrance from the living room, Mair opened her eyes. She was very weak now and felt herself ebbing, although when she had telephoned her father she had made no drama of it. There was no purpose any more in calling Doctor.

Vera was dishevelled, she observed, her dress smeared and pulled at, as by twigs or brambles. She wondered where Idris had got to, but did not say anything. Vera paid her no attention, but Mair followed her through eyes half-closed brushing herself down with her hands and straightening her dress and then drawing herself up so that her breasts stood out under her frock like two fists. Then she crossed to the spigot and rubbed her face clean with a plastic sponge left on the trivet. Now she took up Mair's own bag and rummaged in it until she brought out a lipstick. Mair could see her cross to the harmonium and sit before it on the stool, which she bolstered with a cushion from the settee. For a mirror was set in the headboard of the harmonium above its music-stand, and however dim, the light was enough for Vera to smear her lips by. The band of vermilion gave Vera a clown's mouth, but she gave herself a whore's leer in the glass, delighting in this image of herself. And Mair guessed. It was all she saw.

The mob of drunken farmers in their motley of vehicles turned off the road into the driveway that, in the language of the knighted architect, inflected with the contours of the land. They did not trouble with any car park, but ranged their vehicles in line before the power station's actual gates like an investing army of mediaeval times with their siege-machines before a stubborn fortress. Some of them relit their resinous torches. The sight of the place after the long hour's trail through the night re-aroused their defiance. Yet the vast implacability of it, the ominous vibratory hum with which it filled the night air, did in the same instant demonstrate their declared aim of 'storming' it as something other than feasible. At least they would spoil for a battle with the enemy if they could draw them out. And sure enough there emerged from somewhere a few unarmed guards in uniform to gather agitatedly behind the gate and the wire-topped high-paling steel fences.

The besiegers needed a champion: they had one in Idris Owen, and they heaved him drunkenly atop the gatehouse roof. He too was drunk, but not so drunk – whatever the liquor in him – to drown the secret ferment that possessed him, giving him his force and giving him speech. He stood there with the huge immaculate bulk of the building looming behind him against the night sky. But he too looming, ape-like, woolly – for he had lost his cap – half blocking the blank ghostly façade.

All at once floodlights illuminated the entire perimeter, and a raucous cheer rose up as if the lights were a signal of combat engaged. Idris turned to the throng of upturned faces and rallied them in his own language.

'Now they can see who we are! The sons of Gwynedd!'

Vera was startled by the sound of a vehicle, then a car door slamming. The cottage door was pushed open, and when the old minister entered there she was in sudden alarm to face him.

'Oh!' he exclaimed. 'It's you, Vera. What have you done to your face, then? Playing games?'

He glanced across at the figure of his daughter, her eyes half-closed, on the day-bed.

'And Idris?' said the old man. 'Still up at the fire then?'
She gave him a slow leer. 'He's gone with the men, I expect.'
'Where to?'
'There was talk of Llangower.'
'At this time of night?'
The leer spread. 'He 'ad a bit, you know.'
'And Mair?'

Vera looked towards Mair as if noticing her for the first time. The minister unwound his scarf and crossed to the day-bed.

'Mair?' he enquired softly.

She did not respond.

One arm lay on top of the sheet in the warm little room. He raised it gently, and the hand fell limp. The old man's face went dark. He touched her eyelid with a finger tip. It did not flicker.

'You must clean up your face now, Vera,' he said. 'The time's gone for playing now.'

'They can see the faces of the sons of Gwynedd to whom the land belongs,' cried Idris. 'The sons of Gwynedd and the sons of Llewellyn and Glendower by whose leave they are here. But by Llewellyn and by Glendower, that leave is about to run out. We are cancelling their licence! We have revoked our toleration!'

He could feel the spirit of *dyfal* descending, giving him wing to soar and defy.

'Their stifling laws, their throttling language – they shall carry them back across the borders.'

Cheers and jeers at the uniformed guards greeted each sentence.

'They have supposed they can murder us by stealth. They blight our air and poison our water in the name of their cheap English deities of efficiency and progress. Tonight they are hearing the voices of the gods who have slept too long. As the very sky is our witness! We shall be rid of them! We . . . shall . . . be . . . ourselves!'

'Open the gates!' cried one of the farmers.

And the cry went up, 'Open the gates!' repeatedly, from the whole throng, and the few still on the tractor-seats gave rhythm to the chorus on their horns. Some of the farmers began to hurl insults at night-shift staff who had emerged from the building to stand in doubt and curiosity behind the guards. Someone called to Idris to go down over the gatehouse and open the gate from within, but Idris's attention was caught by the lights of two vehicles approaching at speed along the driveway, one of them a police car with its blue light flashing. They pulled up beyond the range of floodlights and he did not see who got out.

'Open the gates!' the chant continued, alternately in Welsh and English, roared through the iron palings.

Then all at once, looking down, Idris saw Mair peering up at him, pleading. She was like a face seen in a vision whom he could not reach with words. Yet it was not Mair; it was Myfanwy, pleading with him above the tumult, but the plea was not in her voice, which he could not hear, but in her face. And beside her, Gerry. So the men saw Idris kneeling on the gatehouse roof to catch what this woman was saying to him. But he could not.

Idris turned to Gerry beside her, and called to him over the rampage.

He put to Gerry the single interrogative, *'Mair?'*

Gerry, full of anguish, was nodding to him slowly.

'Gone?' cried Idris, in English.

By now a single policeman had gained the roof and was standing beside Idris, who himself had regained his feet. But neither had touched the other.

'Listen,' he cried in Welsh, in a vast and terrible voice. They all looked up at him, and in seconds the tumult was raggedly extinguished. They saw their hero suddenly and inexplicably changed. The policeman was standing away from them with his head lowered.

Idris gathered himself with immense effort.

'We came here,' he said to them all – and they were so silent now he need scarcely raise his voice – 'we came here to tell these people that it is not their world but ours.' There was only the hum of the power station for answer.

'It is our home, for so long as we want. It is their world.'

He drew the knuckle of his wrist across his eyes.

'It is our past. It is their future. The past is dead. The hills have buried the past. The word for home is buried with it.'

One of the power workers from behind him called out jeeringly, 'let's hear it in a language we can understand, brother!'

Idris made as to turn towards where the voice came from, where the charge hall rose a hundred and eighty feet. In a voice that carried his last cry across the whole assembly, both sides of the fence, he repeated in English, 'In a language they can understand? Yes. *Their* world. Their *future* . . . If you will not speak their language, be dumb!' Then back to his own people. 'Until the dead rise!'

There was a strange silence. A single Welsh voice called, 'Traitor!'

Idris faced in the direction of the voice, shaking his head, and there were no others to take up that cry, for they were stunned, and in great awe at what they had done and where they were, yet were still close to him, holding to him still, and holding him up there, even now in his devastation and his distress.

And as for him, Idris, his eyes were raised now towards the high far horizon, the line of black against the night sky, scanning eastwards and racing along the tops of the overlooking land. But he could catch no prick of light. For the great fire is sunk down now to a throbbing heap of mighty embers. No one remains there. It is all abandoned . . .

Wait a moment. Is there not some motion, after all? Withdrawn a bit, where the glow from the embers just reaches into the first of the high oaks and their protective saplings? A motion only, a choric shifting? A rhythmic motion of limbs, black against the glow of the embers? Gone before it may be properly ascertained? And whether of beast or men would defy proof yet defy denial.

Lady-killer

[i]

It was nice to have the parson visit us, even though he did little more than hesitate by each bed with a cheery 'How's things?' He said it in such a way that if you had replied 'I'm dying' it would have seemed all part of God's bright plan, which he would have capped with an apologetic titter. He was a trim man with almond eyes and a monkish fringe, and although he must have been nearly fifty, his face had no lines that you could see and his little mouth was like a child's. That was the remarkable thing about him. He seemed to have got all this way through life and nothing had happened to him. Certainly he must have been without sin, but that must have been mostly because he had been without temptation.

The only bed he stopped at was the one nearly opposite mine. He would pull off his gloves, unbutton his heavy clerical cloak – it was winter outside and a particularly hard one too – and settle down beside the bed for five or six minutes. From where I lay I could only see his back-view or his half-profile. That bed was occupied by a patient who was surely sicker than any of us. In fact, he was the only one of us who it occurred to me – in an undefined way – really might die, even though the common ailment of all of us in this ward hardly constituted terminal illness. He lay in bed all day staring at the ceiling, apparently wide awake, but quite motionless. He read no books, took no newspapers, never put on his radio headphones, and when the television came on in the evening it just as well might not be there. The only times he came to life were to be offensive to the nurses, who were obviously frightened of him. Once he brought out a little tin from somewhere, rolled a cigarette and started smoking. This was strictly against regulations. The rest of us were aghast. When one of the nurses happened to come in and ordered him to put it out, he took another deep draw. She actually had to pluck it from his hand.

Sometimes, waking at night from the discomfort of my legs, I sensed that he too lay awake, his eyes open on the dim ceiling, just as he did during the daylight hours.

No one else visited him except the parson, and he received each of his visits in exactly the same way. He would stiffen under his sheets, his stare would intensify, and his mouth tighten under his beard. When the parson spoke to him in an undertone he would never glance at him, and his response would be an abrupt and aggressive monosyllable. None of this seemed to affect our man-of-God's cheeriness, which absorbed everything like the very finest soft tissue, although the almond-shaped eyes under the monkish fringe would sometimes take on a sort of humouring concern, like one responsible for someone else's difficult child, and every now and then a small frown would appear only to disappear a moment later without a trace.

One afternoon the parson brought him some sort of document to sign. It took a while to persuade him to do so. I couldn't imagine what it could be or what function he might be performing for him. At first I presumed he took particular trouble with that patient because, as the visiting hospital cleric, he judged him to be in special need of companionship and spiritual sustenance. Then it so happened that he was passing my bed with his customary 'How's things?' just when the patient opposite was irritably resisting a nurse's attempts to plump his pillows and make him more comfortable. The parson caught my eye and confided, 'Always was like that, even as a lad.' He tittered, and added, '*Spoiled.*' And the tiny shake of his monkish head said that this was a cross he had long had to bear – however gladly.

Only then did it dawn on me that they must have known one another all their lives. Nor was he the hospital's padre, I perceived: he came on these visits expressly to visit the man opposite, and simply took in the rest of us as pastoral fodder, as it were.

This was surprising, because the patient opposite gave me the impression of belonging nowhere, a man without antecedents or definable social status, about whom one could tell nothing. Whereas the parson was utterly placeable: you could have described his wife's sensible shoes and have a confident guess as to his table-napkin ring. Indeed, the patient seemed to me as if he might have been brought in here from some home for the destitute. It was the way he ate that gave me that idea. When the meals came on their little plastic trays with their bowl-shaped partitions, he would pause for a moment, staring at the tray, and then fall to like an animal, very rapidly, gobbling up everything except, I noticed, custard. I even thought I saw him shovelling down the portions in a random order, starting with the chocolate shape and *then* to the moussaka. Of course, the food was fairly unpalatable, no better than any hospital food, yet he treated it with contempt, like so much fuel to keep him alive until the next supply.

There was also a mystery about his ailment. The rest of us had trouble with the arteries of our feet and legs, and some of us were to have by-pass operations in that region of the body, or were in the post-operation stage. We shared notes on our ops and prognoses. Of course, the patient opposite exchanged no information with anyone, but there were signs that whatever was wrong with him differed from the rest of us. He was there before I arrived, and an operation had evidently taken place since from time to time a surgeon – although not he who had tackled our by-passes – came to see him, presumably to inspect the progress of his handiwork behind the curtained screens they put round him. He was still unable to walk, and when he reached the stage of being able to visit the toilets in a wheelchair, the hospital provided him with outsize plastic slippers to cover his bandaged feet.

Then one of those inexplicable 'general post' change-abouts took place. The man next to me went home and the bearded patient opposite was moved across to take his place. It was an uncomplicated transfer for him because he had no possessions whatever – no photographs or books or vases of flowers. Not even (so far as I could perceive) a wallet or purse, although there was a little pile of loose coins left over from a pound or two which I guessed were provided by the parson. (I noticed the ward sister had called in a male nurse to see to the move.) He protested, of course, with flaring glances and interrogative grunts to the nursing staff. The vacancy he filled alongside me was the corner bed, and I guessed the staff had decided to put him there because being so uncommunicative he would thus deprive only one, not two, fellow patients of neighbourly conversation. If that was the reasoning, it turned out differently.

I do flatter myself I am a good listener, and I have noticed that even those I do not know at all intimately have a tendency to confide in me. Mind you, I have sometimes suspected that far more confidences are vouchsafed than those who receive them suppose to be the case. As for my new neighbour, however, I have no doubt. He began to take to me because he had to. He had a story to tell, and he must tell it now. It was late afternoon on a cold, bleak Friday and against the dark roofs of another wing opposite we could see the rain becoming undecided as to whether to fall as sleet. All at once the voice beside me said,

'I'm going out tomorrow.'

I was astonished. They were the first words he had addressed to me since moving across the ward three days previously, the first words, so far as I could recall, he had addressed to *any* fellow patient. His announcement was clear and unmistakable. And as I have said, he seemed to be the sickest patient of all of us. I responded instinctively, 'I beg your pardon?' and he repeated at once, but conspiratorially,

'I'm going out tomorrow.'

The tone of his voice made me ask, 'Do they know?' The only answer to that was a glint in the eye. He saw me catch the glint. A finger went to his lips, and a slow grin spread under his beard like a face at the window of a house you thought was empty.

'But can you walk yet?' I enquired.

'Better than they think.'

I was being admitted to a plot: that was evident.

'Where are you going to?' I felt bound to ask.

'Out,' was his mysterious reply.

'Why not wait a bit longer?'

'Sunday,' he said. 'Monday'll be too late.'

'Too late?'

He didn't want to answer that directly. After a careful pause he said, 'You want to know why, don't you?'

He was watching me carefully, and I wondered whether the purpose of this strange intrusion was to lead me on and then snub me with silence. And yet something about his voice – a well-spoken voice, incidentally – suggested a pleading need. I answered, 'Yes,' as blandly as I could. I saw his eyes go dark. I knew at once he had a story that must be told, and that it was I who had been chosen to be led through dark and terrible caverns.

'Do you know Saudi?' he asked. I confessed that I did not. 'A pity,' he said.

'Why?'

'It would make it easier to understand. It was where it all happened.'

'What?' I enquired.

He pushed back the bed-clothes and swung his bandaged feet to the floor, pulled his hospital dressing-gown around him, and sat himself down in a chair alongside my bedhead. To my disgust, he pulled his tin from his dressing-gown pocket, calmly rolled a cigarette, and lit up. I didn't mind for myself, I'm bound to say. But what would the other patients think, or the nurses, of my condoning a flagrant breach of regulations? I stared at the ceiling, as if I had hardly noticed.

His name was Roy Fryer, he said presently. Oddly enough, I hadn't thought of him having a name. A name implied so many things. A provenance, for instance, a mother and of course a father, a baptism perhaps, years ago, though how many, I realised, I could not guess.

He could be anything between his early forties and sixty. Naturally he had a name. Everyone did. And a life that had gone before . . .

The point at which he chose to begin was, it seemed, just a few years previously in – of all unlikely places – a splendid modern hotel in the Saudi Arabian capital city, Riyadh. 'You know about the great oil bonanza?' he asked.

I told him I remembered it all happening, not so long ago.

'It was my last throw,' he said.

The way he had sat himself was facing me and the wall behind me. I looked down now that his thin cigarette was finished and realised that he had fixed his eyes on mine, but eyes that were without any expression. They were not even 'glittering' like the Ancient Mariner's. By contrast, it was their very emptiness that held me: the eyes of a dead man in a body that still lived and had a story to tell. He seemed to me now like someone who had come back from the dead, but unwillingly – back to a world that bore no meaning for him.

'You know,' he said, 'those very modern international hotels? I had been there a week already, spending about three hundred dollars a day just for the two of us to stay there, me and Peverill. Then the girl came in.'

There he stopped. He stared puzzled, first at his lap, then at the wall or through the wall.

'That was the beginning of the end of me,' he said. 'That girl.'

This hotel (Roy Fryer said) was the only top-class one yet opened and if you wanted a government contract you had to stay there. You would not get the respect otherwise. So the prices were sky-high: three hundred dollars a day for the two of them just to lay their heads on the pillow. It was a superb place. Monumental splendour. Soaring columns of dark marble, and at their feet clusters of leather armchairs, deep and soft. That's where Peverill and he were drinking apple juices – 'cider', the waiters called apple juice out there, which was ridiculous in a country that forbade alcohol. Four dollars for a couple of apple juices.

He saw the girl first. He had glimpsed her before, down the two broad steps to the great foyer. He said, 'There's that girl.'

Peverill would never notice a girl. He never noticed anything. That was where Peverill was lucky: nothing stirred him. If the roof fell in he'd brush the dust off his jacket and go and find somewhere safer to sit. Fryer told him she was the prettiest woman he had seen in that hotel in four visits. Peverill actually put his glasses on and twisted round so that his nose and his chin and his Adam's apple were all in the same line.

'Hard-boiled, I'd say, Roy.' That's what Peverill said. Hard-boiled.

She looked Irish to Fryer. Good colouring: petite, snappy. She was with a fat Arab he couldn't identify. He supposed she was a high class call-girl, and he told Peverill they ought to get into that racket – get out of printing into call-girls. His agent Siriani had told him of a middle-aged Saudi prince who at last got away to London on the loose and had procured a young lady for five days in the hotel suite, a Yorkshire lass, and when the five days were up she held out her little white paw and he dropped in eighty thousand quid. He borrowed Peverill's pocket calculator and worked out that at the absolute minimum it cost him five thousand quid per roll in the hay and some of them would be gaspers. ('I thought, I wish I was a whore,' Fryer said, and held me with that same utter emptiness.)

He was like that, in those days. Easy come, easy go. He liked the ladies. They liked him. He was a good-looker. He had the knack. He had a wife and children, mind. He had a wife and children, in a manner of speaking.

Fryer stopped here and looked about, up and down the wall again, seeming to search for them – the wife and those children – to prove what he said was true. Only when he knew he couldn't find them did he resume.

'Wife,' he repeated with a little jerk of the head. 'And two boys.'

Siriani came up and plonked himself down beside them. He was a Palestinian – Fryer's agent, everyone's agent, you could say. He depended on Siriani. He had a sly face and flat hair, brushed across. One thing you always could be sure about Siriani: you were never getting the whole truth out of him. Of course Fryer asked him again when their contract was going to be signed and Siriani said it had to go to His Excellency the Minister to initial and then to the Monetary Agency to endorse and then back to the Minister to sign. It could take another fortnight. That meant another five thousand dollars in hotel bills.

'Mr Fryer is not patient,' Siriani said to Peverill in his slimy whiny Levantine way. 'In Arabia it is no good to hurry. If you hurry, people ask themselves, "This gentleman, why is he in a hurry?"' Siriani infuriated him when he spoke like that, so plump and safe. Almost certainly Siriani knew they were backs-to-the-wall, had to land that contract if the company was to survive that summer. Fryer had promised the men at the works he'd come back with the contract. Siriani had sussed all that out. He was tormenting him – took pleasure in it.

But after he'd seen the girl he felt differently. With a girl, you see, he wasn't so afraid. A girl made a man a man.

Siriani knew her. Fryer asked, Whom did she belong to? Siriani – (did I know what he said?) – he said, 'She is the sales director of an earth-moving company based in Kuwait. She has got for her company a very big contract.'

He couldn't believe it. He had never heard of such a thing out there in Arabia. The Arab she was with was one of her fellow directors. Siriani said they had a special name for her: al Khattira. (Did I know any Arabic? I shook my head.) It meant, the Dangerous Lady. Fryer asked why *dangerous*. 'You want to meet her?' Siriani said.

Well, he brought her over. She was like a flame in the dark, his dark of course. He would have me understand he had no woman at that time. Lynette, his wife, she had gone off, if I wanted the truth – he couldn't blame her. He wasn't much good without a woman. (His blank gaze moved slowly towards me. 'I'm already beginning to tell you about myself,' he said.)

This woman was called Felicity Flynn. Sales director of an earth-moving company! It was unheard of.

He said at once, 'You're Irish, right?'

She was surprisingly quick to come back, 'I've never set foot in Ireland. My mother wasn't Irish, not Irish at all.' He didn't know then what lay behind this. (Again I got his eyes in which all experience seemed to be cancelled.)

Siriani explained she was born and bred in the Gulf. Fryer asked her if she had married an Arab sheikh yet, and she told him, very assured, that she hadn't married anyone, if that was what he wished to establish. So he asked her, casually, if she shouldn't be providing a second generation of Gulf English, for one's parents must be allowed the ancestral role, one's mum particularly.

'My mother isn't alive, Mr Fryer,' she cut him off. She had eyes like an unscalable wall of ice. And all the time he was powerfully attracted by her, *challenged* perhaps, for the very reason that he couldn't seem to make any impression on her. He told her he'd heard it said she was a very astute businesswoman. 'That's Mr Siriani pretending to flatter,' she laughed. Yet she had secured her company a contract, had it all signed up, with the Ministry of Public Works. A *woman*. Lynette, by contrast, never took a blind bit of interest in his business, used to pretend she couldn't understand why he did it since he didn't enjoy it, as if money for the school fees and the housekeeping and the holidays and the Rover 2000 grew on trees. But then, Lynette never challenged him to anything, never expected anything of him . . . except that he should be happy. Whatever that meant.

Felicity Flynn said, 'Mr Siriani tells me you're in . . . what was it?'

He replied, 'I was just saying to Martin here' – that's Peverill, his technical director – 'I'd rather be training horses as I did as a youngster. But it's printing. We've installed the first Arabic computer setting in Britain.' It'd been his idea.

'You find much demand?' she asked him.

He told her it was quite a contract: posters and booklets for the Ministry of Pilgrimages. But they hadn't signed yet, not quite yet. Then Peverill, being a fool, told her what it was worth – 'getting on for three million'. So she asked, 'Three million what?' Riyals, Peverill said. That was less than half a million quid. Fryer was well aware that Miss Flynn's earth-moving contract would be worth far more. And this was the woman he 'needed', Fryer explained, needed 'for himself', to get him through the coming few days of dreadful waiting for the Minister to return from the royal court in their summer retreat. Perhaps even longer than that, he couldn't tell.

I think Fryer must have seen a frown catch my brow. For he interrupted himself. 'You don't follow me, do you? What I am saying? I tell you. There was something about this lady. Every now and then I would come across a woman whom I knew I could – what's the word? – rise to. A woman to give me power to be my full self, to banish my . . .' He stopped. 'Banish my fear.'

Another moment's hesitance allowed me to say, 'Fear of what?'

He seemed surprised. 'You don't know fear?' His eyes began to roam the blank wall, then came back to me. 'A man needs a woman to be a man. Agreed? I see you frown again. It is not unusual, to respond instantly, take the gamble. I had learned about women as a boy, you see. I learned it from my mother.'

He blew his cheeks out, as if disguising a breaking of wind, and then I saw his lower lip clench beneath the beard – assert itself. I tried to let my face betray nothing of what passed through my mind at this curious pronouncement.

*

When Siriani got up to go (Fryer resumed) he made one of his awful homilies. 'This is Arabia, Mr Fryer. It is not Leathurr-head. I am an Arab. I understand these people. So does Miss Flynn. You must be patient. I leave you in good hands.' As he waddled off in his Italian suit, tight across his rump, he turned and smiled at her, the two of them 'winking across at each other like false lights luring a ship on to rocks'. (That was the striking simile Fryer used.)

Then the lady asked, 'Why Leatherhead?'

It was where the boys were at prep school, he explained, one of the most sought-after in the country. 'I've got two boys,' he told her. 'Thirteen and twelve. Bang-bang. Danny and George. Wonderful boys. Really wonderful boys.'

But she took no cue. She was setting out Fryer's miniature backgammon board. It had been a hopeless business trying to teach Peverill backgammon: every time he threw anything interesting, Fryer had to make the move for him. But he could see by the way she set the board that she knew the game. And here Peverill took his cue to leave them, saying he was getting in a shower before supper. So they were alone.

He offered her a cigarette, which she declined, and when he lit up himself, his hands shook. He had to have his fags, he explained, doing business in Riyadh, the Arabs playing cat and mouse.

'And you're Mr Mouse,' she said.

Of course, she didn't know the half of it. Next weekend his wife was taking the boys out and he hadn't even paid the fees. The following weekend was half-term – one was meant to pay before term begins. And they'd had such a to-do getting the boys accepted, the school being so sought-after. Lynette would know about the fees because she'd ask. She'd dig out the bursar and *ask* him. And then of course there was the company. The machine shop was on a three-day week already. Another couple of weeks in the hotel with the contract unsigned would just about wipe them out.

Fryer's gaze fell on me again. There was no pain in it, but no resolution either. There could have been no human brain behind the eyes, or if there was its function was to cauterise the humanity in him with its crystal memory. 'I told you it was my last throw,' he said.

I nodded.

He asked her if she really understood the Arabs. Honey-sweet one moment, arrogant the next. You think everything's agreed, then it's all in the air again. They couldn't answer a telex, so you fly out for an answer. Eight hundred pounds for an airmail stamp.

She reminded him it was his backgammon move. 'What's Siriani on?' she asked. Seven and a half per cent, he told her, and she tutted at its steepness. What was our profit? We'd be lucky to break even, he said. He simply wanted to get a foothold in the market. She frowned. He told her he had a bottle of whisky in his room. She retorted, 'What's the point? It's the quickest route to gaol. Can't you get along without it?'

Friday week, he explained, was half-term. His turn to take the boys out. He couldn't miss that. When he was sitting out there in the desert he kept thinking, 'They'll never be thirteen and twelve again.' And he took out a photograph from his wallet to show her: George and Danny, and their mother. Danny was the horseman, took after his father . . . George the swimmer. George could do anything in the water. All this wasn't quite as true as it ought to be, but he was aware of Felicity's interest this time. He protested to her that they didn't let them use the hotel pool, though he knew the answer: they believed the sight of a woman in a bathing-costume would release uncontrollable lust. In this . . . this suffocation, a pool would double one's chance of survival.

'It's all you're really intent on, isn't it? Survival,' she said.

She was looking at him now, and he felt her attention revive him. With her at his side, he had decided, he could secure the contract, turn his company round. With the right woman to believe in him, he could do anything. (I, for my part, wondered what had become of the photograph, for there was not a sign of any photograph by his bed, and his possessions were almost nil. Or Danny and George, for that matter, for no one ever paid him a visit, except of course the parson.)

When Felicity took herself off (he said), he did some desultory arithmetic on his calculator. Then he began stabbing at the calculator blind, pretending that the final number would be the money he would make out of the contract. It was like his mother in her decline, opening the Bible at random and finding the 'guidance' she supposed she needed in the first verse her eye fell on. He was just pretending, mind. But his mother, at the end, had got sucked down into religious goo, had persuaded herself there was really something in it.

When he opened his eyes there was Siriani settling into the armchair opposite him. 'Mr Fryer,' he said. 'I have not so good information. There is also a Japanese proposal. The Ministry of

Pilgrimages is also studying this proposal. The price is twelve per cent under your price.'

'That is why,' Fryer said to me, 'I went to see the execution.'

[ii]

All the time my neighbour had been speaking, I questioned whether he was a madman. His narrative up to this point was quite coherent, though it was difficult to see where it was heading. My doubts arose only from the contrast between his total reticence previously and now his determined loquacity, and from the curious fact of his own – what shall I call it? – *distance* from his compulsive account. I felt he was passing his story to me like a man ridding himself of a burden. It was connected with his original extraordinary announcement of his unauthorised departure on the following day.

'You are wondering,' he said, 'why I should wish to attend the execution. I will tell you this. I did not know at the time. It was only when it happened that I found out why.

'Oh, I was not the only one. There were several hundred besides me, but they came for different reasons, public reasons. I was the only Westerner, mind. They were all standing there in great clumps in the square outside the big mosque downtown. Restless, expectant. You don't know Riyadh, you said. Justice Square is in the old part of town, and the space is flanked by low-class flats with balconies and open-fronted shops below. One side is taken up by the governorate which is built in the Turkish style in two shades of stone. Opposite that, across the open space, is the mosque itself, and in the space the big square clock tower and one very tall solitary street lamp.

'When the crowd heard the police cars approaching – you know how those sirens yelp – they opened up to make a wide hollow square of which the single street lamp was the centre. Now the soldiers file out from somewhere, with their machine-guns, and one arm swinging right up to the horizontal, as if they know a bit of drill though they're really very scruffy. They halt and form an inner lining to keep the space clear from all us people.

'All the while, the voice of the preacher from the mosque is being amplified across the crowd from the minaret, and makes an echo against the governorate building. It is a terrible rasping voice.

'At my feet an old woman has a plastic bowl with blocks of ice and cans of Merinda and Vimto and Kaki-cola. She is the only woman I can see. I can smell gardenias. The old woman makes me think of my mother. I would like to crouch down beside her. I can see the rings on her fingers. Her hands are the only part of her flesh I can see, because of course she is veiled, but I would like to come under her veil with her. Can you understand that?'

'Certainly,' I said.

'You see,' Fryer went on immediately, 'my mother had died the previous year. When I was young she would say, "Look into my eyes." She would open her eyes wide and I used to imagine myself drowning in them, for they were just like the sea, just as beautiful. That would be when I was about ten or eleven. I was tall and strong for my age, and I heard someone say I would grow up to be a lady-killer. I asked my mother what that meant. Sometimes after that she would call me, My little Lady-killer. Or, My wee king, because of my name, Roy. I was an only child, you understand: the other child in my family was my step-brother, with whom I was obliged to share my existence, like it or not.

'Well, it happened that the ranting voice suddenly stops. Then all at once, the call to prayer. And everyone has to find a space to pray as the Muslims have to, bowing and kneeling, kneeling and bowing, all in the direction of Mecca. I can see right over all these people to the black sealed van parked in front of the governorate building. Here were men, you see, telling God – if there is one – that he has made a mistake, which they will correct for him.

'Just as soon as the last response is given, there is a desperate scramble, everybody getting back into his sandals and scrambling and jostling to get into position to see. The old men are ferocious, shoving and butting and wriggling under the shoulders of their fellows to get nearer the front. Some have climbed on to the bonnets and roofs of the parked cars.

'Now the black van's door has opened and a very small figure has descended, all in white, with a pure white headcloth tied so low over the forehead that it has blanked out the upper part of the face including, of course, the eyes. Now the crowd makes an involuntary surge, like a dog on a leash, and I have to go with it. And you know, I do not yet know why I am there at all.

'The little man, the victim, a common miscreant, a rapist or some such, is young and dark-skinned. He is led forward, barefoot on the scorching macadam, between a pair of policemen – his wrists tied behind him, of course. When they reach the lamp-post, they all halt.

Then the police withdraw, and the little man, blindfold and trussed, is left there entirely alone in that empty square ringed by the soldiers and hundreds and hundreds of us people who are entirely silent. So what does he do?'

Fryer turned to me, but as if he too were blindfold, and again I sensed that I had no function for him except as a listener. He had not even asked my name, for instance. He required nothing from me but attention, to be a mere passive agent by which he might be absolved of certain memories. I said, 'I don't know.'

'He sits,' he said. 'He sits suddenly. You know how an infant that has just learned to stand will suddenly drop to a squatting position. That is what he did, and settled there on his backside like a baby on the floor of its mother's kitchen. Then comes the executioner. Down the steps of the governorate building, a big man in a black headcloth and a black muslin gown, and in his right hand an unsheathed sword lowered to the ground. As he approaches – I suppose it was at a command from him that we could not hear – the victim stirs himself and reassembles himself into a kneeling position. The executioner taps the back of the victim's head with the tip of his sword to tilt it down and expose the tendons of the neck.

'I do then glance at the clock in its tower. It reads twelve-twenty-eight. And beyond that, I see a traffic signal turning from red to green. I suppose we have all held our breath.

'When that sword swept down and took head from body, I knew why I had come here. *Envy*. That makes no sense to you, does it? Envy. It almost stunned me, I can tell you, jolted me off my feet. And meanwhile the rest of them, hundreds of them, were applauding, clapping their hands wherever they had enough space to do so. Why? Because for them that sword had given a sharpness to their right to be alive. That little fellow, so much meat on the tarmac, was their evil, their weakness, their unspent lust. So much meat. I understood then that it was always necessary for someone to be a sacrifice.

'And there was the black executioner strutting back to the governorate building with the sword held up prominently before him now, like a penis just spent. They were all purged, see?'

The ward nurse coming round with the tea trolley was perplexed by what she found. Fryer had stopped speaking as soon as he saw her approach and sat there, alongside my bed, with his gaze fixed on the blank wall above my bedside shelf. 'You're not meant to be out of bed, Mr Fryer,' the nurse said, but I could detect that her concern was mostly for me. Typically, he gave no response. 'Did you hear me?' demanded the nurse. Knowing she would get nothing from him, I gave her a little nod to show that I was all right. Even so, she put his tea down on the locker beside his bedhead, where he could not reach it from the chair in which he was ensconced. He ignored it, and waited till she had completed the tea-round and left the ward before he resumed.

Returning to the hotel from Justice Square, he lost his way. Riyadh at the time was in a frenzy of re-building on its own site. The Inter-Continental lay on the perimeter of the city. He chose to walk, and his route took him into a maze of encampments and shanties of Yemeni labourers who provided most of the construction work force. Moreover, something had happened on the way.

The sundown call to prayer was sounding from all across the city as he entered the foyer. Peverill evidently saw him at once from his seat in the atrium behind the foyer, where he had been awaiting his boss while chatting to a couple of visiting English office furniture salesmen. Peverill was startled. 'I was streaked a bit with sweat, you know,' Fryer said. 'Dishevelled. It's a dusty place. Of course, I hadn't eaten all day.'

But there was something else.

'I was carrying a lizard, what they call a *dabb* out there – quite a fat, chunky thing, about eighteen inches long. There was some blood oozing from its nostrils. Peverill seemed very shocked. "You mean, you've walked with that thing for three miles?" he said.

'So I told him, it wasn't heavy. A couple of pounds. I wanted to give it a chance to recover. I found some boys stoning it, purposelessly. A group of Yemeni boys.

'The hotel staff got upset at once, and the English salesmen were quite ribald. One of them said he knew the locals ate these lizards, he had seen them in the market-place. They had two pricks, he said, and in front of everyone speculated why, and how, such lizards made love, whether "the missionary position or like doggies, one little doggie pushing the other little doggie all the way to St Dunstan's". Of course, he thought he was very funny, and tried to inspect it. Quite a little crowd gathered. Then some sort of manager came up and ordered me to take it out. But I refused. The manager got heated, and Peverill pleaded with me to let him take it out. I still refused. Then I heard Felicity's voice. "Did you bring that *dabb* in here? I'll take it." I was quite shocked when I realised she was there.

'I told her, "Some children were stoning it. You can't let people kill defenceless creatures." And she said, People often do. Then Siriani seemed to be among us. "Why are we fighting, Mr Fryer?" Felicity explained I was trying to save its life, but Siriani was quite angry and very firm that I should throw it out. So I repeated that I had stopped the children killing it.

'"Nevertheless it is dead," Siriani said.'

When Fryer looked at it again, he saw that it was dead.

'You see,' Fryer explained to me, 'they thought I was mad. Do you think I was mad? They knew where I had been . . .'

I recognised a gravity in his eyes. It was that same sort of look that enters people's eyes when, unexpectedly, they are about to break down and weep: all at once one realises they have entered a quite different, hitherto hidden context of involvement. This was a test of my attentiveness, of my right to hear his story, however odd or inconsequential or ridiculous. Apart from the glint of conspiracy when he had told me of his impending departure, this was the only moment in which his eyes had told me anything. I said,

'Not mad at all. I understand completely.'

He seemed at once relieved, but still suspicious of my ability to keep listening and following him.

Siriani (he said) then told him that he had come to say that 'His Excellency' the Deputy Minister wished to see him the following day, Saturday, the first day of the Muslim week. Did that mean that the Japanese proposal had been rejected? Certainly not, Siriani replied. His Excellency would discuss the price.

Fryer had arranged to take the evening meal that Friday with Felicity. Somehow, after the lizard incident, he did not know if she would hold to it. However, around eight p.m. there was a knock on the door of his room, and it was she. He even persuaded her to enter. He had out an illicit whisky bottle, of which he had extracted a couple from a friend in the American Trade Mission.

He was surprised she had come in, surprised that she had come to him at all. She took no drink herself, but watched him while he poured himself another. She sat at a distance from him on a chair. She was not dressed seductively, but sharply, efficiently, in contrast to his 'disorder' as she called it, his impatience, his hectic emotion. 'You cannot expect to be a businessman in the Middle East and represent our Dumb Friends' League.'

'You're a tough little lady,' he told her.
'You think so?'

Then (it seems) he began to spill it all forth, how he'd flown out four times, each time expecting them to sign. He *had* to be home by the weekend: it was half-term, the boys got out on Friday. If he went home without the contract, he went home to wind up the company. He would be finished. Wiped out. His house was pledged against the overdraft, the bank had the key. The boys would have to be taken away from school. No home, no school. Lynette, who had left him, had a bit of money: not much, but a bit. The boys would live with her and go to a day school. He himself would go on the dole.

And who would want the ex-managing director of a bankrupt company, who had no interest in business life anyway? He never wanted the company in the first place. He was really happy at the stables training two-year-olds. The business was dumped on him by the family – his father's family, to be precise. His father had left it to him in his will, though of course he knew it had been coming to him. 'You'll be your own master,' they said. It was quite the opposite: it became a tyrant.

Yet even his mother had urged him to take it on, she who had quit his father when he was a little boy and married her cold and boring widowed officer with his own cold self-satisfied little boy from his first marriage. His mother had always been proud of her own son's 'expectations'. 'Such a catch you'll be,' she used to say. 'Such a lady-killer, and money too.' She used to build him up, secretly, in rivalry to her stepson, because the stepson was always the good boy and her 'wee king' was always in trouble.

He had any number of girlfriends, and then he had married Lynette. The strong one. She made his home, the home for their boys. She was the only woman he ever wanted to bear his children. But he couldn't give up his old ways; he couldn't or just didn't, who could tell which? He had girlfriends. Always someone on the side. He tried to be careful, but she always got to know. They would talk it over: it was fashionable to talk everything out, in the Swinging Sixties. Can you talk back what's gone, what's been destroyed? In the end they tired of talking. They had the best sham marriage in the whole village. When Lynette walked out everyone was incredulous – almost everyone. They didn't blame him, they blamed her.

And here Felicity, sitting on the edge of his bed, said, 'They should have blamed *you*?' Despite the hint of scorn in her voice he answered, 'Of course they should.'

He had asked for it. Lynette walked out about the same time as the company's biggest customer, literally, walked out. There was no other bloke. He never quite thought she would. But when she made her mind up, she made her mind up. She told him she'd hated him for ten years. She remembered the day she admitted to herself she hated him because the admission came to her as a huge relief. Then she wearied of living off her hatred and wanted to go away and not have to think about him at all. She'd planned her exit for several weeks and had rented herself a little house elsewhere in the county. She'd been quietly digging up all sorts of plants from their garden and transferring them to her new garden when he was away at work. She said she knew he'd never look after them anyway, and the proof of it was he hadn't even noticed they were gone. The day after she left, the removal men came in their van with exact instructions as to which bits of furniture to take, with drawings by her of each piece. She always was pretty damned efficient.

Then (Fryer said) Felicity let him kiss her. They fell into a deep embrace. (I tried to imagine the actuality of this – for he was speaking of only a few short years previously – in that bedroom. I am familiar with the extravagant luxury of the modern hotels in such places: they flatter their guests by treating them as millionaires. Could such a husk of a man as I had before me, with a half-spent tin of tobacco as his only chattel, have filled such a role in the arms of an attractive and ambitious young businesswoman? I caught the sour breath; I peered at the hollow bearded face and the lost eyes and obliged my imagination to cast him thus, for there could be no doubt as to the truth of his account. And my imagination failed me altogether.)

Suddenly she pulled away from him, though he tried to hold her, his 'need' for her (as he said) 'so fierce'. She broke the embrace and stood up, straightening her clothes. Had he alarmed her?

Not in the least, she told him. He was rather drunk, she declared, and clammy, and stank of fear. She despised men who depended on drink, she told him. And here, in Riyadh, the whisky was madness. If they caught him with it, they'd throw him out, and that would be the end of any contract, the death of his company. What was all this talk of his – and he took such risks? It was contemptible, pathetic. Did he really want this contract? He was a travesty of a man. If she were the Saudi Minister she would disqualify him on grounds of character alone. He deserved no contract. He wasn't a *man*.

At last he turned on her. A lady sales director of an earth-moving company. What species was that? 'Al Khattira'. Was that a name to be proud of ? A sixteen million contract for shovelling shit and not a husband in sight. No wonder!

He had shouted after her, for she had crossed the room to the bathroom to see to her hair. She came to the doorway very cold, with glittering eyes. He could see she had found his bottle of tranquillisers: she had them in her hand. Then she repeated, almost in a whisper, *Did he really want this contract?*

'Why d'you ask?' he said. And after a long, strange silence she replied,

'I have a proposition.'

'A proposition? Concerning you?' He assured her he wanted the contract.

She looked at him hard in the eyes. It was a proposition of a most unexpected kind. It was that, if he won the contract, he would also win her body.

Fryer turned to me and said, 'Am I boring you?'

I protested at once that that was not the case at all. I was absorbed in his account – how could he suppose otherwise?

'Because,' he replied, 'you cannot believe that any woman would make such a proposition to me, let alone such a woman as I have described to you. Or you will suppose, if she made it, she could not have meant it. Am I not right?'

But I denied it vehemently, naturally. 'I have no doubt she was in earnest. It is strange, of course, but plausible. Strange but plausible.'

She was in earnest all right (Fryer continued). At once she began to go into the detail of his tender, in the light of the Japanese having quoted twelve per cent cheaper. What was his most expensive item? Paper. Had the Saudis specified the exact make of paper? No, but he had. Was that price specified in his tender? No, it was in the total figure. How much cheaper could an approximately comparable paper be obtained for? Perhaps eighteen per cent, but it wouldn't be as fine a job. So what about the colour processing? He subcontracted that to a dependable firm in High Wycombe. But were they the cheapest of the dependable processors? He had dealt with them for years. It'd be a breach of trust.

'The world is not an English prep school,' she rounded on him. 'Don't go somewhere down the road. Go abroad, go where the exchange rate is good. Listen to me. You're to have your new quote fully typed out tonight for tomorrow's meeting with the Minister. It's not yet five o'clock in London.'

It was a lot more complicated than that. Yet it was achieved nevertheless. At the Saturday meeting he risked a verbal promise of a fifteen per cent reduction in their price and by Monday night they had figures in from paper manufacturers and Italian colour processors that showed it was possible . . . and they could still make a profit. To his surprise the men at the works at home had agreed to forgo any union-dictated pay rise until after this job was completed, so Fryer had been able to drop the escalation proviso which the Saudis had always jibbed at. He and Peverill had worked round the clock, spending without restraint on telexes and telephone calls. Fryer amazed Peverill. He had never seen his boss like this before. He didn't know he had it in him. Fryer, for his part, said nothing to Peverill about the girl, nothing about the other 'contract'. And meanwhile Fryer had not seen her or had any contact with her. Only Peverill, hurrying through the foyer, had run across her by chance, and Peverill had reported – for Fryer questioned him – that she said nothing, just gave him a 'funny smile', that's all.

Fryer had Peverill agree they should say no word to anyone until all was signed. But they could – they really could – be on that Thursday flight with the Saudi contract in the bag, perhaps the first of many. That evening, late Monday, he fell to talking with Peverill, and he told him the truth about the boys, how the two-home life was beginning to act upon them, cripple them. George had lost his place in the swimming squad. Fryer was sure it was to do with Lynette and him. He wasn't swimming as well as he did two years previously. (It was he, his father, who had the pool in the garden: George swam with him.) There was no other explanation. And when he had bought Danny the ideal horse he hardly seemed to care.

Peverill said, 'What is it you want then, Roy?'

'I said,' Fryer retailed, '"It's not a question of what I want, or Lynette wants. There's another will at work that belongs to neither of us individually, but that both of us made." That's what I told Peverill. But Peverill didn't grasp it. So I tried to explain. Fourteen, fifteen years. It's a long time together. Something grows on its own, despite. The children, that's obvious. Those two boys. We made them. They belong to themselves, of course, but they belong to *us*, jointly, whether we're speaking to each other or not. A will for us, jointly. It hangs about.'

Fryer stopped. His gaze was on me again, then through me to the wall, or beyond, I couldn't say.

'I told Peverill,' he resumed, 'something I hadn't told anyone else.

'Lynette was always the one for the flowers, I've told you that. She knew the name of every flower in the garden, there must have been a hundred. I liked the trees – that's what I liked. Some of her flowers grew up my trees. Clematis, jasmine. It was the shrubs that brought us together, you can understand that. Especially the flowering shrubs. But that's not the point.

'What I went on to tell Peverill was what had happened the previous summer. It wasn't long after Lynette had taken herself off. She was living about forty-five minutes' drive away. It was my turn for the boys: they were with me. It was in the evening, the boys had already gone up to bed. There were only the three of us in the house. It was quite late, but there was plenty of light still, plenty of light. I'd had the turf people over all that day. I simply couldn't look after Lynette's old flower beds – there wasn't time, apart from anything else. So that day I'd had most of the beds turfed over so all that would be needed for me to do would be the mowing.

'Well, I poured myself a nightcap and went through to the kitchen to give it a splash of water, and I looked out to the garden and there was Lynette, standing there about twenty yards away on the edge of the new turf, quite close to the gap in the hedge. I thought, what's she doing, coming over at this time of night, without any warning? How extraordinary of her.

'I decided not to call out, though the window was open. I went back to the living room with my dram, and out by the French windows to invite her in. I couldn't just leave her there. But when I came around the edge of the house on to the lawn, she wasn't to be seen. I went through the gap in the hedge and she wasn't there either. There was nowhere else she could have gone in the time. I thought she might have crouched down to dig up a plant she had forgotten. I searched all round the garden and even called her name several times. Then I went up to the boys just in case she could conceivably have got into the house. But they were sleeping peacefully. She wasn't anywhere.'

Fryer rubbed his eyes, in a slow, deliberate motion.

'Did you ask her,' I said, 'when you next saw her?'

Fryer took his time replying. 'That's what Peverill asked me,' he said. 'But how could I? If I'd been mistaken, she'd think I was mad. I just mentioned, "I've had the beds turfed over." And she just said, "Oh."'

I asked, 'Did Peverill have any explanation?'

'There wasn't time. Because Siriani came up then, and plonked himself down beside us in his way, and began to say that he had a *feeling* His Excellency The Deputy Minister was pleased, but he hoped His Excellency would not decide to squeeze us more. "It is his job to squeeze," Siriani said. "It is his patriotism."

'I was disgusted by that. I felt quite sick with shock. I told Siriani it would break us, he knew that. And that set him off into one of his horrible phoney speeches. "Not break you, Mr Fryer. You are a rich man. Your own factory. So many staff. You live in this beautiful hotel with your assistant awaiting His Excellency's decision. I expect in your room you have your whisky, very secret, at one thousand riyals a bottle on the black market. It is a matter only of *how* rich. Correct? That is why the ladies come to you, because you are rich."

'He was baiting me, of course. He was as sly and sharp as they come. "How do you advance with al Khattira, the Dangerous Lady? If you were not rich, she would not take the dinner with you, provide the advice. You are a lucky man, Mr Fryer."

'Peverill said perhaps it was because Miss Flynn was lonely. He meant well, Peverill, even if he was a fool. Siriani said, "With all respects to your boss, Mr Peverill, Miss Flynn Khattira knows surely many Englishmen in this city who are young and beautiful as she is. Mr Fryer was also young and beautiful once, but now? Look. A little bald and when worried enjoys an execution but would also rescue the *dabb* from the execution. She chooses him for something else than not to be lonely."

'Peverill said, "Roy always gets the girls." This allowed Siriani to get the point of his knife in elsewhere. He said he was surprised I had time for such things as getting printing contracts. I should leave that to the Japanese, he said, "who pay very good commissions".

'What did he mean by that? More than seven and a half per cent? I smelled something here. When shall we have the Minister's decision? I asked. Thursday? (That's the last day of the Muslim working week.) "Thursday, insh'allah," Siriani said like a serpent, squirming out of his chair. "Saturday, maybe."

'Saturday was too late, I reminded him. And he said, Too late for what? Al Khattira would still be here. "Too late for my children." "Ah," he said, "your children and your wife. You have planned a picnic?" "Let it be Thursday, Mr Siriani," I said. And he was back like a snake: "For ten per cent?" I felt sick with outrage. "We have agreed seven and a half per cent!" Siriani went soft, suddenly. You can never tell with these wogs. "Never mind," he said. "If my children are not eating as well as yours, it is my patriotism!"

'He was playing with me, do you see? Because on the Thursday, what do you suppose?'

The same meaningless stare. I searched his eyes for a clue – a glint of triumph, a shadow of failure. Here was a man who had spoken of shock and outrage, of desperation to save his company, of imperative concern for his sons' half-term, of wild desire. And this long, strange, tortuous narrative of it all in which he had so purposefully entrapped me. Yet in his eyes the same nothing. Nothing.

'How can I guess?' I pleaded.

He said, 'We won the contract. We got the signature.'

I confess I experienced an unmistakable sense of anticlimax. I forced a smile. A happy ending. And yet . . . and yet . . .

The flight home, he explained, was at midnight.

'Of course,' I intervened brightly. 'There was the other contract. Al Khattira!'

Fryer nodded politely, as if to acknowledge my attentiveness.

That Thursday evening, having left Peverill at his supper, and paid his bill and packed his bags, he knocked on the door of Felicity's room. It was about nine p.m. They had made no precise assignation, but he knew she was there. She looked . . . breathtaking. Not dressed overtly to seduce yet, somehow . . . breathtaking. He told her, 'I came to thank you.'

She walked back to the desk where she had been at work on some papers. She asked him the time of his plane, and he told her from the doorway he would have to be off to the airport within the hour. She said, 'You can wait here if you like. Put your bags down.' He had his suitcase, an overnight bag, his briefcase and a plastic bag. But he said, No, thank you.

'You see' – he explained to me – 'something had changed. At least I thought it had. I had decided not to stay. Just to say thank you.'

'What happened?' I asked. But there was no need to prompt him.

'I'll tell you,' he said, 'exactly.'

[iii]

'She said, "Mayn't I see the contract?"

'I had to show it her. I came right in and closed the door and took it from my briefcase. She studied it carefully, clause by clause – it was in Arabic and English alongside – right down to the signature on the last page. "Such a little mark," she said. "It calls for some celebration. What's that in the plastic bag?"

'It was a bottle of whisky, unopened. I was going to ask her to give it away to someone. I couldn't take it with me. She fetched two tumblers and poured a peg for each of us. She kicked off her shoes and curled up on the bed. "Here's to your reunion," she said, raising her glass.

'You see, she knew. How she knew, I could not tell. She knew what was in my mind at that time. She seemed to know how it all lay between Lynette and me, though I don't remember having indicated anything more than that we were living apart. That was a shade uncanny, I admit, that she had sussed out so much. Or had she been chatting up Peverill?

'I drank the toast, and she said with a smile, "People never can quite remember why they needed the broker once they've done the deal."

'I began to tell her I was well aware that she and I had a deal, when she cut me off. She said, "You've got your little contract and you've turned over a new leaf and your life is full of meaning again. You're going to arrive at Heathrow tomorrow morning and you're going to drive down to your wife first and propose to her that you and she together take the boys out for their half-term. Because you've turned over your new leaf."

'It was uncanny, because it was almost exactly what I had decided. Perhaps it was still not too late – for Lynette, I mean.

"The conquering hero," Felicity taunted I could hear it in her voice. She came across to the easy chair I was sitting in and kissed me full on the lips. Just for a moment, but I felt her tongue. Then she sort of twisted her body in front of me and settled on the floor at my feet, resting an arm across my knees. She said, "Drink up. What makes you think she'll have you back? That she'll believe you this time? That you can bring back to the marriage bed its sanctity? What makes you think you can keep to such a vow? Your little penance, your self-denying ordinance, will last just so long as you're in doubt . . ."

'I got up from where I was and walked about the room. It was scattered with feminine things, feminine scents. She was taunting me, that I wanted her, that I wasn't man enough to go through with my side of the bargain. And I did want her, I'll tell you frankly, I wanted her fiercely. She was a very attractive woman. My getting that signature on the contract was like being released from a sentence of death. Or rather, release from a sentence of wishing to die. That was the condition I was in. All my senses were intensified, primed, you know, ready to explode.

'She picked herself up off the floor and sat on the bed, with her legs curled under her, and continued goading me from there, following me round the room with her eyes as I strode about. It would have been such a small thing, to take her there and then, to silence her pretty mouth. Stopper her.

'But I kept my head. I said, Why should she pour scorn on one more attempt to restore my marriage? What was it to her? I was on the plane to England that night. I would probably never see her again. She had done me a grand service, put back my courage, perhaps even saved my business. Could she not just accept my gratitude? After all, what could I mean to her?

'I was really very nervous, very excited. I said all that, but I was feeling something else: I was walking along a very very narrow plank with a terrible drop on either side, and what I had to do was keep walking and keep talking and not look down. Then all at once I realised she was crying. When it had begun, I don't know. But she was crying now, as if at the flick of a switch. She had toppled on to her side and was weeping into the pillows. So of course I crossed to her, to comfort her. I was astonished, I am telling you.

'I sat beside her and pulled my handkerchief from my breast pocket for her: some black seeds fell out which I had forgotten I had folded into it. I tried to quieten her, though I was astonished at it all. After a while she said, very quietly but clearly, "Do not go back to your wife. You will destroy her."

'Why should she be so intent on saying that? And why should she take such a line, seem to care so much? I know women; I've told you that. I was familiar with their complex changeability. I'd come across all sorts of irrational female logic. But this? Then she began to tell me something.

"I told you my mother was dead," she said. "I didn't tell you how."

'Of course I said, "Tell me." I had an arm about her, to give her comfort.

'She said, "My father was a flyer. He was in the RAF at Habaniyya and then in the fifties he joined the little outfit of DC3s that turned into Gulf Air. He was a great one for the ladies, as they say, a great one for the ladies.

' "My mother knew, of course. Once – I remember it terribly well – he said he was going away for four days, and he was actually seen in Kuwait, where we lived. Mother had been telling a friend that he was in Tehran or Beirut or wherever and the friend said she'd seen him an hour before. Kuwait was a pretty small place then.

' "When she couldn't stand it any more, he sensed it. He came home one night and told Mum he was never going to betray her again. She believed him. She really believed him. I know quite a lot about it because I was the only child, and though I was only fifteen I looked quite grown-up and had a lot of dates.

"Yes," she said, "Mum really believed him. And when she discovered it wasn't true, that he'd meant none of it, she went to the Indian pharmacy and bought six bottles of aspirin, and swallowed them all, and walked out – straight out of the house we had – into the desert, in the middle of the day, and walked and walked and walked, and do you know how they found her? By the smell! By the smell!"

'She was weeping terribly now. In my arms, you understand. I turned off the light by the bed, to shield her eyes. We lay beside each other for a while, I don't know how long – I'd lost track of time rather – and then we began to make love. You know why? Perhaps it's not so obvious. Because at that moment, after what she had told me, I loved her. I really *loved* her. I felt for her, completely. I felt all the betrayal of women by men, I felt all that terrible suffering, I felt all that smashing and pulping of love. How could I put that to rights with this girl? How could I expiate it? With my body. It was all I had. There was more love in that act of loving in that bed than any in my whole life.

'She lay in my arms, and quite some time later slipped out of bed and went to the bathroom. I heard her moving about the room and asked what the time was, and she said there was no hurry, it wasn't late, and came back to bed. She came across the black seeds in the sheets, and I explained I had collected them from a flowering shrub in the hotel forecourt for Lynette. She said a shrub like that would never survive in England, but I told her Lynette always had a hot house or a sunroom which the frost couldn't get at. But she insisted that it would never survive.

'Then she said, "People don't change, Roy. You're not going to change. I'm glad you got the contract. But getting it won't have changed you." She sounded quite gentle and sincere. Then she said, "You know how you got that contract?"

"Because we cut the price," I replied, "below the Japs."

"Partly," she said, "but also because I told Siriani that if you didn't get it I'd tell the whole expatriate community that he'd been acting for two bidders for the same contract. Which he had been."

'I whispered, "Al Khattira," and she laughed out loud. Then I looked at my watch and I suddenly realised how late it was.'

★

Fryer stopped here. There was more to be told, that was obvious. But he had come up against some sort of barrier. The face which had shown nothing all through this long narrative now looked somehow darker, or narrower. More utterly spent. More fathomlessly void. He fumbled for his tobacco tin. For a fraction he caught my disapproving glance, but looked down, choosing to ignore it. I too looked away, turning my head up the ward, to demonstrate my disowning of my neighbour's unsociable behaviour. But the other patients seemed absorbed in their own affairs. A few were engaged with visitors, others in a world apart with their headphones, or engrossed in magazines. With remarkable swiftness he had rolled a fag and lit up. In four or five draws it was gone, finished. I saw him put the butt back into his tin. By the time the odour of the tobacco reached any of the others the clue to its source would have vanished. Then Fryer resumed.

'It was before they built their new airport, which I've heard is one of the wonders of the world.

'I was very very late. Peverill had been waiting for me, searching for me. Of course, he'd no idea where I'd got to. We got there in a taxi about ten minutes before take-off, ten minutes to midnight. I knew it was bad because there were so few people about. And I heard the announcement telling passengers to board the aircraft as soon as I got inside the airport building. I had my three bits of baggage and left Peverill to pay for the taxi. I went straight to the check-in counter and the goon on the other side said the flight was closed. I told him it was still on the ground and I was getting aboard, with my friend. He repeated it was closed and I told him he could count my cases as hand-baggage and I could walk straight on to the plane, why not? Then Peverill came rushing up to say the taxi-driver was holding on to his bag and was demanding fifty riyals and he hadn't got fifty riyals. The proper fare was twenty, and that was all we had between us. So I rushed out of the building and down the steps and tried to yank Peverill's case out of the taxi-driver's hand, but he was strong as buggery and wouldn't let go. So I shouted to Peverill he could get Monday's flight, I had to catch this one. It was the boys' half-term, I couldn't possibly miss it. I told the clerk I'd fly without any bloody baggage, my friend would bring my baggage, I would go empty-handed. I'd been there on government business and I had to get this flight. The booking clerk said again I couldn't, he wouldn't let me, the flight was closed. I picked up my briefcase and went for Emigration, which was right beside. I was wild. I had to get on that plane now, somehow, I had to do it, the boarding entrance was only just beyond Emigration. Then somehow the clerk came round in front to block me and I hit him. I hit him quite hard. A soldier came out immediately from Emigration, in a white tin hat, with his little machine-gun, and that stopped me. He stuck his machine-gun right into me. The booking clerk said, "Has he been drinking?" He stuck his nose in my face and told the baggage loader to open my cases. I immediately said, "I apologise, I most sincerely apologise!" The clerk said, "This is a very bad mistake," and I repeated my apologies but he wasn't having any. Of course the soldier didn't understand anything except that I had hit the clerk. He was just a *bedu* anyway.

'I heard Peverill say, "Oh God, Roy," and I looked round. The baggage loader had opened my overnight zip-bag on the scales and the first thing he had come across was the half-empty bottle of whisky. I knew at once that was the end of everything. The contract was dead ... prison ... and everything else became terribly clear. Everything. All at once. I heard Peverill repeating, "Why did you pack it, Roy, why did you pack it?" He was always a fool, Peverill. I told him, "Not me, Martin. Felicity." She knew what she was doing. They would have found it in my overnight bag at Emigration anyway.

'I wanted to die then. The soldier still had the gun in my stomach and I started pulling at the muzzle, deliberately pretending to pull the gun away from him. I heard Peverill shouting, Roy, Roy, and then the plane's engines started roaring, and I kept pulling. He was only a small *bedu*, and at last he pulled the trigger. It was only a little burst. It didn't kill me, did it? It got me in the groin.

'Even so, it ought to have killed me. But it didn't, did it?' (There was just a shadow of irony in his voice.) 'It seems a long time ago now, but it isn't really. Three or four years. I've lost count. You want to know any more?'

[iv]

'You'd better finish,' I said.

'Finish?'

The story had been harrowing enough to this point. Yet I realised I was no wiser as to how it all bore on his plan to leave the next day.

'Is that what you're in here for,' I asked. 'Complications from that injury?'

'Not at all,' he said. 'There are no complications left, as you call them. They got me to their big hospital downtown, the rough and ready one. Shemaisi. They operated that night. It was quite a mess. They took out three bullets, an Egyptian surgeon. Nothing wrong with him. But the nursing was terrible. The wound went bad and they had to cut my balls off. No, it wasn't a form of punishment, they were very sorry about it. One had been damaged anyway. As it was, they had to take them both off.'

It seemed to me an appalling outcome. Yet there was no plea for sympathy in his voice or manner, not a vestige of such a thing.

'I'm sorry,' I said. He turned towards me with a look almost of surprise.

'The British Consul,' he said, 'was really good. He got the Saudis to waive all charges over the drink. You know what they're like over liquor. Of course, I had to be flown home under escort, as if I was a dangerous maniac.

'Lynette took me back, you know. Into her own house. The bank took our old house. The firm went, of course. The boys came away from school early. They're . . .' He paused, frowning at the wall. 'I couldn't stand it, though. Maybe you would think differently. But I couldn't, that's all there is to it. So I went away. I've been gone some time now.'

He seemed to have finished all he intended to say. He twisted round to look at the rest of the ward. Everything was as one would expect. The nurses were beginning to bring round supper. The television had been switched on: it was a Bugs Bunny cartoon, kiddies' bed-time stuff.

'And you're not going back there?' I ventured.

'Where?'

'To Lynette.'

'Oh, no, no, no, no.'

'Then . . . ?'

'Nowhere,' he said 'That's why . . .' and completed his obscure message by putting a finger to his lips.

There was something he seemed to presume I had grasped, but I HADN'T. Yet there was a limit to the questions I could go on asking. I tried one more. 'What are you in for?'

'Frostbite of the feet,' he replied at once. 'They took off a toe. Listen,' he continued directly, deliberately moving me on, 'if I were to ask you to lend me a fiver . . . even a couple of quid . . .'

'That's all right,' I said. 'For tomorrow?'

'Exactly.'

I had a five pound note in the wallet by my bed. I was surprised how quickly and surreptitiously he took it from me. 'Give me your address,' he said. He stuffed the note into his tobacco tin, and climbed back into his bed. Because the suppers were arriving.

All next day, the Sunday, he behaved as he always had done before, lying back, staring in front of him, or at the ceiling, doing nothing, saying nothing. I noticed that he ate every particle of food put before him. Except the custard on the top of the trifle; he scraped that off.

Of course my mind was full of his extraordinary narrative, and of the fact that he had told it to me. Why had he done so, and in such careful detail? It was not sympathy he wanted. That was evident. What *did* he want? What could I do for him? Presumably he would be gone that day, as he had covertly announced, though he seemed to have made no preparations. And what of that unexpected answer, 'Frostbite', thrown out so dismissively? Though I was beginning to put two and two together.

Returning from the toilet after lunch I said to him quietly, 'Is there anything you want?'

'Want?' It seemed to make him think. 'I've got all I want now.' I remarked the 'now'. For what might have altered for him lately to allow for a 'now' . . . unless it was that he had told his tale, as he had never been able to tell it before? Could that be it? And here was that same slow grin I had seen just once before, the previous day, when he caught himself referring to a 'self' he doubted he was entitled to, and here too a word to add to his 'all I want'. '*Nothing.*'

Towards evening it became clear that the hospital staff were preparing for his discharge the *following* day, Monday, and that someone was coming to fetch him, though I was puzzled as to who it could be. It did not square with the intention he had vouchsafed to me, and I even wondered if I had surrendered the five pounds unnecessarily. A nurse brought him various garments – trousers, a jacket, a pullover and so forth – evidently for his approval, as if they were not his property but from the hospital pound. These were put beneath his bed in a very battered suitcase which I supposed did indeed belong to him. But no shoes were provided – his feet were still protected with some kind of elasticised socks. Apart from that there were only the outsize plastic slippers.

The lights went out later than they did on weekdays, because of the ITV Sunday film. I supposed that Fryer must have had a change of plan. Anyway, I was soon asleep.

I was awoken at about four in the morning by a suppressed flurry of consternation right beside my bed. One of the night nurses and a sister were in urgent whispered conversation. When the sister saw that I had woken she immediately said to me, 'Did you see Mr Fryer leave his bed?' I could see beyond them that the bed was empty, although the suitcase was still beneath it. I shook my head. I had slept soundly all night, I said. Then they too thought of the suitcase, and looked inside. It was empty. They immediately hurried out, and I heard more urgent conversation, and telephonings in the ward office outside. Half an hour later a doctor came with the same night nurse, and they searched Fryer's bedspace and the bed itself with a torch, evidently for a note, or some other clue. There was nothing.

By ten o'clock a new patient had been put into that bed. Then at ten-thirty the ward sister came in with the parson. She brought him direct to my bed. 'I'll leave you two together,' she said, and withdrew.

The parson looked a little flustered, as if he had splashed some tea on himself, or had mislaid his spectacles. 'How's things?' he said.

'Very nicely,' I assured him.

He took off his scarf and began to pull off his gloves, finger by finger – the forecast had said cold. He kept his anorak on (it wasn't the clerical cloak today), but unzipped it. 'May I?'

He settled in the chair Fryer had occupied on the Saturday. Something made me instantly wary of this special treatment.

'Your friend has' – he cleared his throat – 'discharged himself, so it seems. I hear you and he had a good talk.' I received a bright inquisitive little smile, and the familiar titter.

'That's right.'

'He didn't say where he was off to?'

'Not a word.'

'Or ask for your address, by any chance?'

'Address? I didn't give him my address,' I answered truthfully, if obliquely. 'We weren't that close.'

'You didn't give him any money?' The word 'money' inducing another titter.

'Oh no,' I lied without a moment's hesitation.

'Well, he can't have gone far. He only had a few shillings.'

Whether, in the fine balance of things, the grain of relief at Fryer's supposed proximity outweighed disconcertedness at the likelihood of finding him, was difficult to assess. For he resumed almost at once; and I had begun to guess at something.

'What did he have to talk about? If I might ask?'

'Printing,' I said. 'He was very knowledgeable about printing.'

Lady-killer

'Extraordinary,' the parson said.

'It was particularly interesting to me,' I explained, 'because I am a writer.'

'Oh really? What is your name?'

I told him.

'Should I have read you?' The titter that followed here was a brightly guilty one.

'That's difficult to say . . .'

'You see, Mr – the name was, you said?' He hastened on, 'We had planned to bring him home today. My wife and I. We had everything prepared to welcome him. His own little room.'

'Home?' I said.

'Yes. My home, of course.' He did not seem quite sure how to proceed. 'He always was an awkward one, always a trial. This is quite typical of him, quite typical. I shouldn't be saying this, of course – I shouldn't be thinking it – but he'll have done this to aggravate.'

'What?' I returned.

'Oh dear, discharging himself. Disappearing like this. It's extremely cold, of course. And what could he have done for shoes?' I too had become concerned for his footwear. 'There's no end to the trouble he's put us all to. No end to it.' He paused amid a forest of little crosses. 'All that business in Saudi Arabia – you don't know about that, I suppose. It was in the newspapers. His wife agreed to take him back – it was most noble, most *noble* – and after a few months he just walked out.'

'Where to?'

'That's it.' The monkish fringe gave a little shake. 'He just went on the road. Disappeared.'

'You mean, became a sort of tramp?'

What distance, I speculated, might Fryer have put between himself and this hospital with my fiver? Or even for part of it.

'Tramp. Yes.' The little frown was gone as soon as it came. 'We didn't hear of him from one year to the next. We couldn't trace him at all. His poor wife. And his boys. I hesitate to tell you; the upset, the shame, I'm bound to say. He'd left money in his bank account, you know.'

'Good gracious. How much?'

'There was nearly a hundred pounds. There was nothing anybody could do about it. You see, I'm responsible now, after his wife got her divorce for desertion. She had to, of course . . . for the boys. I'm next-of-kin.'

'Really?'

He had gathered himself for the little plunge.

'Indeed. Related. Brother – step-brother, to be exact. My father married his mother. We grew up together. From the age of six. Different surnames naturally. But when he disappeared I informed the relevant authorities.'

'What for?'

'Should he turn up. We just had to wait and wait, not knowing what might happen next. Then the police telephoned me at two o'clock in the morning. Two o'clock in the morning.' My expression told my sympathy. 'Only a month or so ago. He'd been found in an abandoned railway shed with frostbite. He'd have died if they hadn't brought him in.'

'And he'll have gone back on the road?'

'What else? In this weather, too. He won't survive, of course.' It was exasperating. 'And why? *Why?* his own little room, quite out of the way. We'd decided to buy him a budgerigar. I'd told him about it. It's quite typical, don't you know.'

'I think I understood,' I said, 'he was castrated.'

'Oh yes, yes,' the parson confirmed, widening his almond eyes. 'There was that too. Surely he didn't *tell* you, did he?' That really was the last straw.

Territoire Inexploré

[i]

As to the break-up of marriages, Pat and I have a rule: we decline to apportion blame. We reckon it's as hard to trace the source of pain, of loss, of emptiness as trace the source of love. These things are too secret; not only secret, but mysterious, even to the protagonists, like that mystery, for example, conjured between drum and the black hands that beat it in tribal Africa. Love and loss of love between man and woman belong to the dark world, the land of magic, of spirits, which those of the Christian tradition perceive as either good or bad.

One can't follow into that world. One can only observe the consequences and wonder. For us mortals (*pace* the global masonry of psychologists) it will always be unexplored territory. We can speculate, but we will never know how love and pain can change places in an instant; how couples who personify true love, who have found the Philosopher's Stone (which turns all to gold), who are packed with optimism, courage and even a measure of humour, who are devoted to one another and their offspring, one day out of the blue bring their indissoluble union to the divorce courts in a state of inexpressible grief, anger, astonishment and hate.

As for ourselves, well, in the fashionable jargon Pat and I enjoy an 'open' marriage. Sometimes I catch in others' tone of voice a presumption that our marriage is in some way of inferior consequence to their own. As if they possessed the gold, commanded the magic . . . while Pat and I were two people of middle age who happened to lodge at the same premises and took turns to feed the dog! It makes me smile and I guess it makes Pat smile too. Even in the case of Rowlands vs Rowlands we decline to award points. If I may say so, I call that pretty civilised.

For Rowlands vs Rowlands is a case of unusual vividness, and I can hardly claim to be unacquainted with the facts, insofar as 'facts' signify. Such is the distancing of time – for all this belongs to a generation or more ago – I ought to be able to retail it with the dispassion of a professional chronicler, however fraudulent.

★

Facts. In those days, young men had to spend a couple of years in the armed services. After basic training and the Officer Cadet School, Victor Rowlands embarked for Malaya to command a platoon of guardsmen. Later, when he was being instructed in the niceties of agriculture and estate management at college in Cirencester, his great-uncle died and he came into three hundred acres of north Oxfordshire not far across the border from his native Gloucestershire. He had known the place from earliest childhood. It was there that he took his bride, after a famous courtship that had continued throughout his two years at Cirencester. June's own family came from Warwickshire, so the newly-weds were settling half-way between their ancestral shires.

By common consent, they were an ideal couple. They did up the place charmingly. Her mother gave them a fitted kitchen and they extended the kitchen into the dining room to make the place easier to run without living-in staff. They kept three horses, hunted regularly with the Heythrop and were a credit to the neighbourhood. They were wonderfully proud of one another, and their home was aglow with their cheer.

June was lovely in a way that only English women seem to attain. She had 'good bones' and that flawless English skin which used to be likened to alabaster. I once heard her called 'Victorian beauty': I guess what was meant by that was not just her impeccable lines and thick coiled hair but an unassailable purity, of heart and body alike. She was 'Monday's child', her mother would remind those who came to court her, 'fair of face', but she might just as well have been Tuesday's: she was 'full of grace', and possessed the talent of promoting it in others. She *expected* good in people. When Victor entitled her 'the most beautiful girl in the world' it was no banality of a man in love but apt words for June through and through. The other girls during her last year at school would have understood him exactly, as she played her 'cello at the concerts. The colour of her eyes, for example, belonged to a porcelain of extreme rarity. I suppose that could be said of everyone's eyes, but with June's you noticed it, you thought of the porcelain. Meeting someone she was fond of whom she had not seen lately, her eyes would make an instant search of the other's, and the gentle complicity thus located would remain their common base.

She supposed there was no one her eyes could not plumb. People were deep, she knew that, especially the shy ones. Everyone had something they held back; even Victor, though not shy, she sometimes thought of as shy in his way. People confided in her: she had discovered that. They trusted her confidence. Sooner or later they would share their little secrets, their tears and fears and hopes.

After all, she had known love all her life, was fully formed by love; her mother saw to that. She knew Satan was in the world, for she had been told so, and sometimes read of him in the newspapers and Charles Dickens. But she also knew she had grown up beyond his reach: that was her privilege. With privilege went responsibility, of course, and her responsibility was to dispense goodness and understanding from the Satan-free stronghold of her inheritance.

Her country upbringing was well furnished with adages of Victorian propriety. Next to godliness came cleanliness. Mrs Do-as-you-would-be-done-by governed the main areas of human relations. However lissom on the tennis court, she herself would describe – a little daringly – the proper female physique as 'carrying all before her but with something to fall back upon', as if her sex was still in crinolines and bustles. She herself eschewed artifice: even coquetry was suspect. It was quite enough to have been born Monday's child.

The accompaniment of an absence of deception was an unsullied loyalty to those she elected to love. Was it this that withheld Victor from telling her about Vivienne? It was accepted that when Victor was in Malaya there had been a 'girl in his life', but June had never enquired further, and whenever the subject was skirted it was as if a shadow threatened to cross her; she would turn the talk aside. It was enough for her to presume him not altogether ignorant of women: that was as things should be. Of course, I speak of the early fifties, before the rage for promiscuity. There was no call to be informed of his 'experience'. Was it not reasonable for her to suppose that love, which conquered all, would provide the techniques for its fulfilment? *Their* love wasn't to be compared with any fleeting liaisons of the past. Victor would have concurred. He quoted her a couplet from a poem he had learned at school: 'If ever any beauty I did see,/Which I desired, and got, 'twas but a dream of thee.' In those days the young were obliged to learn off bits of verse.

At moments during their courting Victor had felt an inclination to speak to her of Vivienne outright, to clear the slate in the Tolstoyan fashion. In the glow of her loveliness he wished to assure her of his devotion in every context, to demonstrate how he had sealed up the past for her. He would give her just the outline of that brief passage of his life. It didn't amount to much . . . Vivienne was the daughter of an official of the pre-war British-staffed customs service in China who had died in a Japanese prisoner-of-war camp; mother re-married and kept a genteel home for her new husband, a purser in the merchant marine, and her smouldering little Vivienne. From a chance encounter at a swimming club, she and Victor had fallen for one another with an urgency sharpened by the deadline of his return to his unit in the jungle. The fervid affair occupied the few weeks of the battalion's garrison in Singapore and the sixteen days of his leave which followed. They vowed to meet again in the few days before he took ship for home later that year, when they would 'decide what to do'. As it was, Victor contracted a severe jaundice up north in Malaya and was flown home by RAF transport direct from Kuala Lumpur, yellow and emaciated. It took him months to regain his strength. When at length he came to be captured by his love for June, all that had happened to him in the Far East seemed immeasurably distant in space and time.

Yes, he would rather have told June the story of it: Vivienne was a fragment of his past with a glitter of its own, but she meant nothing any more. June was his love now and for always, without blemish: he hankered after none other. But the occasion did not arise. June saw to that.

The three hundred acres were not enough to support the Rowlandses in their comfortable house *and* a farm manager. The place had been mortgaged to pay death duties. Victor could not risk neglecting the farm. And yet . . . three or four months' absence during the winter shouldn't put too great a strain on his three farmworkers and his poultryman, and June herself would be on hand to keep an eye on things. Moreover, he defended his resolve to return to the jungle on financial grounds. The expedition he planned, he told their friends, was a 'punt': success might net a fortune; if nothing came of it he shouldn't be more than a thousand or so out of pocket. The bank, having the deeds of the property already in their safe, would surely oblige, with the usual masque of condescension.

The jungle in question was not Malayan but African – French Equatorial Africa. A former schoolfellow who had spent his national service stationed in the Cameroons had told Victor of meeting a German doctor on return overland to Europe. This doctor had worked for several years at a hospital sited upriver in a remote region of the tropical forest, founded and presided over by one of the acknowledged sages of the mid-twentieth century. He told of tribal patients contributing to the hospital's funds in gold-dust carried in matchboxes or screws of paper or even leaves. The origin of this gold

Territoire Inexploré

was unknown to the few Europeans working in the area: the natives were vague or evasive as to where it came from. It was clearly alluvial, but due to the inaccessibility of the region no one had traced its provenance.

On a midsummer's whim, Victor wrote to the address his friend had jotted down, and some two months later – it was when he was working fourteen hours a day stooking and threshing and had all but forgotten having written – a reply arrived bearing a West German stamp and a Lüneburg postmark. In painstaking English the doctor described 'all which I can tell' about the gold-dust and even appended a hand-drawn map indicating the course of the rivers of upper Gabon, the disposition of the tribe credited with knowledge concerning the mystery, and an adjoining area which Victor was surprised to see designated 'unexplored territory'. He had presumed that no part of the habitable globe was still 'unexplored'. Had not all been penetrated and mapped by civilised man by now – if not actually on foot, at least by meticulous aerial survey? The phrase must be a fanciful dramatisation.

During the long blazing days of that late summer, his wrists and arms pricked red by thistles in the sheaves, and beer and chatter flowing at dinner-break with his labourers, Victor felt the idea growing irresistible. He brought out the doctor's letter from his shirt pocket and his men read it slowly. They abetted him, particularly his cowman: he had served in the Burma campaign and for him, too, the jungle held no fears – at least, not as to the techniques of survival. He even proposed himself as a companion; but Victor said, No, he intended to go alone.

Looking back now one must wonder why, why young Victor Rowlands, nestled into the life of his native Cotswolds, encompassed by the devotion of his chosen English rose, should become captivated by the prospect of immersion in the forest darkness of the African tropics. He was twenty-four, and so much to occupy him at home. He was not driven by need of fame and fortune. Had not the army already given him a chance to see a bit of the world, sow a few wild oats?

I find it hard to bring Victor alive . . . He possessed a very English, throwaway charm, a loose-limbed fellow, a vein of self-deprecation in his humour and no crack visible in his assessment of himself. I view him as a young man well protected by convention, educated at the same school as father and forefathers where he was known as a cricketer, serving in a socially appropriate regiment and shortly to belong to the right London clubs. He was commended for his perfect manners. 'Manners Makyth Man' school and, indeed, family tradition had urged on him. Once he heard a sermon on that text: the little phrase went deeper, he recalled, than one would have thought. Something to do with a fundamental unselfishness, a martyred Lord, a chivalry that distinguished Man from Beast. Here was more tradition of which it was satisfying to find oneself an heir.

You know the kind of fellow. He took life as it came and life returned the compliment. There was no discernible rebellion in him. At election time he roared for the Conservatives, and June at his side was obscurely puzzled how a doctrine of envy and greed, as peddled by the Opposition, could attract such support. (Would not Lady Bountiful, left to herself, handle the problems of the poor who would anyway, as Jesus pointed out, always be with us?) In due course, she supposed, Victor might stand himself: he was already a committee member of the Hereford Cattle Society, a national body, and he read the Lesson beautifully. She would become a magistrate . . .

They complemented one another so aptly, the young Rowlandses. An ideal couple, following the Heythrop hounds on an October morning. 'If any beauty he did see, 'twas but a dream of she.' Mightn't he have offered the opening of that same poem? *I wonder by my troth, what thou, and I / Did till we loved? Were we not weaned till then? / But sucked on country pleasures childishly?* But of course he enjoyed his country pleasures. They both did, weaned or unweaned.

So why did he know that he *had* to go on this expedition, that nothing would hold him back? Why did he make his preparations with such singleness and intensity, taking no chances with equipment, researching at the Royal Geographical Society, somehow even obtaining a letter of recommendation from the Ministre des Colonies in Paris? Why did that anachronistic little phrase, surely phoney, 'unexplored territory', catch at his mind, give him no peace?

I confess as self-appointed chronicler I know that any explanation attempted would not be adequate, at least, to me . . . however many latter-day discoverers there may be to tell me why. If I am accused of being disingenuous, so be it. Make your accusations, you who delve the mysteries, you who house the Philosopher's Stone in your commodes.

As for June, she took it as a sample of typically male idiosyncrasy. Her younger sister, the brainy one, had quoted, 'Man does, woman is,' and June thought that defined it cleverly. A real man, which her Victor was, had to be up and doing. She looked on the adventure as slightly madcap and was pretty sure it would produce nothing. She said so, but the idea tickled her and during the weeks of preparation she took to calling Victor 'the explorer' in a tone half teasing and half proud. She would miss him of course, and though he played down the danger she knew the element of hazard was part of the appeal for him. Yet her trust in her hero's ability to look after himself was solid. And there was something else. During his last hectic days she had reason to believe that what she most yearned for was occurring: that she had started his baby. His absence would spare her those enthusiastic attentions which from Mama's experience she knew could so easily provoke miscarriages in the early months among women of a certain cast. She said nothing to Victor, wishing to be quite certain of so sacred a prospect before revealing it.

On Victor's early morning departure for London airport, his expeditionary kit was gathered in the hall. He had borrowed a big-game rifle from a grandfather, found a pistol for self-defence, brought out his old Army 'jungle green' uniform (the insignia removed), and obtained such maps as Stanford's could offer. He and June checked his inventory together and completed the last of the packing. The daily-woman from the village had walked up in the dark specially early to get breakfast, which was hastily consumed. The labradors were disconsolate.

Bulging suitcase, rucksack and gun case were already loaded into the Rover when Victor hurried back into the house clutching the overnight bag which in those days the airlines provided. June called to him impatiently: he was shameless in his habit of cutting things fine. He shouted back that he would be just a minute.

He doubled up to one of the attics and shut the door behind him. He knelt beside an old-fashioned leather trunk, unstrapped it, pushed up the humped and heavy lid, and in one corner rummaged through its forgotten wedding presents and documents and ancient toys, swiftly locating a bundle of letters tied with the green lace of an Army jungle-boot. He thrust this little bundle into his overnight bag, and re-fastening the straps of the trunk, bolted downstairs and out to the waiting car.

'I'm sorry, darling. There was something I nearly forget. Away we go.'

She would punish him by her silence, and didn't lean across to peck him on the cheek until they had covered two or three miles. She refrained from asking him what he had gone for. He would have fibbed, of course. He had done no more than act on the thought flickering at the mind's edge since the previous day, namely that if anything 'happened to him', sooner or later June would come across those letters and thereafter they would cloud her recollection of the limpid wonder of their love. That would be a tragedy. I use the word with care. For in June, he knew, that recollection would be her most precious possession all her life, an object of *vertu* that Fabergé himself could not excel: he could perform no more grievous posthumous disservice to the woman whose love was, to him likewise, the most precious thing in the world. Oh, I know he hadn't quite been able to bring himself to destroy the letters he had fetched . . . it would have seemed almost to elevate them; and to entrust them in a sealed package to a friend during his absence, too elaborate a performance. It was only that he had given the matter no proper thought, and had procrastinated; only that at the very last minute did leaving the letters where they were seem a risk not quite worth taking.

It was not until his aircraft reached Brazzaville in Moyen Congo the following morning and he had assembled all his kit in his room at the Relais Colonial, that he brought out the letters. It would have been an easy matter to put them out with the refuse (they hadn't actually provided a waste-paper basket), or to make a little blaze of them in coarse grass . . . He didn't untie the jungle-boot lace that bound them together, but the mere touch of the packet brought to mind so vividly the effect of those pale blue envelopes when the mail arrived in the mess at Kuala Kubu Bharu, and how exquisitely precious that swift, flattened handwriting with its eloquent urgency had been to a lover isolated among boorish fellow officers who ribbed him for his ladyfriend. They had nicknamed Vivienne 'Chinky' because of the suggestion of epicanthic fold over her sly dark eyes, and Victor knew they classed her a common little thing. It was a relief to him to be out of the mess and back in the jungle: he was surprised to find himself more at home there than in the mess.

There was no call to decide just yet. True, if misfortune befell, his personal effects would presumably be gathered up and sent back to June by a conscientious British consul. But the first leg of the expedition consisted of no more than covering the few hundred miles of murram road northwards in a second-hand jeep and could scarcely be classed dangerous. He stuffed the letters into an Army issue waterproof pouch with a flap that was secured with two tapes, and stowed the little package in his case for the time being.

[ii]

The cluster of bitumen, palm-frond and tin roofs crawled up the hump of an island encircled by the great languid river as if taking refuge from the universe of forest. Victor and his jeep reached it by a raft ferry paddled by men whose rate of stroke was given by a drummer raised on a dais, inspired by an inner devil of syncopation and percussive fancy. Each performance of brilliant improvisation was offered to the stream and lost on the air. Several of the paddlers, in cast-off shorts and shirts, were missing fingers or toes, ex-lepers in whom white man's medicine had persuaded the sickness to recede: once blighted and restored by a foreign magic, they had no home now, he realised, save this *grand village*, administrative headquarters of a colonial *région*.

After washing and shaving at the river's edge – for he had been negotiating the wretched vehicle track through the jungle all night – Victor's first act was to call at the *Poste Restante*. The African clerk, whose face seemed a mass of tiny scars, frowned over the miscellaneous pile of correspondence, kept in a shoe-box under the counter. Victor recognised his wife's hand instantly from a single word on a corner of the envelope protruding from the heap. The letter overflowed with joy, for it told him of their child-to-be. The same joy flooded Victor. June wrote of it as 'our love-child', and of 'your gift to me, my one true darling, and mine to you, and God's to us both'. He too could perceive the God-givenness of this child – for a moment it seemed to him a cherub, perfectly formed, wings and all. He saw infinite generations growing out of his and June's love like a tree reaching into the sky with countless branches.

With a light heart he climbed back into the jeep to drive himself up to the residence of the *Chef de Région*, but changed his mind and walked. If the expedition should by chance succeed, it would be for this 'love-child' that he would make his fortune; for his unborn baby would he dare and strive. Surely it was why he was here. On his way by the steep lanes he was followed at a short distance by a skulking cur. One of its back legs was useless and its pelt was a map of red sores. Villagers shooed it away and a child scored a direct hit with a pebble.

The rambling white bungalow was set atop the island's hump. A grizzled black manservant in white tunic left him on the verandah. You could see, all around, mile upon mile of forest. The river beneath moved like a black snake, a snake without head and without tail. Only this little island with its bric-a-brac of dwellings was free of jungle; for all natural creation was comprised of jungle. But for the river, the jungle would swallow everything. The same feelings had possessed him all night on the mean murram road. The great trees touched limbs overhead most of the way, and the road, such as it was, seemed in constant danger of disappearing. The bridges over the countless streams were never more than two flattened parallel logs. He had stayed at the wheel for twenty hours, almost without pause: oh, he wanted to get here, but he had no clear cause to push himself so. It was as if he might be afraid the jungle might close in entirely before he had negotiated the so-called road.

The river was different. The river was in complicity with the forest, but had its own purpose and its own power. For man on this island, the river was both defender and gaoler. Was there not some such snake, in an ancient mythology, that thus guarded the repose of men's souls?

A white man came out on to the verandah gripping the letter from the Ministre des Colonies Victor had sent in. He greeted his visitor with careful affability, a stocky, good-humoured, punchy *Chef de Région*, not yet forty, in baggy shorts and knee-high white socks. White was for good order – white clap-board, white skin, white-painted perimeter stones, the Peugeot white in which he escorted Victor to the government Rest House at the upstream end of the island. As a seeming afterthought he invited the Englishman to share his table that very evening.

Nightfall's speed should not surprise Victor: after all, he knew the tropics. In those few minutes of re-ascending the hump in his jeep the world turned from light to dark, from gleaming sundown to the paltry defiance of man's so very private light. The *Chef*'s bungalow had no generator: kerosene lamps sufficed. They dined off local *grenouilles*, a *médaillon de boeuf*, a sherbet made from locally grown pineapples, and two wines which had endured the long, hot passage from another world. The bungalow seemed populated by innumerable spears, drums, stools, masks, fetishes of dark wood, certain of them straw-skirted. And populated by more than such objects – for the fully animate, also, occupied nether regions of this headquarters station. Two or three half-caste children had peeped at the visitor from outbuilding corners or cassava patches as he had stepped down from his jeep in the vanishing light.

The table was cleared, and when the grizzled houseboy brought an extra lamp Victor noticed his stubbed fingers: he too was a former leper. The *Chef* spread upon the table the latest maps of the area.

There, across a piece of Africa some hundred miles wide, east of a tributary of the great river, Victor was once more startled by the words *Territoire Inexploré*, and in italic lettering each side the further description, *Gorilles et Eléphants*.

The *Chef* offered Victor a cigar which, to please his host, he accepted.

'The furthest point up that tributary,' the Frenchman explained, 'visited by the Government launch, is that point there' – and he indicated a site about fifteen kilometres from the tributary's confluence with the major stream. 'There you will find a timber concessionaire, a compatriot by the name of Marcel. Monsieur Marcel is very strict but quite fair. He will put you up; I will give you a note. Marcel is a good friend of mine. From there you and your porters can start your march into the *territoire inexploré*. Yes, there could be alluvial gold in there. I couldn't say. Certainly gold-dust passes from hand to hand in this part of Africa. Its origin is obscure. Definitely obscure.'

The *Chef* was accustomed to articulating to his Africans in basic French, and Victor found he could converse with him in his school French. 'You should recruit your porters from here, from this *grand village*,' the *Chef* commented, 'not from upriver. The natives there are frightened of the territory east of that tributary. Nobody lives there, so far as is known. But the tribe that live along that river itself are an afflicted people. They are sickly and shy. Difficult people. They are also great cannibals – it is the common sin of these parts. Cannibalism is the most frequent offence in my court session. Each Friday I sentence men for cannibalism. Not for nourishment, you understand, as such. For fetishistic purposes.' The *Chef* drew on his cigar. 'It is said that that tribe outcast certain of their fellows for reasons of superstition, and that these outcasts survive in the *territoire inexploré* by raiding certain of the villages by night and securing corpses, either by murder or by opening graves for the purpose of obtaining human organs with protective or restorative properties. I cannot vouch for the truth of this, but it appears to me quite likely.' He blew away ash which had dropped on the map.

'Contagious magic is universal, you understand. The possessions of the strong or powerful are very potent *nkisi* – tokens, you might say – especially intimate possessions, or parts of the body. Such ideas are not easily comprehended in Europe. In Paris, for example.' He gave Victor a quick combative smile. 'You yourself require to be careful. I cannot hold myself responsible, you appreciate. The territory is not controlled, it is not – to be exact – explored. Sleep with your weapons within reach.' He puffed the cigar ash away again. 'But as a rule, we Europeans are exempt from the influence of spirits. We are, as it were, on a different network: we and our possessions can work neither boon nor bane. As a rule, but perhaps not always. I do not deride the natives for their beliefs.'

He turned directly towards his guest. 'If you or I had a splinter of the Cross, we would treasure it, would we not? Prize it above everything else we possessed for its power for good?' It was not a factor of human life that Victor had considered. The other added unexpectedly, 'If such is true – or if we make it true by the force of our credulity (and who is to tell the difference?) – why should we disbelieve in the power for evil of certain objects? But good and evil, you understand, are concepts of civilisation. Perhaps I should say, *our* civilisation. Here the distinction is different. The distinction is between what has power and what has not. *What* power can reach *where*. *I* have power, yes, of course. But it is power of a certain style, upon a certain plane. I do not have pretensions to power where it really counts, not in this region of the globe.'

Somewhere in the recesses of this rambling structure, and the outbuildings, Victor had come to suppose, resided a common-law African consort. Here was a colonial method, he realised, alien to the British experience. What District Commissioner would keep his job with his own piccaninnies running around the house where the national flag flew? The vaunted *mission civilisatrice* was altogether more primitive, makeshift, *compliant* than what he had encountered in Malaya. Life was cheap and justice rough. All around him, unequal deals were being done with a pitiless nature. Since the rains had begun, so he learned, the road to the coast had become impassable: the river sufficed even if it took several days. The hospital erected by the world-renowned sage approximated a native village in order to entice the sick, so the theory ran, by the customary. It could be approached up its backwater only by dug-out canoe. The only school for many miles was attended by a tiny fraction of the children of the region: in the *Chef*'s own words, it was like '*une petite lanterne dans la forêt*'.

As Victor descended the hill, his headlights caught the crippled, scabious dog.

Among the sloping lanes of the village the young Englishman became a familiar figure. The natives supposed him to be a trader. They knew of only three species of white: traders, missionaries-cum-doctors, and administrators. They guessed he would open a store: that was it, he would open a store. That was why he seemed to be assembling a team. He needed staff for his store.

They responded to his charm and his youth and his natural command. He had no need to go looking for Africans; they came to him. He would descend to the riverside market where the goods were ranged in handfuls on banana leaves on the trodden earth: white cassava roots, grey and glutinous manioc, strips of crocodile flesh, pyramids of flying ants and dried locusts. The Africans came to him instinctively, gathered about him, competing for acquaintanceship. He needed to cross to the hospital, they found him a dugout and formed a clamorous crew. They brought him his letters from the post office, with his home tribe's chieftainess's head on the stamps. They volunteered to run back with his own letters home (it was hard to keep June abreast of all this) which left by river.

He kept his purpose dark. He masked it by chatting easily on every sort of local topic. In such a way he learned what little there was to learn about the gold-dust, which indeed many of the natives possessed in small quantities. He claimed to be writing a book. The Africans presumed him to be dissembling cunningly, perhaps hinting at the making of an accounts ledger, since that type of book was the only one they were aware of except the Bible, which had already been written, even in their own vernacular. The white missionaries at the hospital were more familiar with book-writers. They believed him. Their bizarre encampment was short of patients but rich in philosophic nostrums, and hence books, several of them by the hand of the sage.

The old man himself – theologian, musician, saint – demonstrated to Victor the irreconcilability of white and black by clouting one of his walking patients, a leper on the mend, with his stick and marking the man's failure to protest, let alone to retaliate. Black submission, white will. His method of demonstrating the point surprised the young Englishman but gave emphasis to the manner in which the egalitarian views he had arrived with had made their escape. The books by which the sage had broadcast his reputation spoke of the assertion of the blind elements: *On the Edge of the Primaeval Forest*, *More from the Primaeval Forest*.

Humankind was here on sufferance, its clearings of space barely tolerated. This place was indeed 'primaeval'; it belonged to the beginning of things, as did its people, squat, puzzle-eyed, simian, not so much *homo sapiens* as one of the contributory strains. Darwin's men. Victor marvelled that the *Chef* could even have brought himself to couple with such a species, wondered, even, at the versatility of the primate gene that allowed for the cross-fertilisation of such remote phyla.

He himself could feel a sexual recognition only of the few half-breed girls who hung around the bar where he drank his Primus beer in the evenings. He supposed they were offspring of timber concessionaires or traders or even colonial officials of an earlier generation. One such attracted him sharply: the fluidity of her movement and the dumb thrust of the rump within the paler skin reached the base imperative within him. She seemed to link him – of the refined, the dominant race – to the primaeval world around him. Jiggling to the gramophone, she made the simple, liquid snatches of repeated tune her very own to soften and allure . . . but he supposed she must have the clap, for which (I remind the reader) there were then no sure, swift cures. It seemed to him natural that the accepted profession of half-breed girls should be prostitution for the passing whites.

I sense I am better succeeding, now, in bringing to life the chief character of my narrative. Is he not taking flesh? He felt so himself, a fresh manhood supervening, which he would one day carry back to his wife. Oh, indeed. He wished nothing of this further self to be denied his darling wife. Give him time, he would refine for her and share with her this recrudescence of the elemental. He loved her, was committed to her, she was a context for his endeavour, a justification, a repository of his pride. She deserved the best and the truth of him, not least the grandeur of his lusts, even if the detail of his experience could not be relayed in all its rawness in letters home. But he could tell her of the dog. The maimed cur plagued him with its hopeless suffering. It hung about him, but always at a distance. If ever he tried to approach it to within several yards it would cringe away and lollop off on three legs, half-starved and suppurating, holding his eye with a pleading, accusatory gaze. He yearned to shoot it with his pistol. It surely belonged to no one. It could distinguish the white skin or the white scent of that species of humankind that did not drive it off with stones. It had learned that, of this species, the stranger would for a while respond to the scale of its misery.

One afternoon in the rain, which shut down native activity, Victor set out with his pistol to put an end to it. To pity a beast distinguished a civilised man. He could not find it. Then he came across it in an open space, enclosed by native huts and banana groves, at the top of the village. It was standing there on its own, lop-sided and rain-drenched, as if waiting for its executioner. It was a bitch, he saw. It watched him closely as he took out his revolver and loaded two chambers. The thought returned to him: What if it *does* have an owner? What if a false owner furiously presents himself after the deed is done, demanding compensation? Who is watching from the huts? He was not man enough to kill it.

A week later Victor had recruited his porters, or rather his fellow-porters, for he intended to carry his own share. First was a sturdy young Ibo, son of the principal trader in the *grand village* who had brought him up to speak not only the language of their homeland in far-off Nigeria, but real English, *pidgin*, and French. Victor had already won his admiration. Next there was Mba, a tribesman of massive build from further north, a version of Umslopagaas, in Victor's eyes, of the Alan Quatermain stories by Rider Haggard on which he had been reared. Mba was recently married; he was unwilling to leave his bride alone so soon, and so she was to come too.

Victor laid out his expeditionary equipment on his bed in the Rest House. It consisted of tinned foods, salt tablets, medical kit and water sterilisers; ammunition for game rifle and pistol; a kerosene stove, lantern, matches, and torch; an all-purpose penknife, and his Malay *parang* (a machete); the panning equipment and empty containers; water bottle, groundsheet (which doubled as a poncho), mosquito net, camera and film; and, for currency, tobacco, salt, and a bottle of powerful resinous alcohol. As for the waterproof pouch which contained Vivienne's letters, he put this aside with items of clothing and books in the care of the rest house servant for his return in a few weeks. The letters' destruction just now would be an exaggerated act. Why trouble to deny a past he had grown beyond? Although his mind would be easier if they were beyond reach, they recorded – indeed themselves comprised – something once inexpressibly precious. Perhaps he might re-read them (which he had never done since each was first received) before he parted with them for ever, but there was no time for that now. In any case, it would be ludicrous to suppose their survival implied a betrayal of June. That evening, on the very eve of the expedition proper, he sat down and wrote a letter to June, packed with all his activities and redolent with tenderness, which he posted that night.

The *Chef de Région* had placed at Victor's disposal an elderly river launch to carry the party upriver and into the tributary to where M.

Marcel, the solitary European, worked his timber concession. It would save days of laborious paddling into the current. The dawn mist had not risen from the matted rim of forest across the slumbering river by the time the party of four and the *Chef*'s boatmen were assembled on the landing stage and their packs and chattels put aboard. It was the sweet hour of the tropical day, that the sunrise itself bisects. Only then, reviewing the inventory, did Victor consider he had packed too little film.

He hurried back up the three hundred yards of the island's steep riverbank to the rest house, where the dog was waiting, and at once found the film. Like the letters it was contained in a waterproof pouch. He first picked up the pouch of letters in error, and it was by the merest caprice – should 'something' happen to him in the jungle and his remnant chattels here find their way home – that he thrust that pouch too into one of his capacious bush-jacket pockets.

[iii]

The narrow eyes in their fleshy setting regarded him malevolently across the camp table. There was a sense of threat, too, in M. Marcel's pectoral muscles, which were formidable. Sitting across from Victor at their venison and wine, he boasted that there was no task, no piece of equipment, he could not handle better than his men. He despised Africans, he reckoned that fifty should be shot every day by the authorities, although would that be fast enough to eliminate so worthless a race?

He also detested the English, he told his guest from the English shires. When he first came to Equatorial Africa, ten years previously, he was given a job: put a stop, they ordered, to the hijacking of the company's rafts of timber on their month-long journey floating down to the sea-port. Someone was shooting the natives assigned to pole the rafts off the mud banks and replacing them with his own pair who then delivered the timber, re-branded, to a rival company at the rivermouth. It was an English villain conducting this operation, M. Marcel discovered, when he ambushed the riverside camp where brands were changed. 'What species of man do you suppose he was?' M. Marcel demanded, revelling in his narrative. 'An old man! An old crock of a boozer. Been in Africa since the First World War. Had a native wife at the port. Can you believe it? He'd actually married her.'

M. Marcel's mouth made a circle of clownish astonishment.

'What do you suppose I did? Kill him? Not I. If you have to kill a black, you kill a black. With a white it's different, even with an old crock of a boozing Englishman.' The narrative was approaching its beautiful climax. 'So what did I do? I trussed him up and tied him to the raft so that only his head was above the water. *Eh bien?*' The tiny eyes were all aglitter. 'It was only a matter of time before *monsieur le crocodile* took note and *paff* . . . an old man disappears *sans funèbres!*' His laughter burst out into the surrounding darkness. It was an orgasm of merriment in a man long starved of it. 'Maybe his wife ate the crocodile!' The pricks of eyes produced their little streams of joyous tears.

The laughter left the clearing oddly quiet as if everything in the riverside enclave had listened to it. The forest itself, which clamped them in against the river, was never normally silent, and it was too early for the low murmur of the labourers to have ceased. Victor could see the moon through high foliage from under the edge of the open roof that covered them. It seemed remote and indifferent to this place. It was the white light of the lamp not the moon that made the scars on M. Marcel's forearm look like black ravines under their vegetation of hair.

'Unexplored?' M. Marcel scoffed. 'What do you mean by "unexplored"?'

'I took the word from the map. The recent map.'

'There is nothing in there. Nothing at all. One cannot explore nothing. It's just a word, my friend.'

After they had eaten and drunk, he conducted Victor round the camp with a lantern on his nightly round. The natives got up from their beds or their bowls of manioc and stood silently. Victor's own team was with them, at one end of a long hut. 'You should oblige them to stand when you approach,' M. Marcel counselled. 'They will take advantage of lenience, always. You saw *le grand docteur?*' he continued. 'He'll tell you what they're like. He knows his Africa – a great man, *un homme sensible, hein?*' It was hard to deny he was a sensitive man. Had Victor not read, in the *grand docteur*'s own autobiographic notes, how as a boy in Alsace he had fainted at the beauty of a brass band playing in the public gardens?

'I tell you,' M. Marcel persisted, 'I pay them in alcohol, they prefer it to money. They know they are animals.'

'What do you mean?'

'They regard the gorillas as their rivals, their enemies. They have stories of battles with gorillas, of gorillas ambushing them and running off with their guns and spears. They know they're no different. Their ancestors used to live in the jungle, of course, up the trees. Nowadays they're afraid of the forest. They've abandoned it to the gorillas. My friend, if the gorillas get you, we'll know you've gone native!' He guffawed again, and conducted his guest to the sapling used as a whipping post for the disobedient or recalcitrant. The weapon itself, of plaited hide, was stuck in the lower branches. 'It reminds them,' the Frenchman observed.

'You want my opinion?' he demanded, opening a third bottle. 'You waste your time. If there was gold in there, why would I be here extracting timber? You think I am stupid?'

'The gold-dust must come from somewhere,' Victor replied.

'Everywhere you go in Africa, natives have gold-dust. You are an innocent, my friend. For example, what route are you taking from here?' The eyes watched his guest cunningly.

'I shall march due east,' Victor said.

'Due east? A simple east, like that? Nobody can move through the jungle on a compass bearing. Not even an Englishman.'

'I shall compromise with the game tracks.'

'Ah, compromise with the game tracks. *Eh bien*, why this "due east"?'

'I want to get as far from the big rivers as possible, to higher ground where there could be streams.'

'What makes you suppose there is higher ground?'

'The *Chef de Région* said he thought the land rises . . .'

'The *Chef* believes anything. Nobody knows the forest as I do.'

'What about the natives?'

'I told you. The natives cling to the rivers. They are afraid of the forest. They never enter it further than they need to go for a crap.'

In the morning it was raining: it was impossible even to see across the forty-metre river. Only a trace of superciliousness hung about the corners of M. Marcel's mouth, and as Victor assembled his three porters, he handed his guest two days' supply of manioc wrapped in a leaf. He invited him to stay with him on his return. 'We whites,' he commented, 'must stick together. In a place like this.' He put out a thick paw to be shaken.

Mba bore the three Africans' supplies on his head, in a banana-frond bundle tied with fibre. The girl carried the airline bag, also on her head, and the young Ibo a rucksack. Victor led, with the other rucksack and the rifle, and the pistol at his belt. M. Marcel had appeared to him as a repulsive figure, and the Frenchman's hostility was scarcely veiled. How could the seemingly dedicated *Chef de Région* represent such a monster as a friend? Yet simultaneously Victor felt attracted by M. Marcel. There was an honesty to his brutishness. In the primaeval struggle for existence, M. Marcel survived by his own will and his own audacity. He was less than ten years older than Victor, and most of the year was stuck out all alone in his riverside forest camp, yet he seemed to have lived life in a way that had all but escaped Victor. The various scars on the Frenchman's muscled body carried a story of death cheated. He knew where to find his women as unerringly as his liquor at every *grand village* down the river and every port along the coast. At each leave he would learn of a new child he had fathered. Victor found no occasion to tell him of his own pregnant June in north Oxfordshire.

The instant Victor and his three companions left the wide track made by the foresters and the jungle closed around them, he was aware of its primal force. The experience was not new to him, but in Malaya had he recognised it for what it was? He perceived now that something concerning the jungle had sirened him back to it: an awe, that reached to the bowels, of which in his way M. Marcel too was an exemplar. He recognised now that the jungle was the opposite of its reputation: it was not impenetrable, it invited penetration.

Man feared it; indigenous man could make his life only along its perimeter, on river banks, and by atavistic obeisance. But it was a needed, compulsive fear, as of a blind, indecipherable, archaic god. There was no space for pity, moralism, none of the refined and contemplative conceits of humankind. Whatever was most vigorous, most ruthless, prevailed and survived. When M. Marcel was contemptuously dismissing the possibility of alluvial gold in the jungle while slyly sussing out his intended route, Victor knew his host was acting the only way the jungle allowed. If Marcel were to send a couple of men to track him, or arranged an 'ambushing gorilla' as he had arranged crocodiles to finish the old man, a natural justice would have taken its course. Was man not, at base, another animal, competing for whatever the forest chanced to offer? Might not man, like any other species, instinctively assume his rights within a territory, and exercise them with the required savagery? Why should M. Marcel not see his rights as extending beyond the food of the rivers and the giant hardwoods immediately at hand, to unlocated treasures of the hinterland?

Victor felt not afraid but liberated. Why should his own energy, cunning and ruthlessness not suffice? He was fit, strong and instinctually alert. Now he was interpreting scents and sounds, and little signs like spoor, droppings and snapped stems. He could feel the trust of his team bulwarking him. He could already sense himself taking on the lines of a hero to the young Ibo, and the massive Mba, whose tribe populated the adjacent north, deferred willingly to his judgment.

Victor himself led, compass in hand. They struck eastwards for two days, then south, so as to cross the streams and rivulets which presumably fed the main tributary. The virgin forest, an Eden unwary of men, proved to be a cageless menagerie of animal life. Troupes of monkeys accompanied them through the treetops on a plane above. Forest elephant, whose tracks they followed so far as their direction allowed, were frequently in evidence; so too, by their contrasting scents, were buck, cats (leopards or civets), forest hog. As night fell by a pool, he shot a small buck for the pot. The two shots silenced the forest like M. Marcel's laughter, then the chatter and cackle resumed with an altered tone.

I cannot say whether Victor Rowlands observed that moment of altered tone. It is difficult to be certain what a man's mind takes note of. The activity of dreams suggests it is infinitely subtler than our common perception acknowledges. As Mba flayed the little beast, and his woman deftly knifed up the flesh (she was to boil it all up, piece by piece, that very night), I cannot be sure that Victor's mind did not somewhere record the sudden reduction of a creature of infinite grace, glory, rightness within its dappled world, to man's meat. I *suspect* it did. Victor was not an unimaginative man: rather, it was that nothing had ever been expected of his imagination. If asked what he was doing here, camped round a low fire in the dense blackness of an unexplored tropical forest, he would not have hesitated to answer, 'Seeking a fortune.' Why, please? 'For the sake of my wife, my family-to-be.' His reason was staked there firmly in north Oxfordshire.

Questioned further, I suspect he would evince a little impatience, expressed with a dismissive charm. What more was there to ask? He had this forest to himself. He was master of himself, and master of this place – a trained man, with his compass, guns, his loyal team. Mastery unmakes mystery. But mystery has its methods – the 'low road' in the Highland song, the spirit road, the dream, the magic way. It bides its time.

Setting out next morning he was astonished to see in the soft earth the fresh imprint of a human hand. He stopped abruptly on the track.

A human hand with a deformed thumb! The Africans had come up beside him, gazing at it. The *Chef de Région* had told of outcast tribesmen . . . yet Victor's party was already too far *in*. And what were these fibrous remains, chewed white and juiceless, a creature's breakfast roots? And just further along the track as they resumed, its faeces, resembling the faeces of a man, yet not quite a man's? Surely they would catch up with it and any minute would see it – a gorilla, of course, whose footprint it was – they would spot it ahead on the track, half-turned on an extended knuckle regarding them with a glance of mean, half-human complicity. They did not, but instead it seemed that a few minutes later the creature slipped off right from where it accompanied them on a parallel course, always just out of sight, uttering its cough-bark call. Its man-cousins puzzlingly mimicked it, and thus they continued all day, building an infantile language of mutual inquisitiveness.

Next day the canopy of trees became broken. The ground here was higher, watercourses rarer. Natural glades occurred. And on the seventh day Victor saw unmistakably in the silt of a stream the glitter of particles of gold. Here they made camp for a week. Samples of silt were taken systematically from every stream within a radius of ten miles. At certain points, Victor himself panned the silt until he had half-filled his small tin. It was a triumphant time. Exploitable or not, the presence of the metal vindicated him. Here, in the depths of the forest, the discoverer's rights were paramount. There were none to challenge him. He was Prester John, El Dorado, in his kingdom of trees and beasts. When they awoke each morning they found themselves marvelled at from the trees at the edge of their clearing by a family of rufous chimpanzees. Each evening, after their meal of game stew, Victor worked on his sketch maps by lamplight, inserting six-figure map references. He wrote up his diary, for the story to be retailed to June and one day, perhaps, to their child. He shared his thoughts with the young Ibo, and the Africans asked him about life in England. He drew them a picture of a horse. At night he slept with his weapons beside him: *his* body would supply no tribesmen with fetishes.

Then there was an odd occurrence. They believed, as I have been at pains to explain, that they were now very far from human presence. This was not a territory of pygmies or any forest dwellers. They had marched on, away from the river highway, for several days. But on the last day of their sojourn in the forest depths, they came across the remnants of a native hut. It was a primitive shelter, it had not been occupied for some while, vegetation crowded in and creeper had worked across its thatch. But it was unmistakably the work of man.

It gave them sudden pause. There was a small clay pot, a tiny circle of damp, blackened stubs. If they were alone now, they could not presume it would always be so. This place was known of by another or others besides themselves; known of, and known, perhaps, from long past. Victor Rowlands's presumption of kingship was called into question by this paltry, crooked hump of woven leaves and grasses on a mean frame of twisted cane.

On the second day of their return march westward they struck a river. It was some twenty yards across and would surely flow into the tributary of the great watercourse they set forth from. They followed this downstream for several miles, keeping it in view as well as they could, until at length they spotted the sign they sought – a fishtrap. Soon after a cluster of huts appeared on the further bank, set back a few yards from the river's edge. Then they caught sight of a similar grouping of huts in a compound on their own side of the river.

The white man and three black strangers emerging from the forest were met by the inhabitants in stunned silence. Even the dogs were mute. The very silence communicated itself and without call or whisper men slowly emerged from huts, the women hanging back in the shadows. Men and women moved in slow-motion aimlessness such as Victor recalled from newsreels of Nazi concentration camps. Here was the same spectral incomprehension of eye, the same gaze of infinite emptiness. The grass thatch was musty and grown with weed. From one such hut a withered headman was carried out to pay wheezing respects to the pale intruder and his companions from the feared forest. Something was dreadfully amiss. It took a minute for Victor to grasp what it was. The venereal sickness the whites brought to Africa with shackle, gospel and gun had fixed upon this fag-end of upriver humanity a God-forsaken desolation, and *there were no children*.

One man alone seemed free of the blight. He was stocky and muscular. The skin of his upper body was webbed with a profusion of scars that indicated persistent magical attempts to fend off the scourge. He came paddling across from the further bank with ferocious strokes. Officious, hectoring, accustomed to obedience, he was ugly as much by will as by nature. He made it evident at once the visitors were unwanted. He confronted Victor as a threat to his power. For power he had. Perhaps by virtue of brute strength and vigour, spirit-power rested in him, and thus, amid a people so stricken, temporal power too. He was this community's medicine-man.

Victor's single requirement was a dugout to carry him and his companions downstream to the tributary they had set out from, and thence to the great river and the island's *grand village* – a journey, he presumed, of a few days. Someone must accompany them, both to quell the alarm of the communities they would appear among on their descent downriver and to paddle the dugout back. This village possessed only one dugout large enough for five and only one possible escort: the medicine-man himself. He refused outright. Victor was not inclined to give way, nor was it wise to do so. M. Marcel's warning came to mind, 'They will take advantage of any weakness.' If he wavered here they might never get a craft to carry them . . .

The prestige of a white-skinned man was formidable. But here the species was known only by hearsay and by no structure of authority. With the passage of days, the presence of children might allow a stranger like himself to win *rapport* with a primitive community. Here were none. Following their leader's example the villagers shunned the interlopers and shrank away at any approach. They cooked for themselves. The withered headman proffered manioc, that was all. Only of an evening, as Victor sat on a stool outside their disused hut, writing up his diary, would the men squat in a half-circle to watch this gnomic ritual. From time to time they got up to peer more closely at the movement of the pencil as it made its minuscule scars on the square white leaves of his notebook. Victor's young Ibo, who could read, would indicate a written word and make a sound for it, then turn that sound into a word of language known to the onlookers. They wondered silently. The medicine-man kept away.

Victor himself grew stubborn. He would wait, he would bargain. He had no intention of revealing his gold. Currency had no meaning. Guns, however, evidently did, and in these – the pistol and rifle – the medicine-man expressed a greedy interest. The bottle of resinous spirit also had meaning. On the third morning negotiations became centred on this liquor. At length the ruffian consented: he would accompany the party downstream in the big dugout in exchange for the bottle they had with them plus two more when they reached the *grand village*.

Victor resolved to set out forthwith. But as they loaded the narrow, unstable dugout refractoriness broke out anew right there at the water's edge: the man would only go if he got his first bottle *now*. They confronted one another in argument like two cocks, puffed and contemptuous. Victor in disgust offered a tactical concession: *half* now. Instantly the man grabbed the brown bottle from the rucksack already in the dugout, yanked out its stopper and began to gulp. Victor had to wrest it away – over half was gone in that short moment. Less than two mintues later the party was on its way, the half-drunk tribesman for'ard with a paddle, with Victor's 'Umslopagaas', Mba, in the stern with another paddle.

They rounded the first bend in the river. A partially cleared, once-cultivated patch of steep ground appeared on the right bank. The medicine-man in the bow brought the dugout close in alongside. In a flash he was out of the boat and scrambling up the bank, making for the forest. With a great roar, Mba was after him, all but capsizing the little craft as he leapt from it. He flung himself after the fugitive and caught him in the middle of the clearing. The battle was fought out with hands, teeth and heads – especially heads. It was unequal from the start. The medicine-man was fearless in drink and sturdy but wild and clumsy, Mba by far the mightier in size and muscle. He butted the other mercilessly, to the exhortations of his woman and the Ibo. In a minute or two he had the fellow by a leg and an arm and had flung him into the river. Long-snouted gavial lurked under the banks.

Humiliated and sobered the medicine-man crawled ignominiously out and reboarded the dugout by the stern. Mba took the prow. Victor loaded his revolver and kept the man covered as he paddled. The native fixed the white with a glowering stare. If need be, Victor would shoot him.

Or would he? I have sometimes wondered. I feel I should know him well enough by now to be able to say, in such-and-such circumstances he would kill him, or under such-and-such threat. *If you have to kill a black, you kill a black* were M. Marcel's recent words to him. He did not imagine himself to be bluffing now, with his pistol at the ready. He had shot the enemy in action in Malaya: that was like scoring a half-century for the House team. But this was more particular. He was acquainted with this man, however worthless and despicable. He sat hunched with the revolver in his tilted lap supposing he would use it, but without precision of thought. Despite the man's hostility, he judged it wiser to keep him with them. Many miles of river lay ahead, and so much explanation if they were to travel without any member of this riverine tribe; nor did he intend to *steal* the boat. All that day he never let the man out of his sight. That night, at another village likewise blighted and cowed by the spirits' disfavour, he set a guard over the dugout and slept with his weapons attached to his person.

Next morning their river flowed silently into the main tributary, a secret, willed surrender, the lesser lost within the greater, a life given to whatever is more than life. The placid greater river had its own bestiary: here were crocodiles not gavials, and hippos were in evidence. Human settlements occurred every two or three miles, each half-hour or so of paddling. The dense, implacable curtain of jungle would part fractionally for a tiny track to lead from riverside to a clearing out of sight. Each such paltry community of a dozen huts was linked to neighbours only by the river, and none had forewarning of the inexplicable strangers paddling down the river they had never ascended.

It was at that union of rivers that the letters came to mind. Perhaps the passing out of unexplored into mapped territory prompted decision. The letters had lain in their oilskin bag unconsidered throughout the expedition. It was now or never. With difficulty, given the narrowness and low freeboard of their primitive craft, he extricated them from the bowels of his rucksack. The pouch with its big flap wrapped round was fastened by two tapes. He weighed up whether he might at last re-read them before bidding them farewell. But would it not affront a memory immediately thereafter to cast them out? And might they disappoint? He recalled no phrase, only the shards of joy they brought him in his lonely station upcountry. Sometimes Vivienne decorated them with little pictures – he remembered that. Would they prove banal, their wonder to have belonged only to a passion that was half-childish? It occurred, that early vibrancy, and was left behind. There was no replaying, no merit in putting it now to the test of his maturer scrutiny.

He trailed the squared-up pouch in the dark water, making it skim the surface, then let it go, watching it bob away in their wash and the vigorous paddle strokes of the medicine-man who, facing him, looked at the white man with surprise in his apish eye. The object remained visible, floating awkwardly on the glassy blackness, until a broad, leftward sweep bore them out of sight. No further thought was to be given those letters of long ago. Who was that boy playing at love, mocked by his fellows for his infatuation? What bearing had he on this robust man, emerging triumphant from the unexplored with samples of alluvial gold in his pack upon which to build a fuller life for his unborn child and his flawless wife? The callow past had no rights on present and future. They must press on to the *grand village*.

In his urgency to speed their descent, he allowed night to fall without choosing their resting place. But the moon was full, and every few miles they came on a cluster of fishtraps or a moored dugout, and a moment's parting of the jungle. He himself felt no tiredness. He took the forward paddle, Mba the paddle astern. They kept midstream where the current served them best. When at about ten p.m. moonlight fell on a path between the trees, Victor determined to halt at the very next settlement. Yet was it not already too late to intrude upon a village without grievously alarming the inhabitants?

The next settlement was slow to appear. They paddled on in the darkness, chewing kola nuts. At last they caught sight on the left bank of a single moored dugout. As they drew in towards it, there, to be sure, was the thread of a pathway which the moon revealed just parting the canopy of forest. They came alongside, and secured their little craft. Before rest, food was required; manioc, even a fistful of bananas, would suffice. Late as it was – close upon midnight – Victor led his young Ibo up the track to see what they could find, leaving the others at the river's edge, Mba in charge of the rifle. Victor had his pistol with him.

Within fifty yards, as expected, the path opened into a clearing of a dozen or more huts. There was no sound; no dogs to bark warning, no sign of life. The stillness was of such intensity as to suggest this was an abandoned settlement. Yet there was that dugout. They paused outside the entrance first of one hut, then another, and softly called. No one responded. After half a minute's familiarity with the stillness, a low sound from one of the huts became audible: muffled drumming. The two men approached. Through the reed walls of a certain hut the glow of a fire was just visible. With the muttered throb of drumming was now also discernible a rhythmic stamping of ankle rattles. A partition of slatted reeds blocked the hut's entrance: Victor rapped it sharply. Instantly all sound ceased.

There ensued a frozen silence of several seconds. Then with violent abruptness the partition was yanked back. A grotesque apparition thrust itself upwards at him: a creature scarcely human, squat, daubed, and wigged. It uttered a sharp cry, at which the very walls of the hut burst open on three sides, releasing a scramble of native figures that fled headlong for the surrounding forest.

With his left hand Victor grabbed the creature that had uttered the cry, and drawing his pistol entered the hut. Before the central fire lay a woman, smeared in white lime, and further back two other human creatures, painted up and too sick to make flight. Beside the fire on the ground stood an enamel basin containing a moist and reddish compound of substances; a foul smell filled the air. His captive had turned instantly slack and compliant. She was a hunched and shrivelled woman. Face, neck, shoulders and fleshless dugs were daubed with white lime. Her eyes were ringed in red, and the same red covered her fingers. A civet pelt crowned her head, with a grass wig stained maroon on one side. Neck and throat were festooned with snail shells and stained tufts, and her skirt was similarly of bunched grasses, one half stained maroon. Wrists and ankles were ringed with rattles.

At the sight of this priestess-witch, the young Ibo had taken to his heels. Victor, however, was exhilarated. He at once resolved to expose all he could about this wretched dark rite at full-moon in propitiation of the spirits' wrath, to confound it in the name of civilisation. Still gripping his witch, his 'Gagool', he returned to the river. There was the Ibo, regarding him wide-eyed from the bank. When the medicine-man, cowering with the others in the dugout, caught sight of the witch, he began to utter little exclamations of horror which mounted to sharp commands of dismissal addressed to the woman herself. She hung back limp in her captor's grip. Victor ordered the Ibo to bring him the torch. Only on repeating it was he reluctantly obeyed and the torch handed him at arm's length. 'Sir,' the Ibo said, 'you must send this person away.' He pointed to the forest.

'I shall do nothing of the kind. You will come with me back to the village.'

The Ibo accompanied him like a scolded dog, leaving the others to cower and jibber in the dugout. Victor would have no truck with this persecuting superstition. He strode back to the hut which had been the scene of the ritual. One of the diseased victims was still as he had left her, hunched into her wretchedness, by the dying fire. One was gone. A third was trying to crawl out through a gap in the hut wall: Victor forbade it. He had his Ibo close the gaps in the hut's walls.

There he stayed, covering the three wretches with his pistol. They seemed acquainted with the lethal force of the white's clumped steel. They began furtively to rub off their body paint and shed their ritual accoutrements. The white man forbade this too: he would have them as they were, in the morning he would photograph them. But what had become of the rest of the villagers? He was caught up in a fury of exorcism. By now he had fortified his Ibo enough to leave him on guard with the pistol over the three sickly women. He went out into the compound with his torch. They could not be far. He would gather them in. He had had enough of this cowering at shadows. He would convert by the enlightenment of his inheritance, by light and the revolver. It was his God-granted responsibility. In his own person he was an army of light.

He began to search the other huts. The weak beam of his electric torch picked out stools, clay pots, palliasses. From the hut roofs hung a weird assortment of objects on strings of fibre – gourds, strips of meat, bunches of roots. Foodstuffs were suspended from roof slats to escape rats, he was aware of that; but was this not evidence of black magic, fetish potions of men sunk in darkness? He moved to another hut, ducking to enter. It contained nothing but three black pots. He got a whiff of the same foul pungency as of the hut where he had broken in on them. Then he saw, beyond the pots, the earth of the floor disturbed. Something was buried there. Suddenly he realised: it was exactly as he had feared, as he had feared and as he had hoped. It was customary to bury corpses beneath the family hut, linking material earth with human descent. These savages had exhumed, extracted organs, marinated them in a pungent bark, and by ingesting them made their absurd communion with the life force of ancestors.

Where had they fled to, those dark-ridden, pitiable souls? They could not be far. His frail beam had found a little track entering the jungle. Here was no moon, and almost at once the route became complex and dubious. He required to save the torch; it was his last battery. Moreover, he did not want to give himself away: they could be watching and listening from among the trees. Rather, *he* would locate *them*, perhaps by their sound or by a glimpse of them in some other clearing deeper in the forest, and then surprise, command and corral them by the authority of his presence, conduct them back to their own compound, and at dawn regale them with rays of his own light, exhort them, by some device of translation, however circuitous, through the young Ibo and Mba. He could not abandon them – neither them nor his own profound and given purpose.

They seemed to have vanished. He penetrated further, perhaps three or four hundred yards, it was difficult to tell in the utter darkness. Had there been a choice of ways? He could not be sure. Selecting a jungle foot-track by torchlight is famously tricky, a single beam making so much of the merest curtain of foliage or epiphytes that lightly mask a trodden way. But surely he was still on some path that human feet had pressed? One could not be quite sure of it. Where might they have headed? Diffused to in a random scatter? Or, in the little mass, slipped away to, by a network of hunters' tracks, to cower hidden at a place known only to them and gorillas?

He pushed ahead tentatively and paused to listen. He had his ears, he had his nose. His ears told him he was in jungle, but jungle alarmed and wary and hence peculiarly silent. Frogs were audible; monkeys were whooping from somewhere distant, across the river. No sound from birds, nothing else in the near vicinity, no rustling, cracking of twigs or of dry pods, no whispers of fear or of assault. His nose told him of human presence, of cloth against sweating skin for several days under tropical skies, and an extra scent: a tang of excitement, of chase or pursuit. All he smelt in the blackness was himself.

Pause *him* there. I should be able to read by now my Victor Rowlands, pin him there with spears or darts on his path or no-path in the heart of his forest, give him an obituary of an uncanny accuracy for his unborn child to know him by and his widow to recall him. (For this began, did it not, as an account of a marriage, the contributors thereto, for better, for worse. I set myself the task of explaining the factors why . . .) He could not decide whether to proceed or withdraw. He was unafraid. The vanished tribesmen – were they near or far? – might see themselves as fugitives, to him they were his wards, fellows of this common domain. He was alert, indeed he was intensely alive. He felt a perfect trust of the forest. He knew of men in his platoon on jungle patrol getting lost trying to return from where they had concealed themselves for a morning shit. But he was unconcerned, though without compass, or weapon either. What caused him to hesitate was a sense of having entered the border-land between possession and being possessed. The excursion – all of it, the very penetration into 'unexplored' territory – was an act of daring intimacy, rousing out of ancient quiescence powers by which he recognised himself as never before. In such an act, one is both master and slave.

He went back. His feet better than his eyes held the track. He took instructions from his sense of direction, the proximity of the silent river. He regained the compound, relieved the vigil of the young Ibo, was restored to his pistol.

With equatorial suddenness the sun leapt above the oceanic jungle. Victor ushered his sickly captives on to the compound. He obliged them to re-adorn themselves exactly as they adorned themselves for their nocturnal propitiations. He stood over them as they applied white lime and the deep red juices with despairing slowness. He re-entered the hut. The enamel basin was as immaculate as a chalice. He picked it up, with its dreadful offal and pungent bark, and planted it on the compound. He had his Ibo stand guard on the basin as well as the women. He descended the path to the river. Their dugout was gone. He scanned the expanse of water upstream and downstream.

Then he saw it and its occupants in the shadow of the vegetation overhanging the far side of the river. He yelled across and beckoned in irritation at their cravenness. He saw them momentarily confer; then the two men began to work the paddles. First they paddled upstream against the bank, to offset the lazy current, before making the crossing. Half-way across they appeared to change course again, slightly upstream, and to pause, and the medicine-man to occupy himself with something in the water, then they resumed. On disembarking they straggled behind the white man to the compound.

The daylight was already broad. Night was another place, another world. Now under the steep sun he had the three women complete, miserably, the re-adornment of faces, arms and torsos. There was still no sign of any of their fellow villagers – not a leaf pushed aside, not a call or a drumbeat. At the compound's edge the medicine-man watched with absorbed concentration. When he was satisfied, Victor photographed the pitiable trio. Then he spoke, his words relayed by the Ibo assisted by the great Mba.

He told them he knew what they were at the previous night: they had opened a grave and were making worthless medicine with the organs of one of their dead fellows. The authorities in the *grand village* would be disgusted and angry. They could see for themselves the worthlessness of their attempts to placate spirits that did not exist. Let them regard one another now. (The three wretched creatures stood in utter disconsolation.) What had all this white lime and red stain to do with their childlessness and their sickness? What comfort had this concoction in the basin ever brought them? He kicked the basin with the toe of his jungle-boot right across the compound. Its contents of bark and sludge and flesh flew into the air and spattered the beaten earth. If they were ill, or barren, let them get into their dugouts and be treated by the great white doctor in the *grand village*. Only if he, Victor, heard that the sick were on their way downstream to hospital would he refrain from ensuring that this village was punished for its cannibalism.

With that he marched down the path with his little party, the medicine-man trotting immediately behind him. Throughout the white man's peroration his expression of wild alarm had slowly been displaced by rapt wonderment. It had been a noble performance, a majestic homily addressed to all these dwellers in darkness, to the whole of black Africa, ocean to ocean, however thin his actual audience.

*

The five resumed their journey. They were to spend three more nights in riverbank villages. The medicine-man paddled with sustained energy. With each new nightly halt he became more fully at one with the expeditionary party. He mastered the kerosene stove, he opened tin cans for the first time in his life. He learned three or four words of English and uttered them often, with pride. A clowning humour crept into his ugly face. He appeared to have become wholly reconciled to Victor, even devoted. He adopted the white man's cheerful contempt when the rain came down, and paddled harder.

At each halt, the reach of M. Marcel's civilisation became more apparent with the occurrence of discarded planks or packing cases in the construction of huts, and tin cans and bottles. On the final morning as they rounded a sweep of the river, the landing stage of M. Marcel's timber concession came into view. One of the labourers was working there. He looked up and saw them, shielding his eyes, and waited there ready to greet the white man and his crew as they came ashore. Even at a distance his puzzlement was evident that they paddled on past. He called. Victor waved, and urged his paddlers not to pause. He had no intention of involving M. Marcel in his discoveries.

It was dark again before they slid up against the rough wharf of the *grand village*. The place seemed to Victor to constitute just about all a man required in the refinements of living: a shower, cold beer, the carefree, liquid refrains of bastardised African music, a sprung bed. In the morning at the *Post Restante* he would pick up June's letters awaiting him.

Late that next day he climbed the hill to pay his respects to the *Chef de Région*, who had been hearing cases in court all morning. They lunched at his residence the following afternoon, attended upon by the elderly houseboy with blunted hands. As to gold, Victor reported only that there were traces of alluvial deposits, but he would risk no opinion until an assay was done. Regarding him quizzically, the *Chef* commented that Africa had a way of holding on to her secrets, so that Victor wondered if a defeatism had not infected France's equatorial role at its core. He described the tribe's sickness and his breaking in upon the midnight ritual, but said nothing of cannibalism: he had no wish to be kept back as a witness. None the less his host queried, '*Pas de fétiches?*'

Victor said he noticed nothing.

'That's strange,' the other said, and Victor could see he knew he was lying. 'They cannot make the distinction between the material and the spiritual. Someone as observant as you will have discovered that. In Africa, power resides in things as much as in people.' He motioned to the tribal artefacts around the room.

'You have become *bien assimilé*,' the *Chef* smiled as Victor was leaving. The Englishman perceived a glint of mischief in his host's eyes, and guessed he had already heard that the previous night he had taken to bed the jut-arsed mulatto at the *bar*. He wondered how he knew, for he had been careful not to bring her to the Rest House. They had gone to her hut, primitive though it was: first she had urinated into her plastic bucket and when they lay down together he took her like an animal, thus avoiding the vast mouth and its massive red-stained teeth. Only later in the night could his body reconcile itself with hers and allow full coupling, mouth upon mouth, fur to fur – what they call the 'missionary position'. Oh, they made quite a meal of one another . . .

What impudent little rumour had been wagged and whispered so swiftly up the hill to the residence of these neat white socks? Had the *Chef* heard too that, this same morning, he had shot the dog? (Something about this breezy official he found hard to decipher.) The crippled brute had seemed to lay siege to him since his return, it had even been there on the path through the bananas as he walked back at dawn from the half-caste's hut to the Rest House. It was in a more dreadful condition than ever. After breakfast he took his pistol and in a moment when the creature had twisted upon itself to gnaw at its sores – for this task alone could it still summon momentary frenzies of energy – he shot it in the back of the head and flung the body into the deep grasses. Only then did he realise it was pregnant. Such a creature, pregnant! He couldn't understand why he had hesitated to destroy it when he was here before.

The next daybreak he paid off his African companions and bade them goodbye. An unforeseen attachment had grown between him and the medicine-man. The fellow had made camp in the Rest House enclosure. He had taken his wages partly in alcohol (one bottle only), and partly in money and food which he accompanied Victor to market to buy. He declared his wish to remain in Victor's service, and when told this could not be so entreated Victor to re-employ him on his return. Victor insisted the fellow go back to his own people and not linger in the *grand village*. When the white indicated the possibility of not returning here, he seemed utterly crestfallen, and fell into a mute bewilderment that not even the final parting could penetrate.

Now that the rains had begun it took nearly two weeks for Victor to reach Brazzaville in his jeep. Whole stretches of road were inundated; bridges of pairs of logs, planed so as to carry a truck's wheels each side, were often dislodged. Steep passages had become little torrents, and what had been a good murram vehicle-track two or three months previously had turned into miniature ravines. Other transport stayed put, waiting for the rains to end and the road gangs to get to work again. Victor alone struggled on southward. It seemed the place was trapping him in, holding him back.

Even in Brazzaville there was no quick returning home to his beloved June and his farm. For he must find out how to stake a claim, should the assay of his alluvial samples prove him justified; and he must sell his jeep. Meanwhile he could watch for symptoms of any penalty to be paid for his loins' moments of fulfilment in the *grand village*. (I am glad to say that none appeared.) So another two weeks elapsed before he cabled June that he was about to fly home.

[iv]

Airports, especially those terminals catering for inter-continental traffic, hold a fascination for both my wife Pat and me. We become absorbed by the partings and reunions of others: the crosscurrents of pain and joy, the grief and relief at severances, the expectancies and shynesses between those receiving or giving welcome, the shafts of lust and sometimes dismay. Love plays so many roles, in such skilled disguise, that neither of us wonders at that international masonry of psychologists required to keep track of it.

June was of course there at London airport to meet her Victor. It seemed to him now that he had been longing for this moment for weeks. He glimpsed her silk-scarved head through the customs exit, beyond the barrier. 'Monday's child, fair of face'. Now a mother-to-be. He wondered how long she had stood there, for his plane was several hours late; it was already late afternoon. Their unborn already showed its presence under her winter coat.

A tiredness slightly masked her natural loveliness. So many had been asking about him, she reported: he had become an exploring celebrity. On the two-hour drive home across country in bleak March dusk, he enthusiastically retailed his experiences. Already they seemed oddly unreal; the more he tried to exercise his powers of description, the more they seemed storybook stuff. From time to time she appeared to fall into a reverie of her own. How dreadful it was, she commented, the French colonial authorities did so little for the natives that they let entire tribes grow up without any education. Presumably people like that medicine-man, she asked, had no opportunity to learn how to read, or even hardly to know what writing signified? Victor confirmed that, indeed, he did not.

Because of the baby, June said, as the wheels crunched their driveway, she had made up Victor's bed in his dressing-room. She knew he would agree there should be no risking the baby. She entered the house ahead of him to warm up the meal she had prepared before she left that morning, leaving him to unload the Rover.

How the dogs welcomed him! Under a concerted assault of canine delight, he brought out his baggage and carried it up to his own workroom for unpacking in the morning. But he could not resist digging out the little tin box of alluvial gold he himself had panned in the jungle streams, to show June.

Just as he was leaving the room he noticed the large pile of mail neatly piled on his desk. On top was a bulky package that drew his attention. It carried the familiar stamps of French Equatorial Africa. It had been insufficiently wrapped for its long journey, for the packet had split open along three sides and kept its contents only by virtue of an elastic-band presumably provided by the Royal Mail. Even before he had removed the band, Victor saw the green of an army issue oilskin pouch.

He opened the package in a swoon. The blood drained from his head. Immediately under the tattered wrapping were two notes. One was on the official writing paper of the *Chef de Région, Haute Ogoué*, dated twelve days earlier. It read in French as follows:

> '*Cher Monsieur*,
> 'The enclosed package evidently belonging to you was recovered by my good friend M. Marcel from a strange native he found paddling upstream past his station on the River Ngounié. The native was acting suspiciously and asked M. Marcel for a job, although not sober. M. Marcel had him searched and the enclosed package was recovered from him, identifiable as the property of your good self. M. Marcel had the man beaten but he insisted upon the improbable tale that he had not stolen it from you. Yet what other explanation? I am happy to return these documents to your safekeeping.
>   'Believe me, etc.
>   '*Etienne Lefèbre, Chef de Région.*'

★

The other note was from June.

> 'V – This arrived open, and I read part of what it contains thinking it might be something I should deal with. Part was enough and please don't try to explain. J'

Only the outer copies of Vivienne's letters had been rendered illegible by their night in the river. The adhesive of the cornflower envelopes had caused some to stick together. Other sheets of her writing-paper showed brownish contours from their partial submergence and had stiffened, but were still quite legible.

[v]

June gave birth to a daughter four months later. That child, Priscilla, is now of course already grown up. We see a lot of Priscilla, indeed she gets along admirably with Pat, whom she addresses as 'Patience' (my wife's full name) with the quaintly impudent formality I find so appealing. It was a style little Priscilla adopted in her childhood after the divorce of her parents. At first, I suppose, it was a means of self-defence, a need for containment in secretly endured pain amid the shattered trust of her home. (The farm was sold.) It is her characteristic, charming version of her mother's less humorous stoicism.

For June could never bring herself to admit that things could not be quite the same after the incident of those letters. It was not her way of handling her problems. Heaven knows I tried often enough to talk it out – ah, I see I have let it slip, as I suppose was inevitable, that I am the Victor of this narration – but she would invariably brush the subject aside, claiming she had 'already forgotten all about it'. You see, nothing had disturbed the perfection of our love up to that point, nothing had been allowed to. Ours was *true love*, and true is a word like 'all' or 'perfect' or 'ever' – allowing no ifs or buts, no reservation, flaw, compromise, no change. There was no allowance for it. We had met in Eden, ready-made, before the Fall and before, of course, Mr Darwin. Our problem differed from that of the first inhabitants in that, with them, the one had persuaded the other to partake of the apple. They were both in on it, so to speak.

One shouldn't push analogies too far. For another thing, Adam didn't write Genesis. By which I mean to say that Pat's and my 'rule' of taking no sides in marital disputes may, *sui generis*, have been vitiated on account of the authorship of this writing, if only in what I have chosen to say and chosen to leave out. I have a sense that the June I have described is something of a cypher, that I have built her of little pieces of standard manufacture – arms, legs, a mop of hair comprising a generally acceptable prettiness. I have a sense that there is much more to explain. Of course there is, vastly so. (She too re-married, suddenly, to a wiry little actuary who seems to despise me, pityingly, though I have no feelings towards him whatsoever.) My account has given the stage to that fellow Victor, shamelessly, and left June like a dismembered doll for the masonry to pick over. I know well it is not enough for one to protest, as I believe to be the truth, that *I too saw it June's way*, I too wanted nothing to have changed, I too wanted the shape of love to stay as it was, as June herself had written of it, in serene expectancy, in the letters awaiting me at the *Poste Restante* and occupying the pocket of my bush-jacket as it hung on the post of the half-breed's hut.

Looking back now, it seems that I should have *obliged* her to talk it out at the time. Such hindsight is so easy! June was pregnant, with the fruit of our love; she had 'forgotten' it. What moment was this to risk upsetting her with convoluted explanations? And what sort of explanation could I really have given, carrying little Vivienne's letters with me into *territoire inexploré*?

'Forgotten' meant 'not forgotten', naturally. Once she referred to 'those pictures', and I knew immediately she meant the little drawings with which Vivienne sometimes decorated her letters. I regretted then that I no longer had the letters to refer to – I burned them the very next day after my return to the farm without re-reading a line – for I could hardly recall the 'pictures'. All I could remember were the devices she would introduce in which she made play with our shared initials, sometimes slotting the Vs one into another, sometimes inverting them so that their points overlapped. It was not a trick you could play with every pair of capitals, not for instance with a V and a J. I suppose one could read a spectacular intimacy into what can be done with two Vs. So I told her once, 'I never even slept with Vivienne,' which was true. On our very last night together, on the verandah of her parents' house in Sime Road, Singapore, she allowed me to press myself against her bared tummy, and I experienced . . . well . . . release, like that. But that was all. God knows, it was all. I've never pretended, have I, slinky little Vivienne counted for much.

June looked at me then with a blend of doubt and disgust. *I* remember that look, have remembered it all my life. The damage was done, the alchemy already at work on the system. I remembered having thought as I burned the letters, 'This is like kicking the basin of human offal across the compound.' It was as futile as that. To burn the letters or boot the entrails was like shaking one's fist at a storm – one action on a different plane from the other.

Am I, a grown man, honestly imputing to that pouch of Vivienne's handwriting the power of a *'fétiche'*? I certainly am. When at the opening of this account I made reference to the magical in human intercourse (and perhaps in all creation) I was not intending to be fanciful but to use the best, or only, words to indicate those influences which, by exposure to the light of definition, cease to be worthy of countenancing. I am a humbler man at fifty-five.

What she had read of those 'forgotten' letters was branded on her heart. During the strains and ruckuses of ensuing years (I could fill a book), reference to them specifically or to 'your other life' would be flung out rather like a hunt protestor at a roadside Meet might fling a handful of marbles under her horse's hooves. Once she answered a counter-protestation from me with ridiculous poignancy, that it was just *because* it had taken place before we met, for else 'how easy it would have been for you to have told me'. The truth is, every attempt at explanation would fuel the pain, so I quickly learned to say nothing. And soon enough it wasn't the only issue between us, if ever quite *classifiable* as an issue at all. But I know, I know when she ceased to expect good in me: the 'good' she'd grown up to recognise.

So the burning was too late, explanation was too late; perhaps, I guessed, by the same token (an interesting word) it had always been 'too late' and that is why I didn't fight to save the marriage with quite the tenacity some of our friends expected of me. I guess that what destroyed us was there in our love already. Yet this I will say . . . and Pat, if you are reading this writing be steeled and ready, for *I* don't wish to break our rule of impartiality for you, nor do I wish to catch in your voice that tone we have heard in others' when contrasting our marriage with theirs. Though I have not led a celibate life all these years (as you know), I have never had such love to give . . . wait a minute . . . I have never given so much of myself as I gave to June. That is to say, so much of myself as I took myself to be.

That is not to mean I was mistaken as to who the man was whom June loved; only that the relationship between what one was and what one becomes is as utterly a mystery as between those who love or between whom love has been lost. When I used to read the Lesson, I remember even then puzzling over the affirmation in the Creed, 'I believe in the resurrection of the body and the life everlasting'. Which body of all the bodies I have had, or shall have? And those other bodies of mine, unresurrected, shall they remain dead and buried? I do not deny that young man who went to Africa was anyone but I, nor that he and his wife wholly shared their love. To give your all, that is 'true love'; and even if my words now may carry the timbre of jesting Pilate, inasmuch as there *is* 'true love', I can acknowledge but one. It is the characteristic of the term and I don't use it any longer, do I, Pat? It would make you smile, just as – look! – it has made my eyes brim above this paper on which I write.

Oh, and that gold? The assay turned out positive; indeed the man in the poky office up a flight of wooden stairs in Hatton Garden commented that mine were the richest alluvial samples he remembered assaying. I still have the assay document; I still have the six-figure map references, the sketch maps, the notebook. So far as I know the gold lies there to this day undisturbed, though I can't believe they write '*Territoire Inexploré*' on any part of the map of today's autonomous Republic of Gabon. London EC2 (I got a niche in the City through an old school friend I share a club with) is a far cry from the African jungle, gold or no gold, though I do come across Africans of a sort on holiday. There's a chap in Barbados I feel affinity with who mixes a marvellous daiquiri. Nowadays it's only young Priscilla, and lately her seven-year-old-boy, who keep urging me to get off my middle-aged backside and do something about it.

The Lost Poem

I ought to start by describing the resort itself. It lies in a great parting of the mountains at the head of a long valley. I have often brought the family here before – I suppose I should say 'the boys' rather than 'the family' – but somehow the cluster of habitations is always unexpected. As the road twists up through the tiny snowbound Alpine settlements, you have to persuade yourself there can be anything further up, anything significant, at least for the human race.

In former days, before the days of winter sports, there was surely nothing beyond, no human settlement: no purpose for being there since, beyond the village, the mountains just take off into their own stratosphere of snow and rock, leaving behind the last imperilled pines straggling. The peaks have had names from ancient times, of course – Aiguille Percée, Signal de l'Iséran, La Grande Motte – though the men never climbed them. What would be the object, when survival alone in these highest valleys demanded so much? The surprise is that the developers of this 'paradise of snow' should have extracted from the herdsmen so many names for their ski-runs from the shoulders, cols and declivities among the surrounding alps, in which till then none but the Creator of Mountains (to coin a phrase) and summer grazing chamois had cause to take interest.

All that survives of the village as it was up to the middle of the century is the church and the stone foundations of the few dwellings that hunched around it for security of body and soul in the long isolations of past winters. These dwellings are now rebuilt as *pensions* or converted into chalets for us packaged holidaymakers. And now the place has its own winter radio station, its monthly colour magazine, one five-star hotel, two four-star and innumerable lesser establishments for the thousands that throng it from December to April. It is a resort of some distinction, and I mention something of its past because of the parallel – the parallel with myself, that is.

I cannot refrain from congratulating myself. 'I don't imagine there's any place on earth,' I tell my wife – my second wife, to be precise – 'where we could have found so many old friends at one time.'

She frowns up from her ski brochure. 'I just can't take all this scenic splendour. It's too much. I suppose it might have done something to me once. I'm too far gone.' Angie is only forty-two. She pushes out her glass. 'Can we have a refill, darling?'

This is no time to carp at Angie's alcoholic intake: the ferocious exercise and marvellous air is doing her a power of good. We have had a superlative day skiing the Solaise. I led all the way, skiing just as well as last year. I'm sure of that.

The young mustachioed waiter is hovering.

'Anyone else? Charles?'

My seventeen-year-old son Charles Squire sticks up a finger without taking his eyes off the backgammon game to which he has challenged his younger brother.

'*Twuh*,' I say. '*Twuh kümmels avec les rocks*. "Rocks" is the same anywhere, right?' I always have trouble with the French *r*, though when I was at school they said I had an ear for the language (and I think they were right).

The waiter affects puzzlement.

'*Kummel*,' Angie assists, anglicising the German to rhyme with 'tunnel' but not really clarifying anything. All three of us try it – I, Charles, and his stepmother. *Kumel. Kümmel. Avec la glace. Sur les rocks. Kummel, koommel.* Eventually Charles writes it along the top of the *Daily Telegraph*, and the waiter smiles with wan disdain, repeating the word the Gallic way, with the 'u' as in 'cute'.

'*Twuh*', I remind him.

Long ago I made a vow not to drink after dinner because it was waking me at two or three in the morning, and I would disturb my wife slipping out of bed for a pee and pouring myself a tumbler of water . . . though of course it wasn't Angie when I made the vow, it was poor Bella. But what I call the hard grind of politics has put all such vows in jeopardy: ever since entering the House of Commons I have had to compromise. One simply can't disappoint political hosts. If one wants to stay on top of the heap one has to be 'clubbable' – that's the word that fits. It's a point I have already made to young Charles.

In any case, here in the hotel there is so much racket in the corridors late at night from the young that a visit to the bathroom at two a.m. hardly constitutes disturbance. I wouldn't call the younger members of the family and their friends arrogant but I suppose it's fair to say that their sense of social authority does sometimes spill over into unconcern for the common run of citizenry. Could one say it's the price one must pay for confidence?

'And as for Toby Budd being here,' I remark, 'that really is an extraordinary link with the past. I haven't seen him since Malaya. Nineteen fifty-bloody-one.'

'You know everyone anyway, darling,' Angie finally contributes. 'I don't see what surprises you.' She has a point. A good half-dozen English skiers had called 'hi-de-hi' up at the Solaise restaurant that very lunchtime.

'Last time I saw Toby, I was twenty. That's thirty-two years ago, Angie, let's face it. I'd have recognised him instantly. He's just gone from yellow to sort of white. Hair, I mean. Apart from that, no change. Slightly terrifying, if you ask me, these people who don't show their age. He's with Jill and Nancy.' I'd no idea they knew him. I don't imagine there's any liaison. Nancy's been having a step with Tim Thingummy – that's in full swing, far as one can tell – and Jill doesn't want to know about men any more. I don't blame her after what she went through with David. 'I told them all to pop down for a nightcap. Their chalet's only *cent mètres* up the road.'

'They'll not come now,' Angie says. 'One game of Scrabble and they'll be out like lights. It was bloody hard work today, coming down to the village in that slushy snow. If it's only their third day, they'll be out of puff.'

But almost instantly they are present. Nancy de Retz's twelve-year-old twin girls form the advance party, in their moon-boots and spiky hair. The grown-ups have taken care: both the ladies have worked on their faces, renewed mascara showing beneath the Piz Buin No. 6. Jill Parry-Jones, despite her recently acquired misanthropy, is decked out in a gent's dark green Tyrolean hat, which suits her wit and her strong profile. The *après-ski* Toby Budd is in various shades of ochre – corduroys, polo-neck, suede jacket, pigskin fur boots. He always did have money, I recollect; always a bit dressy.

The backgammon game breaks up. I introduce Angie to Toby Budd, and then Budd to my sons, Charles and Hugo. Jill and Nancy need no introductions, but Nancy identifies her twins. They seem irritated by the momentary attention, and their mouths remain sulky in their dumpling faces. I don't always understand the young. The waiter is despatched for a jug of *jus d'orange* and a further supply of *Kümmels sur les rocks*, which I consider enough in vogue to be welcome unless specifically declined. Angie takes the opportunity of providing herself with a refill, to help 'take the strain' as she puts it.

'I'm sure you didn't want us all, Angie,' Nancy declares, 'but the twins wouldn't go to bed and we daren't leave them on the loose.

Roderick' – that's I – 'just wanted a natter with Toby, I know. They last met on a boat – did you realise? – and Toby threw Roderick's poem overboard. Roderick was very upset.'

So Budd remembers too.

'Roderick never told me he wrote poems,' Angie says. 'Is this true, darling?'

'I wrote the poem Toby threw overboard,' I concede.

'You were dreadfully upset,' Budd confirms, with half a grin. 'I wondered if you remembered.'

The Budds of this world are all the same: they never take an emotional risk in their lives. Half-grin men. The line between cowardice and conceit is not easily discerned.

'What was it about?' Jill asks. 'The "ultimate passion"?' In matters affecting the sexes, her mocking humour is always at the ready these days. Is it not a characteristic of ladies whose husbands have strayed? I have spotted such a look in Bella . . . I wonder if Budd is here on account of Jill after all. He's the sort that likes to hang around women, flattering them, without having to take the plunge. There'd be no plunging with Jill.

The women's voices have become sharp-edged, a shade more blasé, drawing glances from other guests across the lounge. Various other families share the hotel with us – some large Germans; some other English, slightly beyond the pale.

'I used to write quite a lot of poetry in those days,' I admit.

'Why did you throw it overboard, Toby?' Nancy demands.

'Oh, Roderick had been messing about in my cabin. Hadn't you? I was interested in some lady aboard ship . . .'

'It wasn't like that at all,' I say.

The drinks come, with little plastic stirrers topped with the griffon that is the ancient symbol of the district. These touches pass some people by completely.

Charles and Hugo break in to inform me and their stepmother that they are going across to Fred's Tea-Bar, a discotheque the English young in this resort feel obliged to attend. The boys appear to have a multiple assignation with various school friends.

'Can we go too?' the twins plead.

'There's an age limit,' Hugo points out with the assertive roughness of a recently broken voice.

'How old?'

'Sixteen.'

'We're nearly fourteen.'

'You're nearly thirteen, you know perfectly well,' Nancy interposes.

'We'll only drink beer,' they say sulkily.

'They've no right to serve you,' Nancy puckers, though she is only mock-scolding. 'If they get thrown out of everywhere, Charles, bring them back here.'

We wrinklies watch them troop out, with a little bit of surreptitious pride, I confess.

'Hugo's only two weeks into sixteen,' I say. It is good to see Hugo letting his hair down a bit. The divorce turned him so quiet: I reckon Hugo is still finding it difficult to reconcile himself to Angie. Not that he will say so.

It is Jill who persists. 'Now, what happened to that poem? Toby's a well-established vandal. You were rivals for the same girl?'

I try to explain. Budd was then a Captain, a regular, four years older than I who was a mere 2nd Lieutenant National Serviceman – we belonged to the same regiment. We had recently steamed out of the Straits of Malacca, headed for home, and we two were sitting on deck. Budd had fallen asleep in a deck-chair with a book beside him. I felt a poem coming on. I had a pencil but no paper, except for a paperback book I had been reading. I took the paper cover off Budd's book and wrote the poem straight out, scarcely a pause, down the inside of the cover – thirty or forty lines – and the last dozen on the flyleaf of my own paperback. Then I put the paper cover in my own deck-chair and the two books on top to weight it, and in my exhilaration I swung by my hands from a pipe beneath the deck above. Budd woke up, saw his book separated from its cover and my writing on it, and protesting teasingly at my 'scribbling' he held the cover high in the wind – the ship was doing its twenty-six knots. I remember crying out 'Don't!' and Budd kept holding the cover high out of reach. I approached him for it quite gently but at the last second he let it go and the wind snatched it overboard instantly.

They have listened attentively, Budd with the old superciliousness.

'Couldn't you remember it?' Jill asks. 'You had the last twelve lines.'

'I tried,' I reply. 'A few snatches. It was hopeless.'

'I know none of this,' Angie says, swirling the ice round in her *kümmel* violently. 'Teach you not to write poems, Roddy.'

'It did.'

'He's never written me one, the brute. That's for sure.'

'How come Toby looks younger than you now, Roddy?' Nancy enquires.

'Toby's led a sheltered life,' I return jocularly, and Angie simultaneously declares – protectively – that I live on my emotions, I care deeply about things. 'Anyway,' she persists, 'it's only hair.' I am grizzled, and scanty on top. 'Who cares about hair and a little on the tum?' She rolls across the sofa and gives me a pouty kiss on my temple which is bronzed by the sun. We have enjoyed sun every day so far.

Angie is an attractive woman still, and I feel it is an achievement I can notch up that a woman like her finds me attractive. She has kept her figure. Her energy and pluck are widely commented on. Drink and sunbathing have roughened her skin over the years, true enough, though it looks its best just now, tanned and heavily oiled. The drink habit is hardly something I can hold against her. One of Bella's least endurable moral affectations took the form of declining all alcohol at constituency or Party functions. Nor would she accept that in the pressure of politics – the late hours, the hurried meals, extempore speeches – a man needed a drink in reach. Angie, at least, goes all the way to boost my career.

I doubt if these lush outsiders – Budd, for instance, shifting from a sinecure in the Household Brigade to the sinecure of inherited broad acres – have any realistic notion of the demands on a man who takes his public duties in earnest. People forget the Lord Chancellor himself has shed a wife along the line. I have heard him personally lamenting the toll that politics takes on private life . . . Even my constituency committee, who are closer to the realities of politics than many, found it difficult to understand that staying married to Bella was holding me back as an effective parliamentarian. Yet Bella never went near the constituency if she could help it. And when it came to the crunch – the actual divorce, that is – it seemed she had built for herself an indefinable respect.

If only Bella could have taken some of the weight off me!

With Angie, I can leave half the village fêtes to her and the branch committees remain perfectly docile. I never make any reference to it, of course, but I am not unaware that I give Angie status and she isn't going to forfeit it. One knows where one is with Angie. She'd never risk having to go back to the old life – running a dress shop with an ex-husband who was neither one thing nor the other.

It has been said in the papers that the reason I have not been given a job in Government is that I am too 'excitable', 'emotionally impetuous'. All *that* means is that I know emphatically where I stand on the issues that confront the nation, and am ready to give expression to my views without trimming or havering, and at once. I am always snappy with my press releases: the local press, I am bound to say, laps them up (they like to keep abreast of their member's activities). Even the national press sometimes finds me good for a couple of paragraphs. I don't mind it being said that my stock-in-trade is forthrightness; but 'emotional impetuosity' is not a fair accusation.

I was widely taken to task for my televised riposte in mid-election to my electoral opponent's sneer that, 'With great respect, Roddy Squire has blundered into politics to defend the interest of his class, the business class.' At that, I came back vigorously, 'What's good for business is good for Britain, my lad,' paraphrasing the well-known American adage about General Motors. During the period of pillory that followed that riposte (I was blamed, here and there, for helping to lose the party the General Election), Bella accorded me her lofty condolence but noticeably failed to endorse the validity of what I had said. Angie – I was already secretly in love with Angie – would have come out of her corner on my behalf with both fists flying.

The real fault, of course, lay in the fact that the public had been allowed to grow unaccustomed to plain truth.

If, now, with the party back in power, I still do not have office, it is because of the leader's understandable wish to give the more promising looking newcomers a try. Public responsibility will soon thin them out.

Angie is already asleep in her twin bed before I turn in. She is a bonny sleeper – even the young's small hours rowdiness seldom wakes her. I finish off the *Daily Telegraph* in bed. I still feel a twinge of guilt reading the paper in bed: Bella used to object to the practice as uncivilised, and in principle I agreed with her . . . The obituaries are frequently a puzzle to me: the most obscure individuals are sometimes given enormous space. I do wonder how many column inches I will merit, when the time comes, or even now, for instance. The *Telegraph* obituaries are more dependable these days than *The Times*, so far as politicians are concerned.

It's no use pretending I will get a job in Government now. Even so a lot can still be done from the Back Benches to influence affairs – 'make the odd dent in the national story' is how I sometimes put it (I have always had a way with words). At least the PM had me appointed a Church Commissioner. That will be the sum of it now, in strictly career terms, though if I hang on long enough I might pick up a knighthood. If truth be told, as a Back Bencher I am a good deal happier with the Party in opposition: Shadow Cabinet apart, we are all more or less on the same level.

A few hours later I wake from a dream of extraordinary sweetness. A male choir was singing in a cathedral and I had been brought in late to join the tenors. They were giving an anthem with an inspired ascending and descending pattern of harmony, and although the music was new to me I was able to follow my part effortlessly. In my half-awakened state I can recall the melody and the sound of the voices and the exquisite sense of peace that they brought. I feel with a poignant joy that this is the peace of God, a perfection internalised within my body like a sexuality virginally experienced.

Of course the poem that Toby Budd let go overboard was totally inspired also. Last evening, when Budd – as sleek and plausible as ever – said, 'Maybe it wasn't quite the poem you thought, Roddy,' I obligingly concurred, 'Maybe it wasn't.' But I didn't for a moment believe that qualification. I let them half-fancy the poem concerned a woman. It was nothing of the kind. That poem was the culmination of a year or more of intense loneliness and self-searching. My talent for words was all I was left with among my fellow officers in their Malayan encampments. In the army they took me wrong from the first day, and the skills of clubbability I thought I had acquired at the old school deserted me utterly. I would retire to my tent to read and wrestle with my poems. None of them truly satisfied me. I had already written one since setting sail from Singapore, on 'the last sight of Sumatra'. Then came the big one. Its title struck me first, 'The Estuary', and then it came upon me in a rush, releasing me in a single miraculous moment – so it seemed – from boyhood into manhood, the river meeting the sea as life is released into death. It was a single product of all the love, the hope, the beauty and the pain that had comprised my life up to that point, and the experience of joy at having composed it was similar to the joy of the dream I have just had. But the poem had not been a dream, for there it *was*, lying in the deck chair under Budd's book, unchangeable, caught in the certainty of its perfection. When it flew overboard from Budd's fingers, there was a fraction of a second in which I would have plunged after it forty feet from the officer deck into the Indian Ocean.

I went down to my cabin and did not emerge for two days. Or perhaps it was only one day: I cannot be absolutely sure after all these years. I remember Budd trying to talk to me through the bolted door, but I refused to open up. I was in dreadful grief. I wrote a handful of laments, odes for the dead child, but the grief was too great for artistry. I felt my spirit to be irreparable. What had been mischievously jettisoned was the truth of me, capturable only at that one miraculous moment. There could be no more perfection from then on.

I am not being 'emotionally impetuous' if I state that it changed my life. Seven or eight years later, when I was on my honeymoon with Bella in Tuscany, a tear rolled down my cheek when I told her about it. She had loved me more for my telling her of it. Hers was the only balm I have ever sought or received on account of it. But I never wrote another poem after that. Nor have I since cried.

As morning breaks, the sunshine is again brilliant. Angie is first up. She calls the boys by telephone to get them on the move. We have a date in half an hour at the Bellevarde téléphérique with Nancy and Jill and various others. On a day like this she would regard a dawdling start as unforgivable. 'Don't spend all day shaving,' she calls after me. I know it irritates her that the heavy German daughters and their parents are always at breakfast ahead of our lot, even though the crimped mama never skis.

When I enter the breakfast room dressed not in my ski trousers and polo-necked shirt but in my cavalry twill and a tie, there is a chorus of protest. It is Sunday and I am going to church, I explain. I don't mind if I sound prim. A service, I have discovered, is being conducted at ten a.m.: I will meet up with them on the slopes for lunch – at the restaurant on La Grande Motte, or wherever they intend to be.

Charles leads the objections. 'It'll all be Roman here, Dad. What's the point? Surely you go to church enough at home.'

It is perfectly true I am a regular attender at Matins in the constituency. I have had a good singing voice since I was a boy and I enjoy reading the Lesson. Because I prepare the dramatic emphases quite carefully, Bella used to claim that I looked on the flock of St Mark's as one of my political audiences rather than as a congregation. And I do not – to be fair to Charles – attend the constituency's Roman Catholic churches, except during General Elections when the presence of each parliamentary candidate is specifically requested. Once one of my opponents was found to have participated in two Communions on the same day, and I issued a statement to the press expressing surprise at this 'ecclesiastic impropriety'.

'You won't understand a word,' Charles persists.

'God won't mind,' his brother Hugo chaffs.

'Your father's a Church Commissioner,' Angie reminds them.

'Not the bloody Romans,' Charles says.

'Don't talk like that.'

I appreciate Angie supporting me. She knows how close the divorce brought me to losing the job, even though there are divorced parsons these days. It was thanks to Bella keeping it all so low key.

I feel subdued during breakfast. Something has isolated me from them. When they have all gone, I return to my room, spend quite a while in the bathroom, lie down on my unmade bed briefly, then put on my House of Commons Ski Association blazer and walk briskly up the road through the skiers to the church, whose squat spire and campanile beneath are visible amid the higgledy-piggledy of lesser buildings. Even if I have put on a little weight the blazer fits nicely and makes me unmistakably English.

The church bell tolls across a valley full of the cries and gabble of skiers. On three sides the mountains soar. What my wife remarked was true: the setting of this place is unspeakably beautiful. Surely the response of the human horde can be more than to gambol, yelp, take snaps and overcharge one another?

As I approach I see the assembling worshippers breaking off sprigs of evergreen box from a cluster of branches heaped into a wooden trough near the entrance. This recalls to me that it is Palm Sunday. I myself take a small sprig of box, and place myself about half-way up the church near a side-aisle. It is already quite full of folk – the local elderly, a few visiting holidaymakers in ski anoraks, some of the shopkeepers, I would guess, and some ski instructors on their day off. I see nobody I know and I must admit to being touched with regret that nobody present is capable of recognising that a member of the British Parliament is in their midst – a Protestant at that. I am no bigot: my opponents, and elements of the press, try to make me out a diehard, but they are wide of the mark.

I am in fact a 'liberal traditionalist'. I think Winston Churchill may have used the term for himself – I don't mind if he did. The other side have had the temerity to call me a 'pastiche Churchill', a penalty, one might say, for having the courage of one's convictions. (One or two on my side of the House, fellows who clipped the real war and got a lucky break in special operations in the Balkans and the like, have never got over the style and delivery of the Old Man – even the angled mouth and the cigar. Why should *they* get away with it?) The fact is, I have always stood for tolerance. If from time to time I have the bottle to speak up for regimes of known severity (some would say brutality) it is because they are the lesser of available evils. Anyone who knows me properly is aware I am a sensitive man, perhaps excessively so. Churchill was emotional.

It is rather preposterous how these otherwise rational French have to do up their churches like a cross between a Hindu temple and a whore's bedroom. Outside it is stark hewn local stone: inside, a confection of gold pilasters entwined with artificial roses and bunches of grapes, batteries of angels with gold wings, portraits of saints – Peter with his key, John with his book – and of the Saviour in a dozen manifestations, as infant, at his baptism, crucified, ascending, sitting at the right hand of God His Father (represented as a hoary old man). And the paraphernalia beyond the altar rail! It mounts into a complexity of miniature gilt architecture designed without the least shame to dazzle and mystify the uneducated.

The elderly priest looks not unlike God the Father, though much less well endowed with hair, and with a wisdom strained by arthritis and tempered by a cynicism bred of fifty years' attention to the petty vices and repetitious miseries of his flock. He is assisted by a high-pitched middle-aged cherub who sprinkles the congregation with holy water and blesses our sprigs of box.

As the readings continue – given by the old priest, his assistant, and a young man in a sweater from the congregation – my grasp of the language seems to improve. The service is to incorporate the entire narrative of the Passion of Christ. As the whole terrible story unfolds, I begin to recall what made me decide to attend church in this alien place: the sense of irreparable loss that last night's dream left me with. The truth contained by the dream becomes apparent to me with scarcely bearable intensity. Somehow the gift that once was mine has been irrevocably squandered, the vision obliterated for ever.

I feel my breast heave. It is the betrayal of Peter, so precisely foretold a handful of hours – and verses – earlier, *thrice*, before the cock crowed *twice*, that tips me into a remorse I can no longer control. Tears flow down my cheeks silently but unchecked on to my House of Commons ski blazer. I wonder helplessly who might see me in this condition. Are any of this congregation English? I spotted none on entering (one can usually identify one's fellow countrymen). I glance quickly about me, but afraid of being observed I raise the sluices of my eyes to the figurine of Christ crucified, tilted outwards from a pillar just above me to the right. It is a stocky, muscular, peasant Christ, spattered with blood, in a gilded loincloth; but the face is turned away from me.

I file into the sunlight shaky at the knees and with a distant nausea. I feel at once that it has turned colder. There is cloud about, a sort of thickening in the atmosphere over the massif northward. I change into my ski clothes, strap on my boots, and tramp heavily to the foot of the Bellevarde lift. I take the red run down to the Daille chair-lift, and stay on the *piste* down to Val Claret and the foot of the long chair-lift up to the glacier of La Grande Motte where I agreed to join up with them. I am an experienced skier. I haven't missed a few days either at Christmas, or more rarely because of the parliamentary calendar, at Easter, for years. Skiing may be the sport of the better-off, but my theory is that constituents prefer their member to be a little larger than life. Skiing is a lot safer, politically speaking, than blood sports: the only blood at risk is one's own.

I know that something has happened to me but I cannot decide whether it is good or bad, and the demands of concentrating on my skiing save me the decision. If it were not for the vividness of my experience I might put it down to an effect of the altitude, for I feel 'heady' and strangely released from responsibility. Yet it is all the result of some truth glimpsed about myself. I cannot say exactly what that truth is or was, only that its effect is clarifying and cleansing because of the strength of the remorse that accompanied its revelation.

When I find them all in the high restaurant at the foot of the glacier, it has clouded over. The place is packed as the falling temperature has driven lunchers inside from the wooden terrace. There among the group is Budd, in a slim anorak of dark blue and a new-fangled cap. I take their chaff at my ecclesiastical devotions in good part, and Budd brings me a *vin chaud* to help down my *couscous garnie*. Now that I am among them again I cannot but feel a tremulous superiority to all these people. Perhaps it is not that everything has 'given way' inside me, but 'opened up'. When Hugo tries to tell me of a jump he had to make at speed, part of me is pleased that, at last, this holiday, Hugo seems to be coming out of his shell, but part of me is regretful, for I suspect that among all these people only the buttoned-up, inward Hugo might understand me if I tried to explain. The boy has a half-empty glass of *glüwein* in his hand and I want to say, *Don't drink any more of that. You don't need it. You're too young.* But I keep quiet.

It is decided the party should split into two groups: the less skilled skiing the undemanding glacier and the better skiers going all the way down and then exploring the slopes further down the valley. We will take the bus from whichever point along the valley road our final descents take us to, and all meet back at our hotel for a drink before dining.

I lead. I know all the *pistes* and where the lifts are: every now and then I take my group off-*piste*, in relatively easy snow since the deep snow has crusted and more recent sun has given it a manageable surface. Budd accompanies us, spurred along by Angie, for he is relatively inexperienced and clumsy. We reach the top of the Aiguille Percée shortly before the lift stops for the day at four p.m. From there we can ski back more or less directly by the route we have come by, or go over the shoulder and tackle the long run leading further down the valley to Les Brevières. Visibility has become rather poor, and it has begun to snow. I am in good skiing form, and am for going on down to Les Brevières. Angie declares it is getting 'too parky' and is for heading for the nearest 'g and t', but few other skiers are about and she isn't going down alone. The boys agree to accompany her down to Tignes. I like them doing things with Angie.

'What about you, Toby?' I ask.

'If you want to go on down to Brevières, I'll come with you.'

'Your decision, old cock,' I tell him.

At the last moment Hugo calls, 'I'll come too,' and begins to sidestep to where the two of us will begin our run. But I forbid him and Charles calls him back. Somehow I know I can't have Hugo with Toby and me.

The slopes down to Les Brevières are where the weather is coming from. Snow is now falling heavily and making it difficult to distinguish where the *pistes* run. I lead as usual, skiing at my normal pace in runs of a few hundred yards, then waiting for Budd to join me through the densely falling snow. Budd is soon in difficulties, twice losing a ski. I judge from the time it takes him to pick himself up and get his ski back on that he is growing tired. When we reach the point where the *pistes* divide, I take the steeper route. Visibility is down to a few yards and I soon realise that Budd only has my tracks to follow me by: the *piste* posts often go by unseen. When I swing off-*piste* about half-way down, Budd gives no indication of having noticed. At one point, on rejoining me, he says plaintively, 'I hope you know where the hell we are, because I haven't a clue.'

'How could you expect to?' I reply.

Budd falls again. I realise what has occurred when after several minutes' waiting he fails to join me. I hear him calling distantly. I estimate that he is about three hundred yards behind me up the mountainside, and I not far above the tree-line. I face away, downhill, and call with less than full force, 'Toby? Toby?'

This is followed by silence.

I raise my voice a little and call again, but still facing away and still with the same query in the voice. This time Budd evidently just catches me, for I make out his shout, 'I'm . . . here . . . I've . . . lost . . . a ski.'

I ski another thirty yards down the mountain, and resume calling, 'Toby? Toby?'

I can just catch the sound of his shouts, but not the words. I continue calling, making my voice fainter. I ski on down another thirty or forty yards and wait. It is snowing now very heavily: two or three inches have already fallen since the storm began. It is a wonderfully pure, silent, new-born world. The dark line ahead must be the trees. I open my flies and make a yellow funnel. There's nothing so private as a snowstorm. It's cold, really cold, and I tell myself I won't please Angie if I let my old man freeze up. Angie can't do without her zizzipom, though these days I perform as much to please her as myself. It works well on hols – strange beds tend to spark us. With Bella I was never *quite* sure she enjoyed it: up to the period when everything began to collapse, she would quite often make the comment, gratuitously, that the core of her love for me had 'very little to do with bodies'. Suddenly all the yearning, the reaching out, in that remark of Bella's becomes apparent to me. I think, now, Can I myself honestly declare that my love for Angie – and if I do not love Angie, who else is there? – has much to do with bodies?

I fancy I hear Budd calling from a considerable distance above. Then I ski on down to the perimeter of the trees. It is extremely cold on my uncovered head, and my forehead and face ache fiercely. I have a theory that keeping my head open to the elements promotes the growth of hair. Although it is early April, I am well aware that at this height in a cold spell there is little chance of a man surviving a night.

I ski on cautiously through the trees – it is steep here. A sharp twig catches the top of my head and when I put up my glove to the point of pain I find it has drawn blood. After ten minutes I find the *piste* again, snaking steeply through the trees. There is no sight of other skiers. I continue on down to the hamlet of Les Brevières, taking my time. One bus has evidently just left before I reach the bus shelter on the valley road, and I must wait nearly an hour for another. It is less bitterly cold down here and there is no fog, but the light is slowly failing and it still snows heavily. I wonder if it will look more convincing if I try to commandeer a vehicle from Les Brevières, but decide against since the time to show anxiety is not yet. I let several cars go by without attempting to flag them down. I doubt if he would survive a bad night like this even in the bus shelter. He was dressed more for sunshine swank than cold weather skiing, though that fancy helmet would probably help him.

I have heard that to die of cold, after the early stages, is a pleasurable experience: you float away.

Waiting for the bus I am concerned about one matter only, and that is that nothing should happen to let the boys think I could be blamed. They will certainly carry a full report back to Bella, and she by her silences will certainly convey to them what she thinks, if I allow them to give her a chance. I set great store by the boys' opinion of me, I don't deny. I am proud of them both having got into the old school, following the family tradition. I have willingly sacrificed for them. It still surprised me how Bella never seemed able to accept that I entered what she disparaged as my 'business phase' for the sake of the boys. Though my partners, not being in public life, have pocketed a lot more of the profits than me by tax manoeuvres I couldn't risk, I have built up enough for the boys to educate *their* sons at the same place. Such commitment to tradition sets a man to work and seize his chances, it shapes his political philosophy. It is a point I have often used in conversation, and usually it is warmly accepted. Bella would not respond, of course: she had no time for terms like 'political philosophy', and when the boys were little she sometimes said she didn't mind where they went to school. There were moments when I caught myself agreeing with her – just moments.

And now, under this bus shelter, after all these years, I can feel myself siding with her. What does it matter? More than that: has the old school not already taken away something from the boys by putting its caste-mark on them? Have I myself not already persuaded Charles that he belongs to the 'leadership element' (I can see Bella's closed distant face), and that what is left to hope for in this country of ours depends on the survival of that element? I would accuse Bella of being blind to such realities – wilfully so, I would think to myself. Have I not, at this very resort, only a day or two ago, put it in plain terms to Hugo? If one wants to enjoy skiing holidays, do the things one's schoolfellows do, travel, learn a language, find a foothold in the tough, grown-up world, it is no good disdaining success, throwing ambition out of the window, turning one's back on one's bit of inherited privilege, on a decent education, on one's 'network of comradeships'. I felt a low anger at my inability to get through to Hugo, was irritated that things had to be put so crudely. But now I experience a little surge of love for my son on account of that selfsame incomprehension. I think, O God, my God, let nothing happen tonight that will jeopardise my boys' respect . . . least of all, little Hugo's.

God, I say, if you have led me into this, do not forsake me. I am a member of Your flock, a Commissioner of Your Church. None of those whom I depend upon can understand. Angie would never respect me – a successful man, on top of the heap – if she knew I harboured obscure disillusionment, was capable of a great gob of remorse. One has a right to suffer – she recognises that – but in certain recognised categories. A spouse misbehaving, for instance, an offspring going on the drugs, alcoholism supervening, a sudden death, a financial setback. A political catastrophe, even. But not this category. To suffer from a discovery that life is without meaning, or its meaning is far, far removed from the centre of one's concerns and that all hope of recovering it is gone, is no way to hold the respect of a woman like Angie. *She* knows how the world goes round.

Only three others are aboard the bus when it comes. At the next stop it picks up two or three ski-lift operators and at the stop after a handful of late-drinkers and some more lift operators or *piste secouristes*. In the resort itself, I trudge up through the snow to the hotel, park my skis and sticks in the ski-room, shed my boots, and emerge into the hotel lounge with my questions ready for the first person I recognise. It is young Hugo, as it turns out, playing the space-invader machine beyond the bar where the German is at his beer and his wife and daughters at multi-coloured cocktails with sugar round the rim of the glasses.

'When did Toby get back?' I ask.

The boy ignores me.

'Hugo, I'm asking you a question.'

'Oh, hello, Dad. Toby who?'

'Toby Budd. Mr Budd. You were skiing with him till the last run down.'

'How do I know? He's not even staying here.'

'He's coming to dinner.'

'No one's here yet,' Hugo says with a frown.

I cross the foyer to go up to the chalet, but at the hotel entrance run into Jill, Nancy and the twins all dressed for dinner.

'When did Toby get back?' I repeat at once.

'We thought he was with you,' Nancy says.

'You mean, he's not back at the chalet?'

They come on into the hotel, brushing off the snow, stamping their feet.

'He got separated from me coming down from the Aiguille Percée,' I say, looking anxious already. 'I thought he must have gone straight down to Boisses. He should have been back some time ago.'

'Wouldn't you say,' Jill suggests, 'knowing Toby, he stopped by the wayside to give himself a boost. It's a cold night, after all. Maybe he's met some other old friend whose literary creations he's scattered to the winds.'

Angie comes out of the lift towards us in her silvery trousers.

'Roderick, you're awfully late. What've you done to your head?'

'A scratch. Nothing.' My fingers go up to touch it.

'He's lost Toby,' Nancy says.

'Not exactly "lost",' I return at once.

'You should wear a hat,' my wife says, but I am pressing on with my explanation, how Budd followed me half-way down the other side of the Aiguille Percée and then turned off somewhere on his own. 'I waited for him for some time. I thought he'd be bound to be back ahead of me.'

'What d'you mean,' Angie says, '"he turned off somewhere but you waited for him"?'

I give her a stare of remote puzzlement. 'It was snowing heavily. One couldn't see much. He was right behind me, then I realised he wasn't following any more. I assumed he must have turned off on his own. Straight down to Boisses, for instance.'

'The lift men always clear the *pistes* of bodies at the end of the day,' Jill says.

'They clear all the *pistes*,' Angie endorses. 'Maybe he's just missed the bus or something. Let's have a drinkie while we stand by.'

The young waiter with the moustache is hovering as usual with exaggerated patience, and the German family is evidently reluctant to make spaces at the bar. The two lumpy daughters are solidly ensconced on bar stools opposite a notice headed *Protection des Mineurs et Répression de l'Ivresse Publique*. I order a round of cocktails, a brandy and soda for myself, and a fresh orange juice for Hugo.

Suddenly I realise Charles is not with us. 'Where's Charles?' I demand sharply. 'Charles back?'

Hugo says he left him wallowing.

'Don't worry about Toby,' Angie says. 'It can't go wrong these days. It's not even dark yet. Why don't you take up your drink and get changed? If Toby's not here in half an hour we'll ring the chalet and ask them. There's nothing you can do.'

'At some point one's got to do something,' I tell them, getting up.

'What on earth do you mean, darling?'

On my way to the lift I turn to glare at her. 'Call the police, obviously. Something like that.'

The leader of the *Section Haute Montagne*, Claude, is an old-timer. I have seen him around. I know something about these villagers – I've been coming here for so long. He is village-born; as a young man, before it became a ski-resort, he would have set forth on foot each November with the rest of the able-bodied menfolk and walk to Paris, thirty kilometres a day, where he would work all winter as a porter for an auctioneers. In May he would walk back to his family in the village and graze the sheep and cattle on the slopes. Sometimes he would take parties of foreign rich hunting chamois or *bouctin* in the mountains. Now as likely as not he's a millionaire, in francs anyway, though he'd never let on. I reckon he was one of the first to learn English: I know for a fact that when skiing came, he and his sons took it up together. He has close-set eyes without eyebrows, and with the earflaps of his fur hat turned down he resembles an ancestral mountain ape.

He questions me courteously but without any trace of feeling, sitting in a secluded corner of the hotel lounge and refusing a drink. Twice during my account he asks me if I left the *piste* on the descent to Les Brevières; at the second denial, which I qualify by the possibility that in such conditions I might have 'strayed' off it, I let a note of irritation sound in my voice. I won't have this peasant put anything across me.

From the moment we set out at about ten-forty-five p.m. he keeps me beside him.

The team is efficient and calmly systematic. Our bus, equipped with chains, is met at Les Brevières by two manned Ratrac snowmobiles. The bus has been used recently to carry the *secouristes* on a torchlight pageant for the tourists, and their resinous brands have left a pungent scent that brings to mind the Bond Street bath essence Bella used to give me on my birthdays. The Ratracs with their powerful headlights at once set off up the Aiguille *pistes*. Both Ratracs carry the stretcher-sleds known as bloodwagons. The remainder of the *Section*, about thirty men, plus me, take the series of chair-lifts and button-lifts, interspersed with short descents on skis, by which one reaches the top. They carry light backpacks and each man wears an

The Lost Poem

electric torch strapped to the forehead by a leather harness. Several carry shortwave radios. I notice that Claude's ski-sticks, as a concession to antiquity, are of bamboo. I myself wear my torch-harness on top of Angie's woollen hat, with the brim turned down over my ears.

It is still snowing just as heavily; a foot or more has settled since it started in the afternoon.

At the summit of the Aiguille the men spread out at twenty-metre intervals on either side of the *piste* that Budd and I started on, and we ski down slowly, in silence, followed by the Ratracs. The only pair that ski alongside one another are Claude and I: we keep to the *piste*.

After about twenty minutes' cautious descent I say, 'I think about here we may have lost the *piste*: we couldn't see much, *vous compwenez*.'

Claude makes no reply, but blows a whistle and adjusts the line of descent. I look at my watch: it is after midnight. I am feeling light-headed again, with a vague sense of anticipation. It is all a kind of dream. I don't particularly care which way it turns out. I am pleased to be on my own, however. The snow-ape Claude and these taciturn professionals leave me alone. Angie was game, of course, but they wouldn't countenance her coming out. She will be waiting up in the hotel lounge: she is a great one for sticking things out. She was the only other guest left in the lounge when Claude came back to pick me up. The boys had gone to Fred's Tea-Bar, and Jill and Nancy had returned to their chalet in case Budd should wander in late at night with an explanation nobody had thought of. The fat German, with his podgy Brünnhildes and their crimped mama, had been the last to retire, the three females in uncontrollable giggles at the far end of the lounge. It is extraordinary how some people can behave: surely they had wind of what had occurred. 'Wind' is the word: what had set them off was a series of audible farts emitted by father, culminating in a resounding belch as he waited for the lift to take him up to bed, which had the ladies rolling in their chairs, knocking their mah-jong all over the floor. And all the while an Englishman freezing to death on the mountainside.

When we reach the tree-line Claude blows his whistle again and the line pauses.

'Monsieur Squire,' he asks, 'did you enter among the trees with your friend?'

'Not with my friend. I had trees on either side, after I had stopped and repeatedly called.'

'You mean, you were on the *piste*?'

'I managed to pick up the *piste* again, through the trees, if in fact I had lost it.'

'How did you receive the cut on your head, monsieur?'

'What?'

'I think your head was cut.'

'Oh, that was before. Yesterday.'

One Ratrac is directed left, down the *piste*, and one to the right, to skirt the trees. The *Section* itself proceeds to enter the trees, descending with great caution and pausing every now and then to straighten the line. The utter silence of the mountainside, the snug protectiveness of the dark pines, the enveloping softness beneath the aimless drift of the snow filtering among the trees, induce a sense of divine complicity and safety. I feel my naked soul to be in the hands of fate to which I have no choice but to give my total loving trust.

When the tone and quickening of voices – the instantly communicated agitation from the extreme right of the line – indicate that they have found Budd alive, my regret is confused by my perceiving in it an admission that I have been envying Toby his death. As I work my way across to the cluster of lights I would have them all vanish, leave me to muse alone and in the overwhelming cold float away. Claude has immediately despatched three men in both directions to fetch the bloodwagon from the Ratracs.

I feel obliged to have Claude confirm it.

'Yes, monsieur, your friend has survived.'

'That's what I thought he must have done,' I say. 'Swerve right towards the blue *piste*.'

Claude makes no answer.

Budd is far gone yet was still struggling hopelessly on when they encountered him. He abandoned his skis and one stick further up the mountain – long since buried in the new snow – and was floundering through the trees, sinking to his haunches at each move. He was at the extremity of exhaustion and hours of fear seem to have rendered speech a problem. It seems that only when he at last sees me among the faces – the frontal torch impedes recognition – does he regain the faculty of speech. 'Hull-o, old boy. You didn't wait for me.'

'I called and called,' I say. 'I thought you'd gone off right by the slow *piste*.'

'I heard you calling. You must have heard me.'

One of the *Section* is giving him brandy, or some new-fangled restorative. Another is vigorously rubbing his arms and legs.

'Thank God you're safe,' I say. 'It's all that matters now.'
Budd does not reply. His face is needing attention.
We hear the motor of one of the Ratracs, and then its headlights pierce the snow and the trees. Two *secouristes* approach from above, one at each end of the bloodwagon. They wrap the casualty in blankets and strap him under the canvas flaps of the bloodwagon, then four men set off with him, head downhill, quite fast through the trees. They seem to know exactly which route to take. Nothing has to be discussed.

By the time I return to the resort, Budd is settled in the little hospital. He is in need of treatment for shock and frostbite of the cheeks. Evidently an ambulance was standing by at Les Brevières to meet the bloodwagon.

I have ready a little thank-you speech when Claude drops me at the hotel entrance, but the man seems unable to grasp it (the French can be wilfully obtuse). Instead he is asking if I or Monsieur Budd carry '*assurance*' to cover the cost of the rescue. I tell him I really have no idea, and I reckon I catch in the man's little simian eyes a gleam of malevolence.

Just as I expected, Angie is still up, alone in the lounge, still in her silvery trousers. I prop my skis in the lobby, the ski-room being closed.

It is she who speaks first. 'I hear they found him alive.'
She has not got out of her chair.
'Yes, we found him alive. How did you hear?'
'Someone telephoned from the *gendarmerie*.'
'They are greatly efficient,' I endorse brightly, as I pull off my boots and then my anorak and Angie's hat. 'An example to us all. And a country under socialism! However,' I add, 'they seem to want paying.'
'Where did they find him?'
'We found him in the trees somewhere above Brevières. He *is* a bit of an idiot, you know. I can't imagine where he thought he was off to.'
'He wasn't hurt?'
'Not so far as I know.'
She has an empty glass in front of her but seems quite clear-headed. I plump down beside her.
'You must be very tired,' she says flatly.
'Not really. D'you want a drink?'
'Do *you*?'

'What was yours?'

'*Kummel.*'

I wish she would pronounce it as gentlemen do: *kimmel*. It's no use pretending Angie is well bred. But one can't have everything.

'What about Nancy and Jill? Do they know?'

'Oh yes.'

I sense that she ought to have more to ask and I more to narrate; but her response leaves me with no cue. Perhaps because it sounded as if only half of it was spoken: Oh yes, *I'm afraid so.*

I am vaguely aware of a night porter somewhere in the recesses who might bring us a drink. I push myself up and begin to nose about for him, padding around in my socks. *Kummel, koomel, kimmel.* It isn't a thing that matters much. Socially speaking, Angie carries it off. She doesn't get in a lather when old acquaintances fail to greet her in the hairdressers, as poor Bella used to. Angie knows how to play the society game, with all her knives just as sharp as they have to be.

'The concierge has gone to ground,' I report.

'Don't you want to turn in?'

'I suppose there's nothing more one can usefully do. The boys in?'

'Ages ago.'

In our room, there are my pyjamas laid out on my pillow, my House of Commons ski blazer on the clothes-horse. Everything is quite normal. The hotel is four-star, after all.

When she is in her slip, in the bathroom, brushing her teeth, I lay my hand on her rump. 'Oh, honestly, Roderick,' she snaps, 'for crying out loud. It's three o'clock in the morning.'

Oddly, I don't feel tired. There is still something I ought to be doing but I can't think what it might be: all day obscure forces, from within or without, have been bearing upon me, taking over from me. In the hot little room I can still feel the rush of mountain air against my face – or is it the rush of air on a high deck of a ship under full steam? When Angie has got into bed, her light out, there I am in my underclothes sitting at the table under the lamp, writing.

'What on earth are you doing?' she demands.

'I won't be long,' I humour her. 'Just drafting a little something.'

'What for?'

'The local press.'

'Local press?'

'Come along, Angie. The county press at home. Constituency h.q. will push it out.'

'*Now*, for God's sake?'

She is quite justified in her irritation. I shouldn't be doing this at such a time of night, even if the electorate does have the right to know that their member has been involved in saving a life in the mountains. It's just that I have an urge to give an account of it to someone . . . even if it has to be just a few paragraphs for the local press.

'I won't be long, my dear. While it's still fresh in the mind.'

Dear John

The incident of a few years ago now by which Cedric Powell-Bourke might be said to have made his name occurred at the end of his tour of duty as H.M. Consul-General in the Arabian capital where he had already served three years. The Foreign Office rated the case important enough to delay Powell-Bourke's departure for the extra weeks it took to see it through. In that part of the Arab world, personal contact could play almost as essential a part in consular affairs as in diplomacy or business. To expect a newly arrived consul unfamiliar with the vernacular (in every sense) to pick up the threads of the case at so critical a stage would be inviting failure and not fair on the incoming man. Or, if it might make his name, on the outgoing.

Not that Powell-Bourke would have chosen to stay on any longer than necessary. The country was hag-ridden by a bureaucracy of unique intractability. He had heard Head of Chancery liken it to 'Brezhnev's Russia run by Praisegod Barebones'. It was hellbent on turning itself into a joyless paradise, on the whimsical gift of unlimited petroleum from a traditionally glowering providence. The theocratic tyranny of Puritan Islam was combined with an administrative method, inherited from the Turks, of massive inertia.

In the common run of officialdom there was no presumption of trust, and no rewards worth the name were to be reaped honestly. The plum jobs went to the ruling family or their cronies who often became enormously rich. Obfuscation helped. A positive decision could be viewed as the wrong one, inviting penalties; so also, possibly, a negative one. Survival depended on deciding nothing. Pass the matter in hand along the line – sideways, downwards, upwards – on the firm understanding that the buck stopped nowhere. Virtually no so-called decision could be regarded as final, no promise depended upon. The conscientious diplomatist from the Western world found his patience tested severely. Powell-Bourke knew a defence attaché in his final weeks *en poste* who constructed a numbered chart and ritually crossed off another day each evening like a homesick child at a boarding school. Or a convict approaching release.

The consular case in question, therefore, had grown ineluctably complex.

Yet the facts themselves were straightforward. One afternoon the British foreman of a construction team building a hospital at Daba'a, two hundred or so miles further north, knocked off work as normal at about two-thirty p.m. (during the high summer outdoor work began at six), collected his mail from the company office, and returned to his billet. He spoke to none of his fellows. Later that afternoon he started drinking the colourless sugar-based spirit, illegal of course and distilled in secret, but available anywhere. At nine-thirty, after dark, he crossed to the construction site, climbed into the largest earth-moving machine, and before the nightwatchman roused himself to action he had effectively razed the foundations of the entire hospital on which his team had been working for four months.

The man had thus not only disrupted the vaunted Five-year Plan for Daba'a region. By drinking alcohol he had publicly flouted the religious law of the country and insulted the devout principles of local inhabitants. His was an act of violent and ramified sacrilege. It affronted the Ministries of Interior and Health as well as the religious authorities and Allah. It did instant damage to British companies scrambling to win contracts against the French, the Germans, the Dutch, the Americans and the Koreans.

He had been arrested that very night, and though he had not resisted or protested in any way, he was manifestly subject to wild irrationality and his legs were put in irons. He was held for several days in the dungeon of a fortress built of mud-packed rocks which served as the local gaol, until the local Amir's office got around to finding an interpreter through whom he could be questioned by the Amir's *askaris*. The interrogation focused on how he had obtained his liquor, which the prisoner insisted he distilled himself. He was then moved elsewhere in the fortress to a large communal cell above ground among other prisoners, and was allowed to shed his leg-irons.

Meanwhile the construction company reported to the British Embassy that one of their men had been arrested following a nocturnal rampage. Enquiries were made in the capital; in due course the authorities admitted they held such a man and it fell to Powell-Bourke to drive north to try to see him.

The man's name was Alistair McCann. He was about thirty-five years old, the same age as the Consul himself, but in every other respect the two men differed markedly. McCann was a stocky, untidy, rough-cast man with a manner both sudden and wary. His accent was strongly Glaswegian and Powell-Bourke could not help remarking to himself what a peculiarly two-fisted, underdog style of speech Glasgow's Gorbals instilled into its inhabitants. If he had had any education there was little sign of it, though he seemed to be known among his mates as a first-class mechanic. His hands were large and powerful. He gave an impression of force, of someone who from an early age had learned to mistrust life, and to whom the bottle was the one sure comfort. His fair hair was thin across a broad forehead and he looked older than his years.

Cedric Powell-Bourke, by contrast, looked more youthful than his years. He was a dark, narrow, fastidious young man. His tropical suits were made for him, suggesting a private income, which he did not have: a riding accident as a small boy, before his father quit home, had left him with a slight imbalance of the shoulders which required a tailor's attention. His shirt collars were rather high. His vigorous hair was firmly disciplined and parted down the middle. There was something old-fashioned about him in both appearance and manner. He had learned early the professional pitfalls of talking too freely, airing views, saying more than necessary, and sometimes he seemed to be censoring his own utterances with a muscular constriction of lips and throat.

By the time two years were up his colleagues had concluded Powell-Bourke would remain a bachelor. Then he caught them unawares by returning from home leave with a bride. They and their wives were soon commenting favourably on the shy enthusiasm with which Jenny Powell-Bourke took up her role as an Embassy wife and espoused Arab things.

She brought with her a university degree and a solemnity which contained, intriguingly, a strain of wistfulness. And on second glance she was really quite pretty. It wasn't long, of course, before other wives were wondering aloud when the Powell-Bourkes would be starting a family. But Jenny would scotch such notions, with Cedric primly concurring that they would try for a child when they could afford a child.

'Don't leave it too late, Cedric,' said one of the wives, chaffing him, because although he might *look* younger than his thirty-five years, he was already elderly. Perhaps he had always been so, even as a child – elderly in caution and rectitude and bearing. When they speculated as to what had drawn Jenny to him, they decided it was security. Jenny, it was learned, was an adopted child – taken as an infant into the home of a childless couple already in middle life, and now in their seventies.

She had grown up lonely, but loved, the single child of ageing foster parents who belonged, it seemed, to that narrowest of all the definable classes, the lower-middle. The father had been a watchmaker.

She had vouchsafed these facts without embarrassment in a quiet chat over tea-for-two with the Ambassador's wife, who happened to comment that Cedric would give her 'security'. 'Exactly,' Jenny concurred at once, with a frankness and a wistfulness in a quite unexpected combination. She had known Cedric for two years before they wed and when he was abroad he had written every fortnight. Punctiliously. He never missed. She had met him in a railway carriage, she said. She saw him doing the crossword in *The Times*, and asked him the meaning of a word in a book she was reading for her sociology course. In the midst of shyness, the Ambassador's wife perceived, a little spear of audacity. There was more to Jenny Powell-Bourke than met the eye.

As for Cedric, he soon knew that Jenny had raised his stock and had caused his colleagues to reassess him professionally. It called for calibre, of course, to be consul-general in a volatile Arabia scrambling for modernisation: the Ambassador himself had commented so. The not infrequent misdemeanours among the many British artisans and navvies temporarily in the country, and sometimes the consultants and managers, made the job no easier. Even so, at Embassy receptions Powell-Bourke would catch the invariable shift into condescension when an outsider learned that he was serving not in the diplomatic grades but the consular; and it was his fixed, unspoken intention to ascend to a diplomatic function at the first opportunity his career provided.

It was not in Powell-Bourke's remit to feel sorry for people and the case of McCann was not one to excite sympathy. The two men were brought together in a low narrow chamber in the Daba'a fortress. The mean glassed apertures in the metre-thick walls, too small for a man's body to pass through, overlooked the newly tarmacked square and the town's main mosque. A third aperture had been widened to accommodate a raucous and ineffective air conditioner. The room contained three wicker chairs and a wicker table imported from India, some benches, flyblown framed photographs in colour of the present king, the crown prince and two of the three previous kings. It was lit by a single fluorescent strip-light attached to a palm beam across the ceiling.

In the two chairs on one side of the table sat Powell-Bourke and the

Egyptian clerk of the local *shariah* court. Unusually for an expatriate Egyptian, the clerk wore the red chequered headcloth and ankle-length shirt of the natives of the country. Yet when conversing with Powell-Bourke he preferred to make use of the elementary English that had survived from his Cairo secondary school than let Powell-Bourke exercise his own quite competent, if cautious, Arabic. He had an odd reluctance to turn and face his English visitor as they conversed. Instead he darted glances at Powell-Bourke out of the corner of his eye, so that as he struggled to expand on the burdens the wayward laid upon the law-abiding (such as the Consul and himself), Powell-Bourke received the ridiculous impression that he was being drawn into a conspiracy. Then McCann was led in by a uniformed gaoler armed with a light machine-gun. The gaoler withdrew only as far as the doorway where he sat on the floor and picked at his toes.

McCann's skin had already turned that sickly yellow of bronzed men who have for some time been denied sunlight. He was hollow-eyed, clumsily shaven and dressed in the same khaki trousers, sandals and tee-shirt, decorated with a patriotic national map, in which he had been arrested many days previously. A prickly heat rash was visible under the fair down of his forearms.

Powell-Bourke was accustomed to the flood of irrelevant denials, pleas, tears, justifications, and requests for errands that poured forth from those who had fallen foul of authority, when first brought into his presence. Yet McCann showed no emotion and said nothing.

The Consul was ever so slightly put out. Having introduced himself, he now passed across his visiting card which McCann did not so much as look at. Powell-Bourke got down to business. He had borrowed McCann's passport from the Egyptian clerk-of-the-court and began to check through the details for the form he had drawn from the buff folder resting on the wicker table.

'You are Alistair Dougal McCann, born at Sandavore, Inverness-shire, on January 11, 195–?'

McCann's replies to each of the questions were so sullen that Powell-Bourke wondered if the fellow cared one way or the other what became of him. When he asked who his next-of-kin was, he got no answer at all.

The Consul repeated his question and waited. He had done the four-hour drive to Daba'a in suit and tie: it wasn't yet the hottest time of year but the small room itself was stifling and from the Scotsman opposite emanated a pungent, rubbery tang. The odour was as much to do with the man's temperamental condition, Powell-Bourke guessed, as a failure to wash.

'Donald McCann,' he answered at length.

The Consul made an entry on his form. His perspiring hand stuck to the paper.

'Relationship?'

'Son,' the foreman said.

'You are his son?'

'I'm the father.'

Powell-Bourke frowned. 'Surely he must be too young.'

'You ask my next-o'-kin. He's my next-o'-kin.'

'Age?' Powell-Bourke queried, with a tilt of his head and a smile of acidulous tolerance.

'Three years two months.'

'A next-of-kin must be over eighteen years of age.'

'In that case I've no got a next-o'-kin.'

'The boy's mother?' Powell-Bourke suggested, with a different smile, humouring. One had to get the form filled.

No reply was offered.

'Your son must have a mother. Or have had.'

A slight frown and narrowing of the eyes indicated the proximity of a response.

'You have something to tell me,' the Consul said in a kindly manner. Part of his task was to ascertain the truth.

McCann answered, in flat tones, the blue eyes averted. 'His mither's quit. Vamoosed.'

'Your wife's left home?'

'She don't reco'nise me, I don't reco'nise her.'

Powell-Bourke made a note.

'When did this happen?'

Again there was no immediate response and the question was repeated.

'She sent me a Dear John,' McCann said very quickly, his face bunched and ugly.

'Dear John?'

'Thasrigh'.'

It was not a term that Powell-Bourke's life so far had made him familiar with.

'She wrote me,' the foreman murmured, turning his head sharply away towards the light of the apertures.

'Ah.'

It was time for another little note.

'If I may ask, where is the letter now?'

To the Consul's surprise, McCann shifted forward in his chair and extracted from the back pocket of his khaki trousers a mauled, cream-coloured envelope. He handed the rectangle of paper to Powell-Bourke. The name and address had been all but obliterated by sweat penetrating the cloth of the trousers, but the British stamp was still there and postmark 'Glasgow 11 District' still legible.

The letter itself was on two sheets of what stationers call 'vellum', with crenellated edges. Stamped across one corner was a raised design discernible as two interlinked hearts. It bore no address. It was painstakingly penned in a childish hand and evidently the result of several draftings. The consul read as follows:

'Dear Ally,
In anser to yours the children are well. Donny is full of mischeif as ever and Louise has been down with tonsilaitis which has kept me up nights, Mum has been over and says to give you her best wishes, she is upset at what I finely decided but I know its all for the best it realy is. Much as it pains me to say out write I do'nt think I have ever realy loved you though I have tried and tried as GOD is my witniss. I have known it was'nt worth trying no more since your last leave home you was in one of your moods again and on the booze I said to myself I cant stand a life time of this I was too young when I was married I should have listened to what they was saying about you. We should not have had no kids but I love them dearly and whats done is done. As it hapens George Boyd has shown me what love can be, insidently I have moved in with him with the kids so theres no point you writing to the old place because no ones there its yours I dont want to set foot there again even though George says I must when the papers are through and collect whats mine. I am seeking a divorce. Do'nt take this too hard I know you will be upset but theres four of us to think about its for the best you will come to see it like I do.
                    Cathy.'

Powell-Bourke looked up.

'Would you like me to have this translated into Arabic? I think it might assist you at your trial.'

'I don't want no assistance,' McCann said.

'All the same, would you let me keep it until my next visit, if I promise to return it to you then?'

'I dinna want you to give it to the press.'

Powell-Bourke registered shock. 'I have no contact whatever with the press.' In fact, from time to time the press did probe into consular activities, even ringing him up from London. Newspapers at home could cause a lot of embarrassment to the orderly conduct of official business in difficult areas. The uncalled-for intrusions of journalists usually began with the assumption they knew a consul's job better than he did.

'Is there no one else?' Powell-Bourke pressed. 'Your father or mother not alive?'

Again, silence. Out of the corner of his eye the Egyptian clerk caught the Consul's eye with a glint of humorous complicity.

Powell-Bourke persisted. 'You do appreciate, don't you, that as a foreigner here you have very few rights. Very few indeed. If you won't let me help you at all, there's really nobody else who can.'

'They'll no be interested.'

'Your mother and your father, you mean?'

'That's what I mean.'

It seemed to Powell-Bourke that McCann's reply was unnecessarily aggressive, even if all the man was doing was trying to disguise that he had long ago broken with whoever had brought him into the world.

'I've driven a very long way,' it was time to remind him, 'with the sole purpose of trying to be of help to you.'

McCann's attention seemed to have wandered. Then he said, 'I'm aware o' that. I'm aware o' that.'

From time to time the Consul detected a lilt in the man's speech which ran counter to his working-class Glaswegian, like an eddy in a river.

'When-do-I-see-ye-again?' McCann asked in a sort of rushed, aggressive growl. It took a moment or two to make it out.

'A month.'

'When do I come up?'

'For trial? One can't possibly say. It depends on all sorts of factors.'

'Such as?'

'You must understand there's no clear-cut procedure. The decision as to whether you are sent before a local *qadi* . . .'

'Wha's that?'

'A judge – magistrate if you prefer – *that* will probably depend on His Excellency the Amir of Daba'a.' Powell-Bourke nodded to the Egyptian. 'Alternatively His Royal Highness the Minister of the Interior's office may advise the local Amir that your case should be considered in the capital.'

'Wha' will they do to me?' McCann asked in the same flat tone.

'I'm afraid they take a very serious view of this sort of thing. You must dismiss any idea of getting off lightly. In the end they will deport you. What happens in the meantime I wouldn't care to predict.'

'Wha' can you do?'

'All *I* can do is try to see their own legal processes get under way. I can find someone to provide legal advice, but you can't have anyone to represent you at your trial, always supposing we can get it that far – it's not the way they work under Hanbali law, as you probably very well know. Then there's the question of compensation.'

'Compensation?'

'For the damage you did. One can't predict these things.'

'It could run into millions,' McCann added gratuitously, and for the first time he smiled – a hopeless, oddly handsome grin.

'One can't predict,' Powell-Bourke repeated. 'I'll apply to come and see you next month. Once they've allowed one visit they usually allow a second.'

After nearly three years in the country Powell-Bourke knew the ropes and his intervention helped to speed the case of Alistair McCann to trial. So far no word of the incident had reached the overseas press (it would scarcely warrant a mention); and the local – muzzled – newspapers never reported crimes as they were committed, though occasionally they carried official announcements of punishments after they were awarded or meted out, especially executions and floggings. The letter from McCann's wife was duly translated into Arabic, and prepared as a court document.

Powell-Bourke had not made it his practice to discuss the details of his work with his wife of a few months. But he often brought his papers back to their villa in the Embassy compound, and on this occasion he happened to mention the 'Dear John' received by McCann. Jenny asked if she could see it, and he passed the original across to her. Putting it down, she enquired how old the wife was. Cedric recollected that McCann said she was twenty-three.

'There must be about twelve years between them,' Jenny remarked. The same number of years divided her from Cedric. 'If he's someone who's seen life, as you say . . . knocked about a bit . . . he'd have presumably chosen her with some care. Or thought he had.'

'We don't know what led up to this, Jenny.' He glanced at her. 'Do we?'

His wife had fallen silent. After a while she enquired, 'What sort of man is he, Cedric?'

'Uncouth.'

The hearing before the local *qadi* was due the week before Powell-Bourke's next promised visit. At one of the Embassy's 'morning prayers' meetings at which consular affairs were raised, the Ambassador complimented Powell-Bourke on the swiftness with which this particular case had entered the legal process, and expressed the hope that the man could be sentenced there and then, at the first hearing. In the Arab world, essentially *consular* problems had a knack of disrupting normal *diplomatic* intercourse. This particular case was a little out of the common run: one couldn't be sure where it might lead.

'I suppose he actually did what he's accused of ?' the Ambassador wondered.

'He doesn't attempt to deny the charges,' the Consul replied.

'That doesn't precisely answer my question, Cedric.'

'I think there's no doubt he's guilty of everything except possibly distilling his own *siddiqi*. He probably got it from someone else.'

'He's trying to protect a friend?'

'It's not so much that, Ambassador. He doesn't seem to care what happens to him.'

'I see.' The Ambassador was acquainted with the broad circumstances of the case. 'They may want to lock him up out there at Daba'a. Local amirs like to have the odd *khawaja* in chokey – it brightens up their authority. The truth is, things can get a tiny bit out of hand, out in the sticks. Take an idiosyncratic turn. Of course it's an awful bore for your visiting, Cedric. I suppose they've got a prison out there?'

'It's a bit primitive – a Turkish fort.'

The sentence, when it came, was not immoderate by indigenous standards, but contained its 'idiosyncratic' element rather as the Ambassador had anticipated. McCann was to serve six months' imprisonment at the end of which he was to be publicly flogged with eighty strokes and then deported. There was no demand for personal compensation, but the British construction company would have to make good the damage done, and the four per cent penalty for every month by which they were late on completion would not be waived.

When the Ambassador read the memorandum he telephoned the Consul's office.

'Cedric, I want you to do everything you can to have that flogging order rescinded.'

'It won't be easy, Ambassador.'

They briefly discussed the options.

'The local governor up at Daba'a isn't a member of the royal family,' the Ambassador pointed out. 'It's a tribal appointment and the family won't overrule tribal amirs if they can possibly avoid it. He's probably a bit of a diehard anyway.'

Powell-Bourke was inclined to agree.

'I'd prefer you to handle this, Cedric – it's probably going to be your last problem case in this job. Let's hope so, anyway. But if you get stuck you'll let me know, won't you, because if it comes to that I'm quite prepared to see what I can do myself.'

When he put down the receiver, Powell-Bourke reflected on the meaning behind the Ambassador's closing words. In diplomacy, spades were not always called spades: one looked for the nuances, for what was left unsaid. He had always sensed that the Ambassador rated him highly, that he would like to see him in the diplomatic grades. The Ambassador was himself an able man, he did his homework. He would know that, but for a difficult start in life, Cedric Powell-Bourke wouldn't have so nearly ploughed his Foreign Service examination. Hadn't he seen his glance rest thoughtfully, even tenderly, on the slight asymmetry beneath his jacket? He would have risked nakedness for the Ambassador, shown him his soul, he did need that trust so. Was the Ambassador not aware of his father's early departure from the domestic hearth, which occurred so soon after the fall from the pony? Oh surely, surely. Those two facts must lie somewhere in the files.

But there would be no record of the consequences . . . how the marital break-up left his mother so spent that all that remained in her to give went to his younger sister. (Was it giving or clinging? His mother clung and Pauline clung back, taking it as love.) How Cedric was outside, locked out. How in the struggle to make ends meet, he had been shunted from school to school, the schools themselves as unworthy as the reasons for choosing them – their fees were a few pounds cheaper, for instance, or their location sufficiently nearer home to save on travelling. It was only recently that his mother's awe at the single-mindedness which got him into so distinguished a service began to look like spontaneous love for him. But it wasn't spontaneous, Cedric knew quite well, it was too late for that, and her preening among her little bunch of cronies on his account infected him with scorn.

He wasn't sorry for himself, not at all. He had a lonely pride in his self-sufficiency, nurturing it. The isolation and muddle of his upbringing had come close to swindling him of his potential. But challenges overcome made for strength not frailty, and he would offer this secret strength as his tribute of loyalty to the Ambassador, on whose final report his transition to the 'A-stream' *diplomatic* grades would almost certainly depend.

What the Ambassador had just been saying now seemed clear: if Powell-Bourke, unaided, got the powers-that-be to rescind the flogging, thus avoiding the usual ignorant outcry in the British press, the statutory protest by McCann's local MP, and the resulting diplomatic *froideur* towards Britain on the part of this desert kingdom, he, the Ambassador, could hardly fail to support his Consul's application to cross the barrier of those grades. But if Powell-Bourke had to call in the Ambassador, not necessarily so. And if – worse still – if he failed to call him in and the flogging took place with all its knock-on effects . . .

The prisoner remained in the fort at Daba'a. A week after being sentenced he was led into the same chamber as before for a second interview with the Consul. This being a statutory consular visit, only the armed prison guard was present. The Egyptian court clerk was not in attendance.

McCann's head was now shaven and he was kitted out in standard prison garb, the coarse grey ankle-length Arab shirt, the *thobe*. His pallor was marked and his blue eyes had a dazed look.

The Consul offered him a cigarette from a packet brought especially for the purpose, and began at once, 'We're distressed about the flogging part. We're thoroughly irritated by that because we thought we at last had got it agreed with Interior that they wouldn't sentence British subjects to flogging. We're going to try and get that knocked off.'

McCann appeared scarcely to be listening. A disturbing silence ensued. Powell-Bourke said tautly, 'I shall ask the Ambassador himself to come in on this one if I have to.' But the prisoner still said nothing. He seemed indifferent to the Consul's visit. Powell-Bourke regretted having referred to the Ambassador: it was a hypothetical statement, and anyway was such a man worth his own care and skill, let alone an ambassador's? Then he caught the wink. How dare he! There was nothing they shared, no connivance at all. McCann was nothing! Human dross! That his own career should have come to depend on a creature of such negligible value! He wanted to remind him outright: I'm all you have, my good friend. I'm your only chance in this remote and dangerous country with its labyrinthine bureaucracy. It's no matter for winking.

But now the prisoner had a question. Did his sentence date from his arrest or the day of the hearing? The Consul told him that theoretically the sentence dated from arrest but that one could never be sure in practice. One could never be quite sure about any aspect of the *practice* of law in this particular country.

'Look here, Mr Powell-Bourke,' McCann resumed with a frown, which was met by a frown from the Consul, and not only because of McCann's wilful lack of grace. The fellow had started to mispronounce his name. At the first interview he had repeated it correctly, 'Pole-Burke'. Now he rhymed it with 'foul pork' – a nickname Cedric endured at a school where he had risked correcting an older boy. (This time, obviously, his visiting card was to blame.) 'Once I'm out of here, can you promise me I can get straight back home? They'll no keep me hangin' aroun' for exit visas?'

'It's in everyone's interest to get you out as fast as possible,' Powell-Bourke replied. But he knew that if the flogging were to take place it was best not to send a man back the very next day when the prurience of the press was at its height and the man's back would be photographed with its weals.

'Who knows at home?' McCann asked.

'We arranged for one of our people to locate your wife and inform her.'

McCann's jaw was set and he made no response.

'We are obliged to inform someone,' the Consul tried to explain. 'You gave us no other living relation. At least, no adult one.'

'Wha's the point?' he said with his blank stare. Then the wink again.

It was a tic in McCann's cheek, Powell-Bourke saw, not a wink after all. Perhaps he should pity him.

'We advised that any letters should be sent to you care of my office at the Embassy.'

In fact, no communication of any kind had come to him from Britain, no further laborious penmanship on fancy cream-coloured notepaper.

Powell-Bourke proceeded with his questions under the various headings: conditions of incarceration, food, exercise periods, daylight, medical, reading matter, access to the prison authorities.

The cells beneath were evidently archaic, conditions vile and the rights of prisoners – so far as they existed – erratically honoured. Most of the Consul's 'headings' were so irrelevant as to bring to McCann's face a contemptuous grin. He was living 'in a heap' with the other prisoners, and they all shared a 'hole in the floor' as a lavatory. The two small apertures in the outer wall were originally made for cannon to fire through. There was no kitchen in the fort or regular provision of meals: he was surviving on food brought to the other prisoners by relatives and friends, and tins of meat and vegetables sent in by his company. Most of the prisoners were Yemenis and Eritreans – illegal immigrants in search of work. McCann had no one he could talk to, but it struck the Consul that an affinity had grown with a local youth on a rape charge who faced probable execution.

McCann's description of prison life came reluctantly. He repeated he was 'no complaining' and urged the Consul not to protest on his behalf. Powell-Bourke regretted this, since he saw it as a residual duty of the Western powers, and Britain in particular, to remind the developing world of the civilised standards towards which they were supposedly 'developing'. Of course, it was still open to Powell-Bourke to let the appropriate people in the Ministry of the Interior know of his pained surprise that such conditions should be endured by a British subject, albeit a convicted felon, in this day and age in such a country as this. Pained surprise was an effective line of consular stock-in-trade . . . A blood-curdling wail suddenly broke upon the peace of the afternoon, drowning the air conditioner and echoing round the square. The Consul could have jumped out of his skin.

It was only the mid-afternoon call to prayer, stridently amplified from the minaret across the square – the one call of the day that almost nobody obeyed. Had McCann spotted how startled he was, from his eyes? Yet he was surely noticing nothing. There he sat, blank and strained. Prisoners were usually so full of questions, pleas, paltry requests. This man had asked for nothing, no needs, almost no questions – not even as to how floggings were carried out. It fell to Powell-Bourke to volunteer that the traditional restraint upon the flogger should apply, a Koran held under the swiping arm. If it were to take place, it would be an ordeal, oh yes, but the humiliation might prove the worst of it.

'They work by their Muslim calendar, don't they?' McCann asked suddenly. The Consul wondered if he had been listening.

'Lunar months, yes.'

'Shorter, right?'

'A day or two. In six months it mounts up.'

'Can you bring me one of their calendars next time?'

'A *hijri* calendar? I should think that might be allowed.'

On the long drive back Powell-Bourke questioned whether a monthly visit to such a prisoner was a sensible use of his time, what with all his own home-going preparations and the round of farewell parties, not to speak of competing calls of duty.

Getting the flogging rescinded soon grew complicated. The Minister of the Interior was unwilling to become involved, that was obvious. The underling deputed to look after the case stalled repeatedly when Powell-Bourke asked what had happened to their two governments' agreement for a joint committee to consider petty incidents which might jeopardise good relations. Had the agreement not been made at the instigation of His Royal Highness the Minister? And had not the British already named their two members for this committee, and were still waiting for the other side to do the same?

Oh, but was the case a 'petty incident', the official suggested, when McCann had put the lives of innocent local citizens at risk by delaying the opening of the hospital? 'Maybe he will have killed them,' he remarked, invoking the complex English future-perfect. When Powell-Bourke reminded that the construction company hoped to make up the time lost, the underling instantly changed his tack. Maybe the affair was *too* petty to occupy the time of any committee. 'These gentlemen are very important,' he declared. Wearily, Powell-Bourke refrained from questioning the importance of committee members not yet chosen let alone appointed. And yet of course 'His Royal Highness the Minister has this matter under his personal consideration. *Always.*' And the underling ever so slightly adjusted his headcloth to shield his eyes from the garish noonday beyond the window.

On and on it went; from department to department journeyed the ever-growing batch of papers. Tentacles from two other Ministries – Justice and Foreign Affairs – got into the tangle, directly as a result of the Consul's intervention. In the office of the Director-General concerned with Western Europe, Powell-Bourke ventured to recall that on the British Foreign Secretary's recent visit the general understanding was reached that it was unwise for British subjects to be sentenced to a flogging. The Director-General – a well travelled sophisticate – frowned with pity that the Foreign Secretary of Great Britain should occupy himself with such trifles. No wonder the authority of the British was not what it used to be. And he went on, with impenetrable urbanity, 'For certain offences the penalty is made clear in the Holy Koran,' offered with the hands opening and a smile that betokened submission to a Higher Power none could question.

Powell-Bourke was not without sinew. 'The law of the Holy Koran is surely for the believer rather than the non-believer, Excellency?' He had no doubt the Koran had nothing to say about bulldozers and hospital foundations.

'The message of the Holy Koran is universal, Mr Po-will.'

In the course it took the case was not exceptional. Powell-Bourke worked with diligence and consummate patience. The root of the problem was that the local Amir carried a lot of tribal weight in his governorate; he stood outside the ruling family's hierarchic authority, and he was a crabbed and pious old man who regarded any foreign prisoner in his charge as a captive in a covert but ruthless war with the Infidel.

It wound on week after week, month after month, into the long and stifling summer. The services of a local Arab lawyer were obtained. He had a cousin who was linked by marriage to the family of the Amir of Daba'a. The Consul clung to the hope of persuading the Amir that it would save him a lot of bother if he allowed his prisoner to be transferred to the capital. There amid the cosmopolitan air of daily life a less brutal interpretation of the law might eventually prevail. But the Amir seemed intent on keeping possession of his prisoner, and the Arab lawyer – another sophisticate, as adept at switching human values as changing a *thobe* for a suit on a Europe-bound jet – softly explained to Powell-Bourke, civilised man to civilised man, that in those backward parts of the country the people failed to understand the need for Western technicians. They couldn't even grasp the need to build a modern state. The old man, he'd heard, had actually blocked the building of a new prison. In bringing the full force of the law to bear upon an erring *khawaja*, like the unfortunate McCann, an amir could win popular credit. And in the light of the probable execution of a young member of his own tribal community . . . Yet the Amir was *reported* to be taking a personal interest.

Powell-Bourke deemed it inadvisable to try to see the Amir personally: it might well have the opposite effect. Anyway, he would always rather work indirectly, not frontally, whether as a result of his experience of the Eastern method or from a private reticence (he wouldn't say timidity) he was never sure.

He told his wife of the Amir's interest. The case had caught her up from the moment she heard about it, affecting her strangely. It made her pensive. Had it not in some way blunted the gaiety emerging as she settled into her new life? Perhaps she was in awe of what it all might mean to his career. Yet he wasn't sure. From time to time she referred to McCann's character, to the 'commitment' a man must feel to act as he did, questioning – but half to herself. It was an odd word, 'commitment'. For a while she kept pressing Cedric to let her come with him to Daba'a on the chance of her being allowed to visit McCann with him, on and on until he was forced to dismiss so absurd a notion quite heatedly. It was then she rounded on him, suddenly and out of character. 'You don't understand him, Cedric, you don't begin to understand him!'

'What the devil are you talking about?'

'You could never conceive any normal person acting like that – you could never feel strongly enough about anyone!'

'Who suggested he was normal?' he retorted, and saw her scolding herself for slipping in that unneeded word, letting him cap her in argument, as he invariably did. But it wasn't fair of her; she must know that if she stopped to reflect a moment.

Meanwhile McCann had served over half his sentence and the official date of the ending of the Powell-Bourkes' tour of duty was only a month away. The Consul himself had been unable to visit McCann again. He had been so very busy, hardly a minute to himself, and it was a four-hour drive, both ways. In any case, nothing for McCann had been received by the Consulate from home and a company representative on the hospital project had reported that McCann's health was holding. The man was tough, that was certain. Powell-Bourke hadn't taken him the promised *hijri* calendar, true enough, but time remained for that, and no amount of calendars would shorten his sentence by a day.

It was odd that no more letters had come, nor parcels either. Powell-Bourke took it as evidence of the man's unsociable and ruffianly disposition. He was hardly one to collect the kind of friends who would stand by him, he supposed, or keep the allegiance of kith and kin. Yet he was mistaken in assuming McCann had no people of his own, for the Office in London had confirmed locating a parental home of sorts and its 'recorded delivery' letters had been signed for. Nothing had come back from there, not a card, not a message. It tended to bear out Powell-Bourke's view.

It occurred to him to mention this to Jenny. He was nervous of re-arousing her feminine irrationality, but he was on the look-out for an opportunity to make two points: *a*, that nothing was better calculated to interfere with a consul's professionalism than getting emotionally involved, and *b*, he was far from indifferent to the fate of McCann. If it would save McCann the penalty, he thought of saying, he would endure the flogging himself. He did in fact let fall this last remark, but it slipped out at such an unexpected moment – she was just stepping out of the bath – that he found her looking at him in the mirror strangely. He masked his embarrassment by scrubbing his teeth with a thoroughness that prevented his saying more.

Two developments in quick succession brought a new urgency to the case and required the Consul to return to the prisoner. The Ministry of Justice – God knows on whose authority – *published* the fact of the conviction and the sentence, and the British press, of course, instantly took it up.

The Ambassador was on to Powell-Bourke at once to stand-by with reassuring statements on the health of the prisoner, the condition of the gaol, and the consular department's efforts to have a British subject spared humiliation.

The second development was the arrival of a document for McCann from a solicitor in Greenock which comprised the start of the divorce proceedings initiated by his young wife.

Coverage in the British press was mostly brief and factual, but even short reports could make for alarming reading when played back in the local Arab press. Indigenous readers had no means of distinguishing one publication from another; nor were they to know that British newspapers weren't subject to government control like their own. Would that they were, for the irresponsibility of British journalists was intolerable. The diplomatic damage of such play-backs could run into sums, in contracts lost, far greater than anything a drunk-driven bulldozer could wreak. In the present case the lurid editorialising in Scotland's *Sunday Record* and, unexpectedly, the *Oban Times*, could easily be picked up by the Arab Press Exchange and read in the capital as semi-official British provocation. There were plenty of displaced Palestinians around the newsrooms of the capital ready to contribute their tithe of Britain-baiting.

The *Oban Times* had dug out McCann's father, an ex-whaler from one of the small isles of the Inner Hebrides. It was there among the last of the crofting communities that Alistair McCann had been born and spent his childhood. He had gone to secondary school in Fort William on the mainland and soon afterwards – in the colourful phrase of his father – had 'disappeared into the pit of Glasgow'. The family heard he had 'got into trouble' and later that he was married and had a bairn, but he had not been in touch and they had no means of finding him even when his own mother had gone to hospital in Glasgow to die of her cancer.

At 'morning prayers' the Ambassador chided the Consul for not revealing that McCann was an islander.

'He insisted he was Glaswegian,' Powell-Bourke replied, growing hot.

'One can tell from the speech, surely.'

'It's a very strong Glasgow accent, Ambassador.'

The Ambassador looked across at him quizzically – they were seated in a circle in easy chairs. The Ambassador was of Scottish extraction himself. 'He would have been brought up speaking the Gaelic. When he got to the big school and went south they'd have mocked it out of him. He'd have tried to disguise his *bedu* background, and once he'd done time as a youngster I suppose he overdid it and broke all contact. Or maybe the family dropped him. They like to keep the scutcheon clean. And they're slow to forgive in the highlands and islands.'

Powell-Bourke often felt the Ambassador was giving him lessons in the business of life. He did it with his usual transparency and grace, but Cedric wished it didn't have to happen in the company of others. Even his use of the vernacular – 'doing time' – was teaching him, as was interpreting for him McCann's father's phrase about 'getting into trouble'. Was the Ambassador mildly censuring him? He felt wrong-footed among these others – the Head of Chancery, the Commercial Counsellor, the First Secretary, the Information Attaché, the Defence Attaché. Did they see a relevance in all this that escaped him?

'I've got to go up to see him this week in any case, Ambassador,' he said, his throat strangle-tight. 'I'll fill out the picture.'

'In the circs,' the Ambassador said lightly, 'I think you'd better go up tomorrow. If this flares up, we've got to have all the answers. So far nobody's played it back here – we're absolutely sure of that, Gervaise?' he turned to the Second Secretary, Information, an exact contemporary of the Consul, for endorsement, and leaned forward to touch the polished wood of the low table they encircled. 'I fear they will, I fear they will.' And he added, 'If only those fatuous MPs can keep their mouths shut.'

'Some hope,' said Head of Chancery.

'For myself, I'd rather stand back from this affair. Cedric, I'm tempted to enquire whether by any chance you're prepared to stay on two or three extra weeks, if it looks to be what's needed to settle all this. Of course, there's no need to keep Jenny hanging on if she's wanting to get on with the moving in at home.'

Powell-Bourke seized the proposal as the last chance of redemption. Indefinably he had lost ground, he knew. Yet the Ambassador must retain some faith in him or he wouldn't have spoken about 'standing back' or suggesting his staying over to see it through. He was in a private fury with the Office in London. How could they have failed properly to research the man's background, such as a mere newspaper had evidently done in a single afternoon? As for McCann having failed to tell him he had been locked up before, he deserved nothing. Or ought he himself to have deduced this from the man's indifference to the conditions of his imprisonment? Ought he?

The document for McCann from the solicitor was accompanied by a letter addressed to the Consul himself which proposed that he, the Consul, should arrange legal representation for Alistair Dougal McCann if he thought fit. Although contained in a separate envelope marked for McCann, the main document was purposely unsealed, and Powell-Bourke took it back to his villa in the compound to read it without distraction. 'Morning prayers' had left him unwontedly tense, and he didn't feel up to taking it in properly in the office with his consular staff all around him. He could not decide whether there was a note of mockery when the Ambassador was putting him right on McCann's background. It was uncanny how he could 'read' a situation from a few fragments – it wasn't the first time Powell-Bourke had witnessed him at it. But was there *mockery*?

The document from the wife's solicitor mostly comprised a 'statement of facts' of which the intention was evidently to cow McCann into a despairing acceptance of her demands. It 'summarised' her complaints: that he failed to provide for her adequately, abused her frequently in private and more than once in public, 'terrorised' her with threats of violence, neglected their children, was often drunk in the presence of the children, and once assaulted his son Donald. It was several pages long and contained dates and precise locations.

Powell-Bourke passed it across to his wife partly because he sensed she had allowed McCann to assume the status of a martyr, though martyr to what he couldn't say. She read the document slowly, growing pale. When she had finished she put it down between them on the low glass table, Civil Service 'B-stream' issue, without a word. It was one of her gambits – he was already growing familiar with it – to say nothing at all when she had most to say. He debated with himself whether to give her the cue that would unstop her. He suspected that what she had to say would irritate him, but he himself was ready for a confrontation, if such it was to be.

'Well?'

Silence.

'I'll tell Hamid to get tea,' she said, standing.

'I wondered what you thought of our friend McCann.'

'You're not going to take that to him, are you?'

'Of course.'

'You can't, Cedric.'

'I would be utterly failing in my duty if I didn't.'

She left the room and in the kitchen he heard her instructing the servant to make tea. She came back very slowly and then began to move some magazines and a heavy glass ashtray to make space for the tea things. They neither of them smoked but one had to have an ashtray handy for callers.

She said, 'The consequences of showing him that don't occur to you, do they? Your "duty"!'

'I don't really understand what you're saying.'

'That is the trouble, Cedric.' The wistfulness of her face had become wild rebellion. The transformation was extraordinary because the one seemed to be the drastic evolution of the other. It was strange that he had not perceived such a possibility before. She had the ashtray in her hand as if she had forgotten why.

'He's known for four months that his wife has left him,' he said evenly. 'This can't change anything for him.'

'You think not,' she replied, and confined herself to adding with an infinite emptiness, 'Of course, Cedric.' How could he understand, he who had never once made love to her without reminding her they couldn't afford a baby, never had a drink too many, never allowed himself so much as a feeling without weighing the consequences, who would here and now, she wouldn't wonder, jettison everything – marriage, household, mother, whatever – without a quaver, for the sake of the diplomatic grade?

He was still looking at her, head cocked, with a species of pity. Or was it a sneer?

'It's a sickening document,' Jenny said. She lifted it up by the corner in her fingertips as if it was soaked in vomit. 'It's the only reading matter you'll have brought him in four months of virtually total isolation and two months more to go . . .'

'I am taking him a *hijri* calendar, Jenny.'
As Hamid entered with the tea his mistress was laughing.

His wife's bizarre outburst clouded Powell-Bourke's drive to Daba'a the next day. *Of course* he had no choice but to hand the letter to McCann. But he would take the opportunity of commenting that Mrs McCann's complaints were probably only half the story, and that he was aware that quite innocent flurries in a family household could be distorted for the sake of divorce proceedings. The utter injustice of Jenny's outburst the day before served as an example. To a man who had spent hour upon hour, day upon day, in highly intricate manoeuvres to have McCann spared his brutal penalty, it could be made to seem a gratuitous, intolerable *insult*. That couldn't possibly have been Jenny's intention, though he was blowed if he knew what it was. He was none too sure about higher education for women. Least of all sociology.

As it happened he was able to bring to McCann a distinct thread of hope.

Before visiting the prison fortress he called at the Amir's *majlis*, as a matter of courtesy. In the antechamber, the greeting he received from the *aide* was less cold than usual. He got no further than the *aide*, but the Amir, he was told, had expressed the view that if the *qadi* who had sentenced the *Inglisi* were to find cause to review the sentence, he, the Amir, would not stand in his way. Powell-Bourke crossed to the *shariah* court to discuss with the Egyptian clerk what the *aide* said, but the Egyptian rose from his desk at once, and shooting glances from the corner of his eye conducted him along the corridor to his master.

The *qadi* himself was elderly, in poor health and almost blind. Though aware of concern in higher places at the sentence imposed on the *Inglisi* he was puzzled by the cause of it. He had forgotten the circumstances surrounding McCann's arrest and was unable to read the case documents which included the Arabic copy of Mrs McCann's letter with a deposition attached, brought this very day by Powell-Bourke. The Egyptian clerk soon emerged as the key influence. If indeed the matter were to be decided at this level, a moderate sum crossing an Egyptian palm might prove the critical factor.

This thought occurred to the Consul in a rush. He noticed his hands trembling, and in the sparkling new air-conditioned courtroom annexe where the three men were gathered he felt the heat flooding above his white collar. It was probably now or never. Breaking back from time to time into the English which the Egyptian seemed to favour, he made reference to 'special compensation that was surely due in a case that was taking up so much of his time.' But the Egyptian did not rise to the bait, not even with one of his sidelong glances. He decided to drop the notion: bribery was notoriously dangerous. Everyone knew it occurred; baksheesh was endemic. He had heard sales directors who covered the Middle East claiming that no-one got a contract without payola. But he also knew of cases where bribery had landed foreigners in gaol and their companies banned. Presumably an arcane technique went with it. And anyway, he had so little cash with him.

Tea was brought, sweet and clear in little glass mugs which stuck to the mahogany. As they rehearsed the facts of the case, Powell-Bourke debated with himself how seriously the Egyptian took his job. Did a fierce legal vocation possess him? Or was he hanging on in this backwater just to push his children through a couple more years of Cairo schooling than he himself had got? Apart from a pot belly, he was quite spare for an Egyptian of middle years. His mouth sagged in repose. Did this mean he could not be a man of discipline, devoted to the God of the holy Koran? Hard to tell. Powell-Bourke wished the man wore shirt and trousers like any other Egyptian here. This desert *thobe* and headcloth cancelled out the fragments of English they shared, cordoned him off from the brotherhood of foreigners, of fellow Mediterraneans – cordoned him off into this God-ridden community of the barren wastes.

Powell-Bourke found that his hands were still atremble.

Every so often a point seemed to penetrate the fuddled brain of the *qadi*. His head would nod slowly, or both hands would pick up a document like a plate of soup and he would make out a little piece of the Arabic typewriting for himself. But it was the Egyptian clerk with whom the authority covertly lay. That much was clear, even if how to influence *him* was not at all clear. Matters seemed ready to shift. Yet without that little extra push . . .

And now it was already time for Powell-Bourke to take leave of the *qadi* and cross the square with the clerk to see McCann in the Turkish fort. He left his car where it was, under the shadow of the courthouse wall, and he and the Egyptian set off in the heat of the day to walk the three hundred yards. The Consul made considerable play with his regrets over the work that this case was loading upon a man as busy as his good friend.

'It is my duty,' the clerk said.

Powell-Bourke was sweltering alongside him. In the motionless air the sun beat on his head like a drum. Sweat dripped from his cheeks, his earlobes, his chin. His high collar was soaked and his shirt and trousers stuck to his trunk and limbs. He only wished there was something he could do, he said, to reward his friend for this extra burden. *As* a friend, of course.

'It is my duty,' the clerk said.

The *thobe* and the headcloth, the Consul commented, were much the most sensible clothes to wear in this summer heat. Had his friend taken to wearing them because of the climate, he ventured to enquire, or for other reasons?

'Which reasons?' the clerk said.

They reached the fort. McCann was sent for and very soon joined them in the long narrow room to sit opposite them in the remaining wicker chair. A hawk-faced bedouin guard with a light machine-gun squatted in the doorway.

McCann had changed. The immediately visible difference was his acquisition of a broad wiry yellow beard. But the most telling change was in his eyes. Where previously they were dazed, now their look was one of intensity, as if the mind was fixed upon one overriding intention. The tic was gone; he was lean, hard, and unexpectedly bronzed. The Consul could confidently report that his health was holding. What sustained it evidently lay deep in the man. His accent, while still markedly Scottish, seemed to have grown more musical and airy.

Powell-Bourke told him at once that he had brought with him a 'legal document' from home. He could see that McCann immediately recognised what it must be, and making the comments he had planned, passed it across. Taking it, McCann's expression scarcely altered, except perhaps for an intensifying of the eyes. The Consul attempted to offset the document's affront by mentioning that a further hint had been dropped concerning the modifying of his sentence – a straw in the wind. But McCann was already absorbed in the letter, his frown deepening and the fingers of one hand kneading or clenching a fist.

He let him read and read. And he watched him in silence, against the racket of the air conditioner, and remembered his wife, Jenny. What had she meant by that word? 'Commitment'! Was that how to express love to a woman – abuse her, threaten her, get drunk? He saw the man's lips moving as he read. He belonged to a different species, a world apart.

When at last the other was done he broke the silence gently.

'There's no need to reply at once. If you want, we can write back to say you are considering your answer.'

'Will it wait till I'm oot?' McCann looked straight past the Consul at the barred window.

'Probably.'

'Make sure it does, please.'

Please. That was new. Then he met the Consul's eyes with his own wildness.

'Can you guarantee the case canna go forward without my response to these documents?'

'The divorce? I can't guarantee that, but I'll let you know if a reply is definitely required sooner.' What was McCann thinking? Maybe it was the children: were not the frown and fist most fierce when McCann was reading about the neglect of his children and assaulting his son?

'You brought me that calendar?' McCann demanded.

'Oh, yes. Of course.' Powell-Bourke began to search his briefcase, but seemed unable to locate it. 'I put it out to bring,' he chided himself. 'It must be in my car. If I find it there I'll give it to my friend. He'll pass it to you, I'm sure.' He caught the clerk with a fragment of smile.

McCann asked for a pen and paper. Powell-Bourke drew some foolscap sheets from his briefcase and glanced at the gaoler squatting at the door with his machine-gun. He had dropped into a doze. He handed the items across and began to describe all he had been doing to have the flogging rescinded. He said nothing about news of it having broken in the British press, but he did mention he had extended his tour of duty to see the case through.

McCann made no comment and his expression did not alter. All he reverted to was the date of his release and whether he would be deported the same day. The Consul was stung by the lack of common gratitude. Of course, the man knew no better. Or was it perhaps easier for a convict to assume the worst than toy with hope? Maybe that was the intensity: a girding against pain. He couldn't penetrate such a fellow at all.

Just as before, McCann refused to complain of the conditions of his custody. He was now being allowed to work in the inner courtyard of the fortress, which they were paving with cement. The only one never allowed out of the communal cell was the 'poor sod for the chop', the young Arab whose execution was now confirmed. He lived there among the rest of them, but in leg-irons, and on a Friday soon would be led out into the glare and beheaded before the townsmen in front of the mosque. The mosque's minaret, McCann said, was the only object they could see through the apertures in their cell wall. The doomed man was the only subject on which McCann had anything of his own to volunteer and it puzzled Powell-Bourke, this irrelevance, from a ruffian who 'terrorised' his wife and abandoned his parents.

Just as he was being conducted at gunpoint back to the communal lock-up, McCann turned. 'I thought you were coming to see me last month. An' the month before.'

The Consul detected a strand of impertinence.

'If I haven't come to see you as often as I would like, my dear fellow,' he told him tartly, 'it's been because I've been busy trying to save your skin. I rather imagined I had explained.'

But he did not allow the man's offensiveness to deprive him of his *hijri* calendar, which on his return to his car outside the *shariah* court he handed to the Egyptian clerk.

At their late supper that evening, he did not mention to Jenny that McCann had shown no emotion on reading the document from his wife's solicitors, beyond the kneading and clenching of the fingers and a certain wildness of eye.

Nor did he tell her that he had slipped six hundred riyals into the folding calendar with the *hijri* and Gregorian dates, when he handed it to the clerk. The calendar had been in his briefcase all the time. Pretending to rummage for it in his car he had succeeded in shuffling it out and transferring the money from his wallet. The six hundred riyals was all he had – apart from small change for petrol – he supposed about two week's wages for a court clerk. He wondered if he should have rounded it down to a confident five hundred, to make it seem like the 'going rate' for a small perversion of the legal processes.

He did report to her, however, what the Amir had allegedly said, and that he had seen the *qadi*. He had been able to hold out a little hope to McCann.

'How did you find him?' she asked.

'The fact is, he seemed hardly interested in all one has been trying to do for him. Not a word of thanks. Of course, it's well known as a "thankless job". Consul.'

'What *was* he interested in?'

'The exact date of his release. As if it mattered, a day or two either way. And of course these people aren't too good about unlocking offenders dead on time. They can be a bit naughty.' He would have warned McCann accordingly if he hadn't been irritated by his lack of appreciation of his efforts, especially in the light of the risk he was about to run for his benefit. 'And he's obviously bothered about his fellow prisoner who's to be beheaded.' Did he mean 'bothered'? 'Somehow caught up with the wretch. He's a local Arab. I can't say I understand it. What d'you think, Jenny? You're good at this sort of thing.'

She flushed lightly at his calculated compliment. They were on their own now. Hamid had cleared away the meal. 'Don't you think,' she said, 'he feels some sort of identity with the young man?'

'How, possibly? I don't suppose they've a single word in common. The fellow's convicted of rape, something of that kind.'

'They're both at rock bottom. Isn't that it? They're wiped out. Just about, anyway. For a man condemned to death for an offence like that, there's nothing left. He'll have been abandoned by his family, and all mankind. By God, too. You know, before they have an execution I believe the *imam* preaches a sermon which is relayed to the crowds waiting in the square outside the mosque, by the loudspeaker in the minaret. The condemned man's out there, too, waiting for the sermon to finish. Gervaise has heard one. He said there was no prospect of forgiveness, no real idea of expiation. Just a sense of righteousness at ridding God-fearing mankind of a diseased member. It's all pretty savage.'

Jenny's knowledge surprised him: Gervaise had never mentioned to him about witnessing an execution.

'One can't really object to them doing what they think's best for their own people,' Powell-Bourke said.

'I'm not really talking about that, Cedric. I'm just saying that that man's wiped out in the eyes of all his fellows and his God. McCann presumably feels something of the same. I don't know about his God; perhaps he had one as a little boy, long ago on his island. But he's nothing now to the family he left behind there, or his own children . . . or his wife whom he obviously loves.'

'Obviously loves?'

'Oh God, Cedric.'

She got up and for a moment he didn't know where she was off to. Then she crossed to sit beside him on the settee and took his hand. She seemed to be gazing at it. She had admired his hands at their second meeting ever. She had said, You've got sensitive hands, did you know that? and looked straight into his eyes. No one had said such a thing to him before. The truth was, right up to the time of his decision to try for the foreign service he had chewed his nails. When he gave up the habit, the condition of his hands became a kind of symbol of his advancement.

Now he saw the tears in her eyes. And suddenly she said, 'Can't you *see?*'

She buried her face in his lapel.

He lay awake late into the night worrying. He didn't know if it was about Jenny or everything else. There was enough else to worry about. If the transaction rebounded on him it would finish him: the Ambassador would see to that. He would deny it, of course, but nobody would believe him. There would be an enquiry, and it would all leak out. Immunity would protect him from the dreadful physical penalties – seizure, imprisonment, interrogation . . . though one could never be quite sure with these people, a bunch of warring tribes a generation ago. No, but he would be packed off home in disgrace, and it would damage the British reputation incalculably. Echoes would reverberate for years.

He tried to visualise the Egyptian when he came across the money, as he was bound to do – the calendar only had the two folds. If it happened in the *quadi*'s presence, would the old man be too blind to notice it? Or the Egyptian could just pocket the money and do nothing. Then again, had he overestimated the fellow's power to influence matters? But if he had altogether misjudged the man's *character* . . .

Jenny Powell-Bourke returned home to England on the planned date, ahead of her husband. It was not a complicated departure: almost all their furniture belonged to the Foreign Office and the couple had acquired little of anything else. Two or three consuls from the senior embassies had thrown farewell parties for them – staid affairs, although naturally alcohol flowed freely on embassy compounds (it was years since the Religious Police had blundered into a diplomatic function). Cedric Powell-Bourke had grown neither popular nor unpopular during his tour of duty. Mind you, the acquisition of a young wife, and a wife who at second glance was prettier than one supposed and whose wistfulness evoked a protectiveness in the alert male, had caused some to wonder if they hadn't overlooked something in the departing British Consul. His Australian counterpart had been heard to refer to Cedric as a 'dark horse'. The American Consul commented to Gervaise that Cedric was 'quintessentially English', intending it as a sort of two-way compliment which, however,

Gervaise, an Old Etonian, appeared to receive with surprise. The unspoken consensus was that no one knew him much better now than when they first met him.

The Powell-Bourkes' own farewell reception was, they were assured, a successful gathering, despite the awareness that Powell-Bourke himself was to stay on a few weeks more to attend to unfinished business of a delicate nature. The postponement would surely have been taken as an unspoken compliment to Powell-Bourke in the special reliance it implied on the part of the Ambassador. One never knew which way the cat would jump in this country, but the Ambassador appeared to have had no second thoughts: he even saw to it that the Foreign Ministry up the road knew his Consul was outstaying his tour, and why. Every scrap of pressure helped.

Domestically, it was a jumbled period. The new Consul moved in with wife and two children, which meant Powell-Bourke being reduced to a cramped spare room. He was cramped not only by the room but by the sustained apologies of his successor at what he called 'playing cuckoo in your nest'. The new Consul tried to make amends by bringing Powell-Bourke into the family, which destroyed his privacy and subjected him to long periods in the company of his successor's children. He had never been one for being at ease with children. As for his residual tasks, he was lent an office alongside Head of Chancery. As a rule he seldom visited that floor of the Embassy, and it obliged him to carry additional keys and follow certain security procedures that consular officials were not normally privy to.

All this time he was haunted by the six hundred-riyal notes he had slipped in with the calendar. The Egyptian clerk's indeterminate mouth kept returning to his mind's eye. The internal debate was waged relentlessly as to the sort of a man the clerk was. One of fastidious principle? Soft-hearted? Devious? Venal? Powell-Bourke hadn't the least idea. Sometimes he glimpsed his act as one of audacity which would brilliantly pay off: the motto of the Special Air Service, *Who Dares, Wins*, flickered. Yet simultaneously he knew that he had acted altogether 'out of character', and that was a phrase which hung around him more persistently, a phrase which would certainly be used in mitigation at any enquiry into his misconduct. Not that his action could be seen as immoral in intent, far from it (it wasn't as if this place had ever been a British colony). From the British point of view it was at worst a case of *'trop de zèle'*. Yet wasn't that exactly how Watergate started? . . . The hardest part was not knowing – not knowing what the Egyptian had done or not done, or what he might still do – and all this in the certainty that he must face the man again. Powell-Bourke acquired a grey and haunted look. His style of speech became even more stilted, like a man giving evidence under cross-examination.

Maybe a decision on the McCann case had been reached already. Maybe his attempted corruption of an official of the state had already come to light locally. Repeatedly he cursed himself for his recklessness. He looked back on it with astonishment. He'd made a hole in his pocket for the sake of an horrendous gamble. If the flick of a switch could obliterate his folly, he would have flicked it a hundred times . . . On the other hand, if there *had* been a revised decision on the flogging it would be typical of these Arabs to omit to inform the British Consulate. Left to themselves, there was no certainty they would get round to telling the man himself. It was not something Powell-Bourke would be wise to attempt to ascertain over the telephone to Daba'a. He had no alternative but to drive down again.

His next statutory visit fell during the fourth week after the previous one. He made the journey on the very first day of that week, the Saturday. He reached the Amir's *majlis* by late morning.

This time he was admitted without delay into the presence of the old Amir himself, a tiny, incongruous, beaky figure shadowed by his chequered headcloth like an owl in a hollow tree. Various tribal dignitaries, officials, and foreign contractors were already present, facing each other in two ranks of vast upholstered armchairs, drinking alternately mugs of sweet tea and cardamom coffee, waiting for their moment to intrude their request or register their complaint. Powell-Bourke had not previously got as far as the presence of the Amir. He now crossed the room to shake the hand of the old man, who half rose without actually looking at this latest guest, let alone enquiring his business (he was simultaneously engaged on the telephone). The cold *aide* stood behind the Amir. His eyes met the Englishman's but gave no signal of recognition whatsoever.

Powell-Bourke took his seat several armchairs distant from the Amir's desk. He was making this particular call only for courtesy: he knew it was not the place to launch into an exposition of the case in hand. The relevant point of call was the *qadi*'s court, or rather, the clerk's office.

After half an hour of being ignored, except by the tea-boy, he was about to rise and take his leave. At that moment (it was a little uncanny), evidently at some signal from the Amir, the *aide* stationed behind the old man crossed to Powell-Bourke and told him in rapid and nearly perfect English, *sotto voce*, that he would wish to know, as the representative of his country, that His Excellency the Amir had decided the *Inglisi* would not be flogged. This was relayed to him almost as an aside, with no endorsing glance from the Amir at the end of the chamber; and when Powell-Bourke at once proceeded to take his leave, as was clearly expected, by shaking the Amir's bony hand once more and offering a semblance of thanks in his best Arabic, the old man still refrained from uttering a word and caught his eye for no longer than a deadly, penetrating moment.

Powell-Bourke was obliged to call on the Egyptian clerk at the *shariah* court if only to secure access to the fort. In any case, he did require something *on paper* about the reprieve.

This was not immediately forthcoming. The Egyptian declared it was not necessary: the Amir's word was quite enough.

Powell-Bourke replied he did not doubt that; but he had to have written confirmation to take back to his Embassy. Could the clerk himself not give him a note, on the letter-heading of the *shariah* court?

'Who am I to write letters?' the clerk protested mildly. 'I am nothing.'

'Oh, we're both foreigners here,' the Consul concurred, preserving the complicity between them. 'But you can see I must take something back.'

'You do not trust?'

'Good gracious. Of course I do. That's not the point.' He pursed his lips.

'This paper. What should it say?' The clerk frowned deeply as if it was extraordinarily difficult to imagine what such a document might set forth.

'Why don't I draft it?' Powell-Bourke proposed, and did so there and then, in a single sentence of Arabic, addressed to himself, the British Consul: 'This is to confirm that the prisoner A. D. McCann, British subject, is excused the penalty of flogging.'

The clerk gazed at the words in heavy doubt. 'I cannot write this,' he said glumly. 'Not I.'

'Not you, of course,' the Consul conceded at once. He was no greenhorn in this country, when it came to the official mind. 'Perhaps we could just type it – here, right now – and the *qadi* could make his mark.' He gave him a hard look. He had heard it said: once one's started the *baksheesh*, there's no end to it.

Yet an hour or so later it was done – a mark of sorts from the *qadi* whose frosted eyes had not been able to make out the little blur of words.

Once again the two men crossed the main square, flanked on two sides by the fort itself and the town's main mosque. Once again the sun beat upon them with tremendous force; but Powell-Bourke felt an exhilaration he had seldom known, and such was spilling over into warmth towards McCann himself.

A cautious but distinct deepening of intimacy with this Egyptian clerk had grown, so it seemed to Powell-Bourke as they accompanied one another stride for stride. Conversation flowed easily within the narrow overlap of their languages. Just as he supposed, nobody had thought to tell McCann, although the decision had evidently been reached some while previously. Yet it would give him satisfaction to be the one to bring the word himself. After all, it was his personal achievement.

The square showed evidence of a recent festivity. The tarmac was littered with 7-Up and Vimto cans. The two men passed an inverted plastic basin that was split down the side as if someone had used it to stand on. Then Powell-Bourke remembered. Had the execution occurred the previous day, after Friday prayers?

The clerk confirmed flatly, 'Here is the blood.'

A single lamp-post stood in the middle of the square and quite near its foot a sticky patch covered a surprisingly large area, suggesting the body had been allowed to lie there some while. It seemed to Powell-Bourke a slovenly way to run a town – yesterday's washing-up. Maybe they left it there on purpose, *pour encourager les autres*. Goats were browsing over by the boxes at one end of the square: in due course they would work their way across and probably lick it up. Goats would eat anything.

Because his visit was unheralded, the Consul found himself confronting McCann in the inner courtyard of the fortress, where he had been shifting rubble in yellow plastic sacks. It was to be a brief exchange. McCann struck him as shorter-in-the-leg, more ill-bred than ever. But that hardly mattered – he did experience a warmth for the man, a genuine tenderness. Did he not look so vulnerable, filmed with dust and streaked with sweat, under the sullen muzzles of the warders' guns? Poor fellow. Yet when Powell-Bourke gave him his tidings, all he could return was a perfunctory smile under his powdered beard and a muttered 'Good for you, Consul'. Powell-Bourke now experienced a stab of outrage. The skill, the daring, the immense cost in worry and risk, such risk . . . and he could summon nothing better than a graceless smirk and a 'Good for you, Consul'. He didn't deserve it. Powell-Bourke would have administered the thrashing himself, a lesson in sheer gratitude . . . Yet what could one expect? Here was a man incapable of expressing himself, a half-man, such as they shouldn't allow to go abroad. What could one expect?

He regarded McCann now. He did indeed appear diminished. 'Wiped out' was Jenny's phrase – half-way like the man whose blood was smeared on the asphalt of the square. He was sallower and scraggier, yet with that same light as before, like a fever, still burning in his eye. Powell-Bourke had said nothing to Jenny about the obsessive fixity: he'd been too worried himself. He knew of 'gate-fever'. Was this it? Gate fever? The man still had a month to serve.

There was little else to be said. The new Consul would be taking over what was left to do, handling the deportation on the man's release. But McCann suddenly asked, 'D'ye have any other information for me?'

Powell-Bourke was puzzled.

'What sort of information?'

'From the home.'

The Consul was surprised that McCann should consider he had a 'home'.

'There's nothing else,' he said.

The two men shook hands. They had never touched before. It was unreasonable to suppose the paths of two such disparate men would cross again.

On the drive back to the capital Powell-Bourke wished that Jenny were waiting for him. He wasn't blind to her sympathy for McCann and he would like her to see that now. With the burden of official responsibility in the case passing to others, one could make room for a private tenderness. McCann had performed a service for *him*, too, he could accept that.

The whole route between Daba'a and the capital was desert, mile upon mile of merciless desert. It was an utterly hostile place. Every now and then he passed the stinking, putrefying corpse of a camel and the wreck of a car or truck that had rammed it by night. If he broke down here he would be helpless. He could only wait for a passing vehicle, rare enough on this road. His car with its diplomatic number-plates gave him an illusion of protection: that was all it was, an illusion. Alone here in this heat he would be dead in a day or two. A passage of his boyhood came into his mind with extraordinary vividness; an incident, really, rather than a passage. It was of the only time he had left the suburbia in which all his childhood was spent. He went to Scotland on a summer camp, organised by whichever school he was attending that year: it must have been that same year he fell from his horse and his father went off. The boys had bivouacked on the 'bonny braes' overlooking Loch Lomond. He remembered now that world of the promise of inexpressible beauty, a beauty forever unfolding as the weather unfolded, or the day advanced, or as you climbed the first ridge, and the further ridge and yet another ridge higher and beyond.

It was odd all this coming back to him now, in the lone inimical wastes, for he had hardly ever thought of it all those years, and he never day-dreamed. Yet just now it was unaccountably vivid – the sun coming up beyond the water. He supposed his fall and all that ensued had blanked it out. Was it McCann who had sparked this recollection? The lilt of his speech, perhaps? It struck him now that McCann had *changed* during his imprisonment. The wrenching, aggressive slum Glaswegian had melted back to something closer to the airy singsong that must have lurked in Cedric's ear ever since those far days in the Highlands. Yes, there was that strange spontaneous reversion in McCann, surely. Yet McCann could have had no one to speak to these past several months, none but himself, the Consul . . . to whom he had nothing to say. Was that, then, what McCann had grown up amidst as a boy? That inexhaustible, boundless beauty and light, and sounds of a secret burn, and the sea, too, of course, among his isles? The chuckle of the burn and wash of the sea?

And look where he'd got himself now! Oh.

A stone struck by his front wheel rapped the underside of his vehicle violently, jolting the Consul out of his reverie. Certain things were best managed without. Beauty. Love.

The Ambassador was clearly gratified, even if he left Powell-Bourke with the faintest of impressions that he was relieved to see him go. The Foreign Office in London saw to it that news of the reprieve was released, and a paragraph appeared in a few but by no means all the papers that had reported the flogging sentence.

Powell-Bourke flew home two or three days later to the flat that Jenny had leased in Barons Court. He eschewed any show of triumph. They found no occasion to speak of Ally McCann. That may seem surprising, yet it was so. It was behind them; another era, a distant place. Yet Cedric's holiday in Scotland did keep coming to mind – to his mind, privately – and one day, so he promised himself, he would take Jenny there. The young couple spent much of the remaining weeks of their leave having the flat done up, buying furniture at the cut-price places they learned of through breathless, fifteen-second ads on television, but taking much care to match the curtains with the chair-covers. Whichever branch of the Foreign Service was to engage Cedric's talents, they would need a home base they could sublet when abroad.

Jenny could hardly fail to be impressed by the tax-free savings her husband had put aside for their own little home. She need never know there might have been six hundred riyals' worth more.

Then one morning in the last week of their leave a letter arrived in an official Foreign Office envelope. Cedric was at his breakfast, and Jenny brought it up from the ground floor, where the post was delivered. It was one of several letters, for Christmas was approaching already. Cedric went quite pale when he took it, and she noticed he didn't open it at once. So she found some cause that took her into the kitchen for a minute or two. When she returned, she saw it had been opened, cleanly with a knife. And after a moment or two he passed it to her without comment. It was a brief letter, personally signed by the Permanent Under-Secretary, confirming Cedric Powell-Bourke's admission to the diplomatic grades of Her Majesty's Foreign Service. She came round the edge of the table to give him a peck of a kiss, and could not help noticing his eyes were blinking ever so slightly.

Now, that same week, Alistair McCann was due for release. Several days ahead the new Consul had been pursuing the Ministry of Interior on the smooth removal of the unwanted man from Daba'a and his deportation to Britain. He was ready for the usual inertia and prevarication. The accumulation of signature and counter-signature from this, that and the other Ministry, not to speak of the local governorate and the gaoler himself, was notorious. Right up to the putative day of release itself the new Consul, a scrupulous man, had received no guidance from Interior as to what he was meant to do or when exactly the man would come out. It was really too bad, and hardly fair on the convict.

On the actual day came a letter, perhaps the same day as the other letter just described, hand-delivered from the Ministry of the Interior and addressed to the Consul by title but not by name. This letter was opened by one of the Consul's own clerks, an Adeni. To save his superiors time and trouble, he checked the files for the British subject to which the communication referred. Irritatingly, he could find no record of the man on consulate files, and it was this that delayed his passing to the Consul himself the actual letter and the issue it raised, until just before the finish of the day's work at two-thirty p.m.

The Consul recognised the confusion at once. The letter referred to a certain 'Alistair Dougal'. It was a common error among the locals to mistake a middle name for a surname. It was quite bland, and the signature belonged to no one whom the Consul was aware of having dealt with hitherto. It 'regretted to report the death by his own hand of Alistair Dougal whilst in custody' and requested the Embassy for instructions as to what should be done with the body.

The very next day the Consul himself drove to Daba'a.

As in the original incident the basic facts proved to be simple. The day before the prisoner's expected date of release, the Amir of Daba'a duly despatched his legal clerk, the Egyptian from the *shariah* court, to explain to the man the precise terms of his amended sentence. Following the representation of the British Consul, it was explained, the sentence of flogging imposed upon the prisoner was cancelled and replaced by an additional six months in prison. That afternoon McCann had no difficulty smuggling into the communal cell a yellow plastic bag, with which during the night he stifled himself.

The new Consul saw a lot of the Egyptian clerk on his visit to Daba'a and noted with approval the man's unmistakable agitation and distress at what had occurred. The encounter raised his estimation of Arab sensibility in general.

Fortunately for international relations the incident was nowhere reported in the British press, and when Powell-Bourke came to hear of it in the Office in London, he saw no call to share it with his wife. Yet he did puzzle over McCann's impatience to get back to the ruins of his life at home. What difference would an extra six months have made for such a man? No, he wouldn't risk telling Jenny. It was all behind them: McCann had played his part. And anyway, four or five weeks later, just as he had planned, she shyly announced she was pregnant.